Compulsion

Hilary Norman is the author of sixteen internationally bestselling novels, translated into seventeen languages, including *The Pact* and *Susanna*, and *If I Should Die*, a thriller published under the pseudonym Alexandra Henry.

Books by Hilary Norman

In Love and Friendship
Chateau Ella
Shattered Stars
Fascination
Spellbound
Laura
If I Should Die (written as Alexandra Henry)
Susanna
The Pact
Too Close
Mind Games
Blind Fear
Deadly Games
Twisted Minds
No Escape
Guilt

Compulsion

Hilary Norman

PIATKUS

Copyright © Hilary Norman 2005

First published in Great Britain in 2005
by Judy Piatkus (Publishers) Ltd of
5 Windmill Street, London W1T 2JA
email: info@piatkus.co.uk

The moral right of the author has been asserted

A catalogue record for this book is available from the British Library

ISBN 0 7499 0729 0 (Hb)
ISBN 0 7499 3618 5 (Pb)

Set in Times by
Action Publishing Technology Ltd, Gloucester

Printed and bound in Great Britain by
MPG Books, Bodmin, Cornwall

Acknowledgements

My gratitude to the following for their help and kindness:

Sarah Abel; Howard Barmad; Diana Bloch, BSc(Hons) MSc (speech and language therapist, generously sharing her experience); Jennifer Bloch; Sarah Fisher; Gillian Green; Howard Green; Gaby Hart; Russell Jones and colleagues at the Grand Hotel, Brighton; Jonathan Kern (the best!); Herta Norman (still reading for me); Judy Piatkus; Christopher (super sleuth) and Penny Reynolds; Helen Rose (chief problem solver); Neal Rose; Dr Jonathan Tarlow (never fazed); Keith Ward.

As always, characters, situations and the weather are entirely fictitious.

For Charlotte.
Beloved cat and writing companion for sixteen years.
1988–2004

Chapter 1

Frankie was expecting to have to wait until morning coffee. Usual time, usual place: in the kitchen, sitting at the table. Same routine as always.

Almost the same.

The diazepam tablets have already been crushed and mixed with Nescafé – a little more than usual, though the pills don't have much taste – and a level teaspoon of Tate & Lyle granulated at the bottom of Roz's favourite mug (the one from Caesar's Palace in Las Vegas), waiting for boiling water and semi-skimmed milk.

It's the second Wednesday in April. They always have coffee together at eleven-thirty on Mondays and Wednesdays, that being the earliest time Roz feels able to face company. Not a morning-people-person, she told Frankie when she first came to work for her last November.

Five months ago.

'A night-bird,' Roz said.

She likes, as she told Frankie soon after, a bit of a flutter. Perfectly open about it, no false shame, and Frankie liked her for that.

Fact is, Frankie is by now well aware, Roz Bailey is a gambler.

Roulette, mostly, at the Lansdowne Casino in Regency Square in Brighton. Not every night; just Saturdays, Tuesdays, occasionally on Thursdays, almost every single Friday.

She is, she has confided in Frankie, a reasonably successful gambler, has developed a 'system' of sorts.

'You never really win, of course,' Roz said. 'But if you're persistent, if you concentrate and if you know when to stop, you can have a great time and do okay.'

1

Roz is not, so far as Frankie knows, very rich, but she is comfortable.

With a beautiful house, at the top of a hill in Rottingdean.

The best house in the road.

Roz is also unattached. No one to answer to. No one – so far as Frankie is aware – who cares about her. Acquaintances, of course, mostly fellow gamblers at the club. But no one who really *cares*.

That's the point.

The reason for *this*.

That, and, of course, the house.

The two mugs – Frankie's decorated with a black-and-white cat – are waiting on the tray by the kettle on one of the granite worktops in the beautiful grey-and-white kitchen – except that fate has just intervened in the form of Roz coming down twenty minutes earlier than usual and finding Frankie working at the garden end of the conservatory.

'Morning, love.'

'Morning, Mrs Bailey.' Frankie's heart is pounding with shock, but she covers well. 'You're early.'

'Mm,' Roz says.

She's wearing her blue dressing-gown, a velour-type garment with a zip, the kind some older women wear for 'entertaining at home' because of its slinkiness. Though Roz does not, in fact, entertain, nor does she look particularly slinky. A nice-enough-looking woman, waistline probably a few inches more at forty-three than it used to be, dark, jaw-length hair touched up with semi-permanent tint every now and then, she looks nevertheless, some mornings, somewhat the worse for wear.

This is one of those mornings, which could, Frankie supposes, mean that last night – Tuesday – was either a bad and very late night at the Lansdowne, or a very good and late one.

No difference to Frankie.

No difference to Roz either, if she only knew it.

Frankie's mind is on the coffee mugs standing out in full sight in the kitchen, the contents of the Caesar's Palace one looking, perhaps, if one were to bother to look, a bit odd.

'All right?' she asks casually.

'If you like that sort of thing.' Roz is rueful.

'Bad night?'

'Late night. And I couldn't sleep when I did get to bed.'

'Oh, well,' Frankie says, 'at least it's a nice morning.' She pauses. 'Coffee soon?'

'Oh, now, I think,' Roz says. 'If you don't mind.'

'Course not.' Frankie's stomach lurches with excitement.

'Let's have it in here, shall we?' Roz suggests. 'For a change.'

'Fine,' Frankie says, easily.

Couldn't be better.

Could not *be* better.

In the right place.

Roz appears to notice, for the first time, thanks to her gambling-insomniac hangover, that Frankie is holding one of her indoor gardening tools, a miniature scythe, in her right hand.

'Those damn weeds come up again?'

Indeed they have, the second crop this month to stick their stupid, springtime-eager necks up through some of the white-and-navy Spanish stone floor tiles.

'Yeah,' Frankie says. 'Little buggers.'

Roz comes closer, peering. 'I suppose we'll have to take care of the roots.'

'I'll buy some Weedol,' Frankie says.

Roz frowns down at the floor. 'Make sure it doesn't stain the tiles.'

'I'll read the directions,' Frankie says. 'Before I pay for it.'

Roz glances at the little scythe still in her hand, and her forehead puckers again. 'Hope you haven't scratched the stone with that.'

For a moment or two, Frankie's hand seems to itch.

No, she tells herself. *No blood.*

'I do love my tiles,' Roz says.

Her tiles.

'I'll get the coffee.' Frankie puts the scythe down, knowing she'll have to clean it before she puts it back beside the baby trowel by the wall beyond the orchids. 'You have a sit down, Mrs B. You look like you need it.'

In the kitchen, waiting for the cordless kettle to boil, Frankie sees her hands are shaking.

Stop that, girl.

No going back now.

3

She opens the biscuit barrel, takes out two digestives and two ginger nuts, puts them on a pale-grey plate, and the shaking stops.

Could go back if she wanted to.

The water in the Russell Hobbs bubbles and bounces, and the switch clicks off.

Too late now.

Frankie pours, first into the Caesar's Palace mug, then her own.

'As it comes,' Roz always says about coffee and tea.

Good job, Frankie thinks now, adding milk to the coffee, crushed pills and sugar mix.

And then she notices the crumbs.

Two of them, on the worktop between the barrel and tray.

She tears off a piece of paper roll and sweeps them into the palm of her left hand, then opens the pedal bin with her right foot, folds the paper neatly around the crumbs and drops it in.

Except she's not sure, suddenly, if both crumbs went in.

She starts to bend, going to check the floor.

Not now.

But if the crumb is on the Amtico, and if she forgets and treads on it later . . .

Not now, Frankie.

With an effort of will, she straightens, picks up the tray.

Tread on it and one crumb becomes a hundred.

Another voice speaks in her head.

'Stupid cunt.'

Bo's voice.

For a moment, Frankie feels the shaking begin again, and then she brings it back under control.

'Bugger the crumbs,' she says quietly.

And bugger you, too, Bo.

She steadies the tray and, careful not to spill a drop of coffee, carries it out into the hall, and on into the conservatory.

'Here we go,' she says.

Chapter 2

Even now, five years later, when Alex looked at the cooker — at least, whenever it was clean and properly polished and looking its handsome best, the way it was always supposed to be but all too seldom was – she remembered going out to order it.

Three days after Matt's funeral, the day after her mother, Sandra, had flown back to Stockholm, where she'd been living with the latest man in her life, and Alex had been both relieved because she'd gone and ashamed to be feeling that way.

The Aga was her gift to him. Better than flowers on his grave, though she had taken those along, too, that same day, a bunch of delphiniums she'd spotted in Selsdon Road, and which were, had been, his favourite in the wild.

She had taken them out of their wrapping paper and scattered them so that it looked as if a wind had blown them there, and then she had crouched low beside the still fresh and incomparably desolate grave, and told him about the Aga.

'I've done it, sweetheart. In the blue you wanted. Almost the same colour as these.'

She had remembered, an hour or so later, that delphiniums were poisonous, had jumped in the car and driven back to the cemetery to retrieve them, afraid that some bird or animal might eat them, or even (she had always been prey to over-the-top imaginings) that a toddler might pick them up and get belladonna or whatever the poison was on its fingers and stick them in its mouth.

The flowers had still been there, all ten of them, for there was no wind and no creature or human had taken them away, and she

5

had gathered them up and explained it to Matt. Had almost heard him laughing at her.

Almost.

The cooker was what Matt had aspired to for years, though the plan had been to wait till they could move out of the flat over Café Jardin and find their house. Which was going to have at least three bedrooms, he'd said, with a kitchen big enough for at least a two-oven Aga and a long table.

'Long enough for our kids and Suzy and any kids she might have and as many of our friends as we can fit in, but not necessarily all their kids,' Matt had said.

Alex had asked how many children he foresaw them having, and he'd said it was up to her, that he'd settle for any number from one to five, and if by chance there were problems that meant they couldn't have any, he'd be glad to adopt, and if that didn't appeal to her, it was all right with him too.

'So long as I have you.'

Alex remembered crying when he said that.

Less than a year later, Matt had been dead, and Suzy in a coma.

They'd all met on day one at Croydon Grammar aged eleven.

Changing into PE kit for the first time, Alex cringing a bit about exposing her long, spindly arms and legs, darting glances around at the hotchpotch of body shapes and colours, certain that everyone else felt more confident than she did, her gaze had fallen on a pretty, petite girl with long blond hair done up in a messy plait, standing staring hopelessly into her gym bag.

The girl had looked up, caught Alex's eye, and grinned.

'No kit,' she'd said, her voice low and a little husky.

Alex had moved closer. 'Nothing at all?'

'Shoes,' the girl had said. 'Good bloody start.'

'You could share mine.' Alex had looked her up and down. 'Not sure about the shorts, but the top should be okayish. At least we'll both be half right.'

'Why should you get a bollocking too?' the girl asked.

Alex had shrugged. 'They can't shoot us.'

'Okay,' the girl had said. 'Thanks.'

'I'm Alex Harper,' Alex had said, pulling off her top.

'Suzy Levin,' the other girl had said. 'You've got great legs.'

He had been outside, waiting for Suzy after school.

'That's Matt, my brother,' Suzy had told Alex. 'He goes to Saint Aloysius.'

Alex had looked, had seen a boy of about fourteen, tall, with longish dark hair, brown eyes and a warm smile, and had felt herself start to melt.

Suzy had pulled her across the pavement towards him.

'This is Alex, though I think I'm going to call her Ally,' she'd said. 'I forgot my PE kit and she shared hers so we both got into trouble and we're going to be best friends.'

'Cool.' Matt had given his sister a hug and grinned. 'Fancy a burger?'

Food from the word go.

Chapter 3

Nearly done now.

Easy so far.

So fucking easy, Frankie could cry.

Or laugh.

Cry in a way, she supposes, since she quite liked Roz. It's all right to cry when someone you like is dying.

Nice enough way to go, mind. Going to sleep, no worries about what's going to happen next. No fear or pain. Better than what might have come naturally in the fullness of time. Cancer, maybe, or stroke. Or sitting on a plane knowing it's going to crash.

Not very likely, the last, but probably more likely than being murdered, though Frankie's heard it said you're more likely to be murdered than win the Lotto.

Roz would have loved winning the lottery.

Most likely, given time, she'd have got cancer. All those smoky casinos. Frankie's only ever been in one, in Blackpool with Bo, years ago, and she couldn't stand it, the smoke and all the people packed round the tables, standing so close, touching her . . .

Lung cancer, probably.

She's saved Roz that, at least.

Just a mug of coffee – and if the tablets did make any difference to the taste, she didn't mention it – and then just dozing off in her lovely chintz-covered cane armchair in her pretty, glass-roofed conservatory.

No idea of what was coming.

Frankie's been putting off the next bit.

Wondering if she could change her mind, finish it with a cushion

8

instead. Just pick it up, stick it over her face, push it down till it's finished.

But she's always really liked Roz's cushions, knows she had them made by some woman in Hangleton, and Frankie won't be able to ask her to make a replacement, and anyway the newer fabric would never match.

So it's got to be the plastic bag, hasn't it?

Uglier to have to watch, but much cleaner.

A clear winner then.

Frankie often wonders what she'd do without plastic.

She notices just before she puts the bag on.

Two spots of something on the padded arm of the chair.

Drool from the corner of Roz's mouth, she realises with disgust, because there's still a little of it on the unconscious woman's chin.

Leave it for now.

More important things to do first.

She picks up the plastic bag, then hesitates.

If she doesn't clean off those two spots right away, they'll dry into the fabric and mark it, and then, however much she scrubs, she'll know they're still there, like one of those infections they say people carry around inside their mouths.

Frankie looks down at the floor, sees – is almost certain she sees – another spot of it on one of the Spanish tiles.

'I do love my tiles,' Roz said before coffee.

Frankie's tiles now. Or they will be soon.

Soon as she's dealt with this.

She puts down the bag again and goes to fetch what she needs, hurrying, even though there's no chance of Roz waking for hours, but still, she's not going to run any risks now. She tackles the spots efficiently, removing and disinfecting, the new smell far from beautiful, but very satisfactory.

Frankie is very good at what she does.

And now, with that taken care of, she can attend to the other thing.

Chapter 4

It was Suzy who had finally – when Matt was almost twenty-one and she and Alex eighteen – pushed them out of the uncomplicated cosiness of great friendship into what she had always known was inevitable.

'For God's sake,' she'd told them both, separately. 'You know you're made for each other, so why not just stop fucking around and *start* fucking around?'

They had opened Café Jardin a year later – three months after their wedding – renting the flat upstairs. Matt was master of the kitchen, Alex controlled the business and what she called 'front of house', and Suzy, in PR by then, used all her contacts brazenly to plug them. Young as they were, together they had made the restaurant – in Selsdon, near South Croydon – pretty and exceptionally comfortable both inside and out in the garden; flowers for all seasons, a sheltered area and heaters outside, banquettes with plump floral cushions within. And customers had ventured in, swiftly taken pleasure in both the surroundings and, more crucially, in Matt's cooking, and had spread the word.

'*Matt Levin understands food and people*,' a *Time Out* reviewer had written, and soon Café Jardin had sported a waiting list for weekends, Thursdays and Fridays.

Alex had loved working with Matt more than she'd ever loved doing anything, and living upstairs with him had been even better, and though the present had been more than good enough, it hadn't stopped them talking, sometimes, about the future, about the house and the Aga and children and dogs.

And then, one spring Monday afternoon, Suzy had come to pick

10

Matt up to take him to a radio interview she'd set up for him at LBC, and a lorry coming the other way on Streatham Hill had burst a tyre and hit Suzy's car head-on, and Matt had been pronounced dead on arrival at King's College Hospital A&E, and when Alex had seen Suzy later that day in their ICU, her beloved sister-in-law and best friend had been almost unrecognizable, and the world as she had known it had come to an end.

The blue Aga had sat in the kitchen in which it did not truly fit, either in dimension or style, in the small flat above Café Jardin, had gone on sitting and gathering dust, because when the specialist fitters had arrived to connect it Alex had asked them to go away. It had, on the day she'd bought it, been a defiant demonstration of surviving love, an attempt to create a solid, visible bridge from the old life to the new. The reality of the hopelessness of the gesture had hit home within days; without Matt there to use the Aga, it was worse than pointless, it was yet another cruel and constant reminder of the enormity of her loss.

She had, in any case, no appetite, seldom ate at all, and then only as little as she could get down, keep down, in order to survive. Baked beans, toast or, on occasions, a boiled egg. Nothing that required an Aga.

Suzy's injuries had been profound and far-reaching. The facial wounds that had initially caused such distress to Alex and to Lyn Perry – Suzy's and Matt's aunt, flown over in a state of grief and shock from Florida – had been the very least of it, mostly cuts, abrasions and bruising, all of which could be either stitched or left to heal naturally. The damage to Suzy's legs and pelvis, however, was much more severe; would – if she recovered sufficiently from her head injury to become aware of such things – cause her considerable long-term pain and take a long time to mend, and Suzy's orthopaedic surgeon had refused to commit himself as to the extent of her ultimate recovery and mobility.

'She will walk again, whatever they say,' both Alex and Aunty Lyn had insisted, both silently aware they were being unrealistic because the spectre of bubbly, vital, energetic Suzy in a wheelchair had seemed so unbearable to them.

Though not nearly as unbearable as some of the alternatives.

Suzy remaining comatose.

Suzy permanently brain damaged.

'That *won't* happen,' Alex had told Aunty Lyn early on with great firmness.

'We can't know that yet, honey,' Lyn Perry had said.

'I can,' Alex had said. 'I do.'

It was, for the most part, the only passion she had permitted herself in those early days, for if she had allowed herself to feel more – and Lord knew there seemed no space left in her because she was already so packed with blastingly agonizing feelings; but if she had let herself actually *express* any of that, if she had let all that devastation escape from her tightly strung self, she thought she might have exploded into a million fragments.

Which would have been welcome, had Suzy not still been there, hooked up to life support, not yet conscious of how much love and patience and care she was going to need.

Not yet aware that Matt had gone.

No one else left for Suzy now except Alex and Aunty Lyn, who had a husband and two kids and a business to run in Fort Lauderdale.

'If she were well enough,' Lyn had said, 'maybe we could fly her over.'

'If she were well enough,' Alex said, 'I'm not sure that's what she'd want.'

'I know,' Lyn had replied, unoffended, knowing as well as Alex that Suzy had turned down an offer to move into her guesthouse three years earlier, after Gerald and Judy Levin, Matt's and Suzy's parents, had died within six months of each other.

'My life is here,' Suzy had told her aunt. 'My work and Matt and Ally.'

That life shrunk horribly down now, she would discover if she came out of her coma and was still Suzy.

Alex still there for her, but no work for a very long time.

And no Matt.

Most of the time in the early weeks after the funeral and Suzy's first life-saving operations, Alex had spent sitting beside her, talking to her, convinced that Suzy heard her, reassuring Lyn, before her return to Florida, that she would stay the course, would never give up on her.

Nowhere else to go anyway.

She had wandered, now and again, into Café Jardin (shut down by her days after the crash, staff paid in lieu of notice, bookings cancelled), stepping over the debris of unopened post on the floor, walking past the barren, dusty tables into the kitchen, shutting her eyes, seeing Matt again in the place where he had been most in his element, preparing, stirring, sniffing, tasting. Then opening her eyes again, seeing no one, and leaving, returning to the hospital to continue her vigil.

The moment Alex had longed for, Suzy's wakening, had led, with relentless swiftness, to the moment she had most dreaded.

'Matt?' Suzy had said.

The name had sounded unfinished, no 't' at its end, but still, there had been no doubt about who she was asking for, *what* she was asking, and her eyes had told Alex that she already knew, and how could she not know, at least, that something was terribly wrong, when her beloved brother had not been to see her? When he would, had he been able to, have spent every possible second at his sister's side.

Alex had known she had to tell Suzy the truth right away. Stark, agonizing as it was, there could be no wavering, no ambiguity.

She had taken Suzy's hand, held it firmly, looked into her eyes.

Seen some of the light snuffing out even before she had said it.

'Matt died, Suzy, darling.'

'What are you going to do now?' people had asked Alex every now and then.

'I don't know,' she had always answered, which was true. She'd felt aimless, directionless, lost. Pointless.

Until the day Suzy – four months after waking from her coma – had strung together her first entirely comprehensible sentence.

'Food here such crap.'

She had been receiving speech and language therapy as well as physiotherapy since regaining consciousness, and Alex had been observing Suzy's relationship with speech therapist Ginny Khan with particular interest. Fascinated by the steady build-up of trust, the precarious balance between professionalism and intimacy, being privy, finally, to their first major success had stirred her in a way that nothing had since Matt's death.

'How patient are you?'

One of a stream of questions posed by Ginny when, after a fortnight of library study and contemplation, Alex had broached, very tentatively, the possibility of completely changing her life and applying for training as a speech and language therapist.

13

'How determined are you?' Ginny had asked. 'In general.'

'Very,' Alex answered. 'When I need to be.'

'Are you squeamish?'

'Not especially.'

The questions grew harder to answer without consideration.

'Do you have any prejudices?'

'How are you with failure? Your own and other people's?'

'How resilient are you?'

'Do you think you could distinguish between your own goals and frustrations, and your patient's?'

'How do you think you would cope with being ordered to turn your back on a patient before reaching your mutual goal?'

Alex had begun to sag.

'Too hard,' she'd told Suzy later. 'You obviously need to be a very special kind of person, and I'm not at all sure I am.'

'Don't fish,' Suzy had said.

Her voice was still clumsy, but her succinctness undiminished.

'Do you really think I could handle it?' Alex asked.

'On your head,' Suzy had said.

Chapter 5

Frankie looked for a long time until she found Ron Bailey.

Seven clients, to be precise, since thinking up and working out her plan.

She knew, from the beginning, that she would need to be scrupulously careful, that it was vital she avoid the temptation to rush into anything. That she had to be, in all of her working situations, as ordinary as it was possible for her to be. The drabber the better, a woman no one would look at twice unless they had good reason to.

Just the cleaner. No one special.

Not one at all, so far as they were concerned.

They. The haves.

One of whom was going to give Frankie what she wanted.

Which was, simply, what they had.

She picked her shortlist of candidates carefully. Most cleaners tend to work in as many households as possible in a single area, but once she'd come up with her scheme and left Calloway's, Frankie arranged her own working week very differently. One client per day, six days a week, each in a separate town or district no less than six miles apart.

The Calloway factory, just outside Romford, was the last place of work where Frances Rosemary Barnes had figured officially on anyone's books, though even that had been on a casual basis – cleaning there, too, of course, and doling out teas and coffees and sandwiches and sticky buns. And even in those days – before the idea – she had preferred living in rented rooms for cash, never asking for or wanting a rent book, finding landlords who were happy with the arrangement, especially once they realised their tenant was taking better care of their property than anyone ever had before.

That was where it came to her.

In the midst of washing up the directors' Doulton cups and saucers and stainless steel spoons (the workers had polystyrene cups and multi-use plastic spoons). The plan to change it all. And once it was in her head, she knew there would be no turning back. She had to find the way, had to go through with it.

Had to.

Frankie has been a cleaner now for a little over eleven years, started when she was twenty-four, mostly because it was the job she was far and away most suited to, but also because she had tried just about everything else that was available to an unqualified no-hoper.

Shop work first, in a boutique in Romford, where she learned that customers were not always right and often unspeakably rude. Then washing hair in a salon just down the High Road called Gloss, which she stupidly believed might be ideal for her, a nice, hygienic job; realizing too late that some people's heads were disgustingly greasy, with all sorts of life forms living on them, and she tried bringing in her own gloves to use for it, but the boss told her that was offensive to the clients, so she left.

She tried Moons Books next, in Chadwell Heath, because the only significant dirt in a place like that surely had to be dust, and because its customers, she supposed, were likely to be of a better class, but for the three months she was there hardly anyone ever ventured in, so the owner had to let Frankie go. After that she became a receptionist in the offices of Pelhams Chartered Accountants back in Romford, but sitting at a desk eight hours a day trying to smile at boring clients and bosses was unbearable; and anyway, like the shops and the superficially glitzy salon, the offices were filthy, and all Frankie had *really* wanted to do was pull on some extra-strength rubber gloves (and a mask wouldn't have gone amiss) and fill a bucket with Dettol or Domestos or even Jeyes, and get down on her knees.

So that was what she started doing. Getting paid for what she was best at.

Four years of job satisfaction.

Until Bo came along and changed her life forever.

And then, after Bo, after her 'trouble', when it was all different, *she* was different, all hope gone, stubbed out like one of his roll-ups, she'd started working again, cleaning again, and she knew *they* would have disapproved, would have told her it was probably the last job on earth she should be doing; but she had to do something, had to earn a wage, support herself, and there was nothing else, and anyway, she loved it, it was all that kept her going.

No shortage of jobs for her, at least. People were always saying, after all, that good, honest cleaners were like gold dust, and they certainly didn't come any better than Frankie Barnes. She thought, in one of her close-to-happy moments – as close as it was possible for her to come to happiness – that maybe she should have business cards printed with something like **Dedicated to Dirt** on them, except that was the opposite of what she was dedicated to, and **Hooked on Hygiene** might have put them off, and anyway, she didn't actually want cards, nothing in writing, nothing that could lead to 'official'.

Before Calloway's, before the idea, Frankie always used to go for 'nice', or at least expensive houses, most of them in and around Chigwell. Not because the rich paid better; on the contrary, in her experience they were often meaner than those on much tighter budgets. But they did tend to appreciate the way Frankie took care of their homes, and the fact was it was more efficient vacuuming with a Miele or a Dyson, and scrubbing a stranger's slimy bath or, worse, bleaching their revolting loos was more tolerable, too, if you were surrounded by cool, pleasure-to-clean marble or smooth granite. And maybe, in fact, if she had not been seduced by the ad in the local paper, lured by the prospect of more money at Calloway's – Frankie was only human, after all, with bills to pay like everyone else; but maybe if she hadn't left the nice, shiny houses and gone to the factory and grown to loathe that place so intensely, to feel as if its grime-encrusted walls and scummy ceilings were closing in on her – maybe she might never have become desperate enough to come up with the idea.

Though even in the Chigwell houses, nothing had ever felt quite good enough for her.

'I'm not sure what it is you want,' Mrs Binder, one of her clients, had said to her, not unreasonably, after Frankie had told her she was packing the job in. 'It's not as if I'm on at you all the time, is it? I don't check your work, I don't say anything

17

about you having the TV on in all the rooms you're meant to be working in.'

'Not *meant* to be working,' Frankie had said, quite savagely.

'No, of course not,' Mrs Binder had said quickly, flustered, because there was no doubt about it, Frankie was the best cleaner she'd ever had. 'But I'm trying to find out what it is I can do to make you happier.'

'Nothing,' Frankie had said.

But later, back in her rented room in Chadwell Heath, the answer to Mrs Binder's questions had come to Frankie loud and clear.

'Give me what you have.'

Not everything, of course. Not Mr Binder, whom she wouldn't have wanted pickled. Not their spoiled rotten kids either.

Just the house. And some of the money, just enough to pay to keep it really nice. Enough to replace roof tiles when they came loose, or get a bloke in to do the gutters, or paint the outside every few years and do up the inside now and then.

Maybe even employ a cleaner.

Not that she'd trust anyone else to do the job.

Anyway, chance would be a fine thing and great big pink pigs might fly.

That was what Frankie told herself back then.

Until the idea.

Which changed everything.

Change was the operative word. Change of scene above all, and right away. No more grungy factory. No more bleached Essex women. No more Romford or Chadwell Heath.

Most important, no one who knew Frankie Barnes.

She toyed briefly with the idea of the countryside, but the seaside, soon as she thought about it, appealed to her more. There was something liberating about all that endless water and waves and boats and, in season, all those outsiders clamouring to come there, and anyway, she'd read somewhere that, pollution aside, saltwater was basically clean.

Where though? The east coast, so far as she could make out from the nightly TV forecasts, was too cold, and the west seemed even worse. At least she knew bits of the south coast, had been to Eastbourne and Brighton and Bournemouth. She hadn't much cared for Eastbourne and had found Bournemouth a bit snobby, a bit geriatric, come to that, but she'd loved Brighton.

She went to WH Smith and bought a map.

It looked easy enough. Managable, all in a nice straightish line she could trace with her fingers. Worthing, Portslade-by-Sea, Hove, Brighton, Rottingdean, Peacehaven, and Newhaven, though the last, she knew, was a port, because she'd seen adverts for ferry crossings from there, and she didn't fancy a big place like that.

She'd need a car, she decided.

She hadn't driven since Bo.

Hadn't done a lot of things since Bo.

Like love. Or trust.

Or imagine wanting to live with another human being ever again.

Chapter 6

If Suzy had not made quite such a good recovery and, more to the point, if she had not met (at their mutual orthopaedic surgeon's consulting rooms, where he was awaiting the verdict on his damaged knee) and fallen in love with and married David Maynard – a fair-haired, blue-eyed lawyer who spent his working life defending men and women accused of often truly vile crimes, but who had a genuinely strong belief in his clients' rights, and who adored and took the best imaginable care of Suzy – then Alex would probably not have considered taking the job in Hove.

Even so, it had been a wrench.

'It's a brilliant offer,' Suzy had told her. 'And this place that wants you's one of the best, I looked it up. A lot of footballers and athletes have gone there, and David's had a friend to do some checking, says it's rock solid.'

'Are you trying to get rid of me?' Alex asked.

'Yeah, big time,' Suzy said wryly.

Alex had come to the Maynards' ground-floor flat in Roland Gardens off Old Brompton Road for dinner – as she did at least once a month – and to canvass their opinions, half hoping they would discourage her, guessing that was unlikely, knowing the real reason for that.

'Suzy hates the idea of you going anywhere,' David said, pouring cold white wine into slender glasses. 'But we all know this is the first really ace job that's come up for you.'

'And the fact of the matter –' Suzy took over '– is that unless you finally get out of that damned flat, and away from it, properly away, Matt's going to go on haunting you forever.'

That was the nub of it. Café Jardin had long since been sold and turned into a seafood restaurant, and the new owner hadn't needed the flat, though the manager had certainly fancied it, but Alex, slogging her way through her first year at City University, had not been able to face the upheaval of moving – or that, at least, had been her excuse.

'Matt doesn't haunt me,' she'd answered Suzy, more than three years after that, a BSc (Hons) under her belt, and highly motivated, but still living in the same place, physically and, in some ways, she sometimes realised, emotionally.

'Maybe not haunt,' Suzy half agreed, 'but deep down you do still feel – I know you do, Ally, whatever you say – that as long as you stay there, a bit of him's still there with you, and he's not, darling. I wish to God he was, but he's gone forever, and it's high time you accepted that and got on with the rest of your life.'

Alex had fallen silent for a little while.

'If I find a little house and adapt it, will you come and visit?'

'Do piles itch?' Suzy said flatly.

So Alex had accepted the job at the Hove Neurological and Rehabilitation Centre, and found her lovely stone cottage set well back off Falmer Road in Woodingdean, five minutes from Rottingdean and just a short drive from the Centre itself; and the only things she had taken from the flat apart from her clothes and books and personal possessions were the menus of the first lunch and dinner Matt had cooked at Café Jardin, their fat photograph album, his Crystal Palace scarf, and the royal blue Aga.

The cooker slotted in perfectly in the new kitchen at Melton Cottage, looked splendid, made the place cosy, finally fulfilling its purpose, a source of comfort for its owner at the end of long, hardworking, sometimes gruelling days at the Centre.

Her patients were a disparate bunch, made up mainly of stroke and head injury victims, and sufferers of degenerative diseases and head and neck cancers. Alex had learned more than she'd ever believed possible in the years since deciding to change direction, and her priorities had shifted dramatically. It was not so much, she thought, that she had actually stopped being self-absorbed, but in the face of so much suffering, so much courage, so much sheer hard work, it was simply no longer possible to think as much about herself, or even to find time to take care of her own day-to-day needs.

21

'You look different,' her mother, on one of her rare and, as usual, fleeting visits to England, had told her over a lavish cream tea in the luxurious but wonderfully relaxing Victoria Lounge at the Grand in Brighton. 'Too thin.'

'I'm really fine, Mum,' Alex said, layering clotted cream and strawberry jam onto her second fruit scone to help illustrate the point.

And Sandra had peered at her more closely.

'Yes,' she'd said. 'I think you are.' She paused. 'Matt would be proud.'

Five years now since she had lost him. Slipping a little further back into memory now, the man and their wonderful partnership. The love itself still a warming energy inside Alex, but no longer the painful force field it had once been.

Alex dated these days, work permitting.

'Anyone?' Suzy asked regularly on the phone.

Meaning anyone *special*.

'Nah,' Alex always replied.

Their conversations often followed much the same route. Suzy, so happy with David, fervently wanted Alex to find that happiness a second time. Alex told her regularly and truthfully that she was perfectly content, and far too busy to think much about that side of life.

'Never mind content,' Suzy had said a couple of weeks ago. 'When did you last have a good shag?'

So long ago, Alex had thought, but not said, that she barely remembered.

She tried not to think about that, because those thoughts inevitably brought back her longing, still intense and unquench-able, for Matt, for the physical side of their relationship as well as the rest of it. The togetherness, the passion, the constant awareness of the other, the warmth and comfort and confidence they had given each other.

But she had dated a few men.

One doctor, one orderly, one nurse and a social worker.

'Have they passed some Sussex by-law,' Suzy enquired once, 'restricting speech therapists' romantic lives to medical and related professionals?'

Alex laughed, replied that it was simply circumstantial.

'I'm not that likely,' she added, 'to pick up, say, a lawyer, in my line of work.'

'Don't want to bother with lawyers,' said Suzy. 'Not many like David. Not what you need at all, Ally.'

'So what do I need?'

'Someone wonderful,' Suzy said.

Like Matt, Alex thought, but once again, did not say.

Not *like* Matt, really. Just Matt.

Still.

Chapter 7

In the early hours of the April morning after the accident in Luddesdown Terrace, Jude Brown dreamed about Scott again.

Same old dream.

The horrible bumping and the indescribable sound that the car made as it rolled over him.

Their mother's face when she realised what had happened.

What she had done.

Her jumping out, already trembling, the first of her screams as she saw, the screams continuing, pitching ever louder, wilder, as she moved the car off him – off her *son* – her whole body shaking now, like a sapling in a storm.

Nothing then for a moment in Jude's dream. Just an odd blank, like a glitch in a faulty film.

Then the sight of Scott's body.

Looking normal enough. No blood or bruises.

No breathing either.

Jude woke up sweating, the way he always did when he had the dream.

Twenty-two years later, and it came to him less often, thankfully, but its power, when it did grip him, was still just as intense.

He looked around, saw he was on his small couch, remembered abruptly why he'd never made it to bed last night.

Remembered the accident.

The reason, he supposed, for the reawakening of the dream.

They had been restoring the shabby little row of terraced houses in Luddesdown Terrace in Kemp Town for the past several months,

24

and while the completed buildings, newly creamily bright and jaunty, were almost ready for reoccupation, both of the end houses, east and west, were still languishing beneath scaffolding and tarpaulins.

Jude was lucky enough these days to be able to pick and choose his freelance building jobs, having earned a local reputation as an all-rounder whose bricklaying, roofing, plastering and painting skills were all second, if not to none, at least to very few. His favourite Sussex projects to date had been the community theatre in Seaford, the new wing at the rehab centre in Hove, a small but quite beautiful hotel in Newhaven set up exclusively to offer holidays for the disabled, and, of course, the E Gallery opened the previous year by Pal and Eva Hauser in Worthing.

He had taken the job in Luddesdown Terrace because he'd liked the houses. As a rule, Jude disliked too much symmetry, rows of homes uniformly built; but these terraces, though all narrow, with the same dainty balconies on their upper floors and the same number of stone steps leading up from their front gardens, had enough minor proportional and design idiosyncrasies to make him feel fondly towards them.

Which was probably one of the reasons he'd been in a fine enough mood – despite working on pointing (which he did not enjoy) and despite it being a bleak, cold April morning – to have been singing along to the Robbie Williams number being played on Virgin, when Earl Cobbins, working up on the roof, had given a loud shout of what sounded like surprise, instantly and horrifyingly mutating into a scream of purest terror as he had plunged past Jude's ladder, arms and legs flailing, down onto the stone path below.

The sound of his landing was still in Jude's head this morning.

It had been clear, from the twisted position of Earl's body, from the angle of his arms and legs, that short of death itself, it was about as bad as it could be. Maybe worse than death, Jude had thought briefly, Christ forgive him, while Ron Clark, the foreman, had called for the ambulance and Jude and the other builders had squatted and stood around the unconscious man, debating with each other – having established that he was breathing – whether or not to move him into the recovery position.

'Best not to touch him,' Jude had said, going on nothing more than instinct.

No one had argued.

25

'They want me to stay on site,' an ashen-faced Ron Clark had told Jude while the paramedics had loaded Earl, neck braced and body carefully strapped, into the ambulance, 'to talk to the police, but someone needs to go with him.'

'I'll go,' Jude had said.

'Good lad.' Ron had patted him on the shoulder.

'What about his dad?' Jude knew there was no wife, didn't think there was a girlfriend, but had heard Earl talk about his father, who lived in London.

'I've been onto the office,' Ron said. 'They've told him.'

'Poor man,' Jude said, and got into the ambulance.

He had still been at the Royal Sussex County Hospital when Ray Cobbins had arrived hours later, his expression shattered, and Jude hadn't actually spoken to him, because he could see that the doctors and staff were taking good care of him as they explained that Earl was in the ICU and, for the time being, still unconscious. And though it was terrible to realise that Earl was unaware that his dad was now there with him, Jude couldn't help feeling grateful, too, because he'd overheard a doctor speaking about his injuries, and they were as bad as he and the other men on site had feared.

'Spinal and head,' he'd informed Ron Clark on the phone. 'Too early to tell.'

'Bloody hell,' Ron said. 'Poor bugger.'

'Want me to come back?' Jude had asked. 'I feel a bit in the way here.'

'No point, mate,' Ron said. 'We've been told to down tools till Health and Safety clear us, and thank Christ for that, cos between you and me, I don't have the heart for it, I can tell you.'

Jude had gone home to the nice little top-floor studio flat with the too-short lease that had rendered it affordable despite it being in Union Street in the Lanes district of Brighton, wishing (which he seldom did these days, having long since grown used to being alone) that someone had been there to put their arms around him or just *be* there.

He'd made himself a sandwich, but found he couldn't eat it, and he'd turned on the TV, which had got on his nerves, so he'd turned it off again, and though ordinarily when he got time off, he jumped at the extra opportunity to sketch or paint, he'd had no more heart

26

for that than Ron had had for working on the site. And okay, he didn't know Earl that well, had only met him at Luddesdown Terrace, but he liked him, liked his free and easy approach to life, and the fact that he was a grafter too, and since there was no wife or close girlfriend, Jude hoped to hell the guy had a lot of good mates, because if he survived this catastrophe he was going to need all the support he could get.

Now, the morning after, it wasn't just the memory of the accident or Earl's plight itself that was still getting to Jude. It was the memory of Ray Cobbins's face when he had first caught sight of his son. His skin was even darker than Earl's, but in those few moments Jude had seen it grow literally grey with shock, and that, Jude supposed now, was what must have triggered his own memories of his mother after Scott, and the dream.

She had looked grey that day, too, as if she'd begun withering before his eyes.

Had gone on withering for seventy-two more hours.

Until she had tied the belt of a dressing-gown and two scarves together, had gone into their garage, shut the up-and-over door, and hanged herself.

And that had been the end of Jude's childhood.

Chapter 8

Frankie knew, within a fortnight of starting work for her, that Roz was the one.

Woman on her own. Divorced for years. No close relatives. No bloke. Not old enough for a pension. Healthy enough not to have been bothered yet, apparently, to register with a local NHS practice.

Rich enough to go to a casino at least three times a week.

With a house so right for Frankie that it almost *sang* to her. *Gottahavit*.

An elegant, grey stone house on Winder Hill in Rottingdean.

A house with a conservatory.

Not that Frankie has ever thought of herself as a conservatory type of person – but then again, she wouldn't have said that Roz Bailey was, either. Conservatories, to Frankie's mind, are for pensioners with money to spare and too tired to take holidays.

But this particular conservatory had a suspended floor.

With space beneath.

And a trapdoor – neatly cut in the tiles and covered with a rug (white, with just a touch of navy to blend with the rest) and one of the cane and chintz armchairs – to allow access to the pipes and cabling.

Quite a lot of space. Frankie had been down there more than once, to clean.

'No need to clean down there, surely,' Roz said.

'All part of the house,' Frankie said. 'No use being clean above the floor if you're filthy underneath.'

Roz smiled, said she supposed not, let Frankie do what she wanted.

More than enough space.

*

28

She knew that Roz was *it* right away, but she still made herself wait till she could be absolutely sure.

Absolutely safe.

She was going to live here, after all, make this her house, her new life, was going to take over as much of Roz Bailey's world as was practical – though not her actual identity; Frankie knew that was an impossibility, but still, she couldn't afford to take any more risks than were unavoidable.

In five months of waiting, biding her time, nothing changed her mind. Twice a week, on Mondays and Wednesdays through late autumn and winter, Frankie arrived, in the aged silver Fiesta she'd bought after first devising her plan, at the house at the top of Winder Illll, early enough to have time to herself downstairs while the lady in question was still dead to the world from chucking chips onto tables at the Lansdowne. Time to sift through papers in the writing desk and filing cabinet, to log onto the computer in Mrs Bailey's little MFI study (Frankie wasn't keen on MFI, but she didn't suppose she'd ever be spending that much time in there), confident that if, by any chance, the other woman did wake and wander to the loo, Frankie would – having very acute hearing – hear her.

The confidence, in general, stayed with her, grew as time went on, made her increasingly certain that Mrs B really was the perfect candidate, the ideal target. A woman who would not be especially missed by anyone. A woman who had few visitors, who rarely seemed to be invited anywhere. Who appeared to have no dealings with the DSS or even the Inland Revenue.

Frankie had nailed that last certainty down more firmly a couple of months back, telling Roz, over one of their Monday coffees, that she'd spent the weekend struggling with a long-overdue tax return.

'Do you do those?' Roz Bailey sounded surprised.

'Doesn't everyone?' Frankie said.

'Not everyone.' Roz lifted her eyebrows wryly, almost archly.

Even better than that was the fact that Roz had told Frankie she had recently started using her computer for banking, was even paying her Council Tax via the Internet.

'Don't like writing cheques,' she said, 'and I can't stand queuing – certainly not when all I want's my own money.'

'Computer doesn't give you cash, though, does it,' Frankie said.

'No, but you still don't have to queue,' Roz told her. 'Card in the hole-in-the-wall, and bingo.'

Frankie grinned. 'I saw an advert once that said you can play that on the computer too; bingo and all kinds of gambling.'

'I've not quite sunk to that temptation.' Roz smiled. 'Yet.'

Roz never logged onto her banking websites when Frankie was cleaning in the study, but Frankie knew where the other woman hid the little book that held all her passwords, codes and answers to security questions; and in any case, her memory was pretty good when it came to that kind of thing, so even if the book was moved, she'd probably still be okay.

Not that it would occur to Roz Bailey that her cleaner would know how to use a PC. But Frankie did know enough, had learned a bit about computers as part of her rehab when she'd had her trouble and been in the *place*, and most of her Chigwell houses had them, either in the kids' rooms or the husbands' studies, and the office people at Calloway's were always leaving theirs switched on after hours. And anyway, even if Mrs B was careful about accessing her bank and building society when Frankie was dusting around her, she sometimes logged on for shopping while she was in the room.

So. No tax or VAT. A building society with over seventy grand in it and a bank account with just over thirty – and no problems tapping into either of those in the future, so long as she doesn't go over any limits, because the pin numbers for the holes-in-the-wall were written in the little book too. Though Frankie's pretty sure that Roz keeps most of her cash in the safe in the bedroom wardrobe nearest to the window, because once while Frankie was there, Roz disappeared into that room empty-handed and came out with enough cash to pay the gardener after he bought a load of bedding plants; and another time, when she asked Frankie to do more than the usual amount of shopping for her, Roz did the same, went into the bedroom, closed the door, then reappeared with a big wad of notes, gave her thirty and stuck the rest in her handbag.

Winnings, perhaps, in the safe, or maybe something dodgier.

Still, nice to have access to the kosher stuff, too.

'Never disclose your PIN or write it down,' the banks and building societies and credit companies were always telling people, and if Frankie ever has her own PIN in the future, she won't do either. But then she's not an ever-so-slightly scatty gambler, like Roz Bailey.

Though there must, certainly, be a touch of gambler about her,

30

or else she wouldn't be taking this kind of chance. However much she checks, goes through the plan, over and over again, it's still a risk, after all.

But Frankie's not scatty.

Scatty doesn't go with her condition.

OCD. Obsessive-compulsive disorder.

The opposite, she supposes, of scatty.

Her greatest dilemma during the long period of planning was deciding how best to deal with the body.

Not the first killer with that problem, obviously, but that was no consolation to Frankie as she fretted over it. Not a lot of murderers, she supposes, with her particular personal problems unless obsessive-compulsive disorder's one of those conditions that the police look for when they're investigating murders, maybe OCD's actually on a list of 'symptoms', like 'from a broken home'.

Frankie doesn't come from a broken home. Not one that broke when she was a child, anyway, though it's certainly been broken for a bloody long time now, in that her mum and dad pissed off together to Spain at least partly because they wanted to get away from her.

'Can't take any more,' she remembers hearing her mother, Angela, say more than once.

Of *her*, was what she meant.

'Sandwich short of a picnic,' was Tim Barnes's favourite.

Not an original man, her dad.

He was right, mind, she knew that.

Still, no real tragedies in her childhood to explain *this*. No deprivation to speak of. No abuse. She wasn't bullied at home in the ordinary, but in no way dreadful, semi in Clayhall, or at St Agnes School, or anywhere else, come to that; she made friends quite easily, was not the type of person anyone might have referred to as a 'loner'.

Not back then, anyway.

Hard to say exactly when she started being obsessive-compulsive. She thinks it may have been around the time when her periods began, but she's not sure because she didn't realise back then that there was anything odd about liking to be clean, or wanting things to be in their proper place. She knew she was different, perhaps, from a lot of her friends; very different, certainly, from her own

31

mum, to whom hygiene was an alien concept. Not that Frankie can remember really suffering because of that, either, doesn't think she ever caught anything nasty off Angela's mess, though she *was* embarrassed to ask friends home, and maybe because of that she wasn't asked back as often as other girls, but that was no big deal, she didn't really mind.

It all started getting out of control in her mid-teens. The washing and the cleaning and the rows with her parents.

'You're off your head,' her father told her.

'Why?' Frankie answered him back. 'Cos I like things clean?'

'You've certainly got a bloody cheek,' her mother said, 'expecting us to change our habits just because you've got this weird thing about *cleanliness*.' She wrinkled her nose as she said the word, as if it had a stink of its own.

'Better not get godliness too,' Tim Barnes said to his wife. 'Or she can effing leave home right now.'

Whether or not puberty actually kicked off her OCD, periods were a nightmare for Frankie, making her endlessly thankful in later years when she got her change so early. She hardly ever went to school when she was menstruating because she couldn't bear not being able to take a shower every hour. Angela tried to stop that at home too by turning off the hot water, but Frankie just went ahead and showered in cold, and having to use the hand shower in the bath took longer than if they'd had a stand-up one, and the cold water made her gasp sometimes. And in the end her dad, finding it all too much for him, put a padlock on the bathroom door, and Frankie went berserk for a while, and she certainly called *that* abuse at the time, but looking back years later, she supposes they just didn't know what else they could do.

Getting back to Roz, there was never any doubt in Frankie's mind that disposing of a corpse was going to be more of a problem for her than for most. Which was why she went for the crushed diazepam and the plastic bag; she knew about that because someone in the psych unit – the *place* – killed herself that way, got hold of a polythene bag somewhere and hid it, then put it over her head and tied it really tight around her neck late one night, and that was that. Maybe it was horrible for that poor woman, maybe she freaked at the last minute, maybe when it was too late; Frankie has no way of knowing, but at least in Roz's case, she was already out of it because of the pills, so there was none of that, no fear, no panic, just a change in her colour, on her face and lips, and, of course, the breathing stopping.

Everything stopping.

Preparation is everything. Frankie remembers a teacher at St Agnes once saying that about some exam or other, not that she paid much attention at the time. She was right, though, the teacher, she accepts that now, certainly when it came to something like this.

Body disposal.

When her own time comes, Frankie wants to be cremated, but she can't, of course, burn Roz, so she's doing the very best she can, and God knows she's gone to a lot of trouble and expense to get it organised.

The burial space, at least, is free.

Which is more than can be said for the coffin.

She found out most of what she needed to on another computer in an Internet café in Southampton, found a website about alternative and DIY funerals, but most of those seemed to be about the 'green' kind, with cardboard coffins you could bury in the middle of a wood, which was the opposite of what Frankie needed. And there were a lot of people who made what she *did* want, but they would only deliver to funeral homes and undertakers, and it took no end of time and perseverance till she learned that what she needed really *was* available, at a price.

If she'd been able to use a credit card and give an address, she could have bought her coffin over the Internet from America for about fifteen hundred dollars. But of course she couldn't do that, and then there was the confusion about exactly what she needed, and she knew she wanted steel rather than wood, and she thought that a gasket meant more or less the same as 'hermetically sealed', but she wasn't sure, and she began to despair at one point and almost jacked it in. But then she found a firm near Gloucester, gave them her by then well-rehearsed speech about the old family vault and falling on hard times and needing to stick with tradition but having to cut costs, and having used steel for some time, and obviously in a vault it was important to have really good sealing, but all at the best price possible.

'Leave it to us,' they said, and were so polite and kind, except, for a short while, when Frankie told them she wanted to come and pick it up herself; but in the end they gave in on that, too, said they presumed she realised she'd need a van or a really big estate car.

'Of course,' Frankie said.

Nearly three thousand pounds in the end, a real choker. Most of her savings, and even though she knew she would soon have a new supply of cash, it still rankled.

Not that three grand was much compared to the price of any house, let alone Roz Bailey's lovely, *lovely* house.

Gottahavit.

Not Roz's house any more now, at least not in any way that counts. Still Roz Bailey's house according to the deeds, that kind of thing, but that's just paper.

Frankie's house now.

One week since she rented the van – more cash – in Gloucester itself, picked up the coffin, and that made her shudder a bit, seeing it being loaded, even in its wrapping, but still she could see it was the business, would *do* the business when the time came for her to drag it out of the van and into the house.

That time's here now.

After dark, and she's driven the van over from where it's been parked near her lodgings over in Lancing (another poky room rented for cash – the last of those, thanks to Roz), and this is the riskiest moment, potentially, because there's no entrance to the house from the garage, so no point driving the van in there, and Frankie's decided to back up the van as close to the garden gate as she can get it, and take the coffin in through the gate, between the privet hedges and into the house through the glass conservatory doors. And all things being equal, it should be okay, there should be no one to notice her heaving a coffin around because the house is at the top of the hill, and Mrs Osborne, Roz's nearest neighbour, lives quite a way down, with a line of those big tall trees – the ones people sometimes complain about – bordering her property, making the Osborne house almost invisible from Roz's.

Private.

The more private, the better, so far as Frankie's concerned.

Still, it is a coffin, and even in its wrapping, it *looks* like a fucking coffin.

Preparation is everything.

Frankie found a portable platform – like the pallets they used at

34

Calloway's – last month at a DIY near Southwick, and she had the lads at the firm in Gloucester load the coffin straight onto that, and there's a ramp, too, to make dragging the thing out of the van and into the garden a bit less of a nightmare. And thank Christ for the years of cleaning, all that bloody good exercise.

'Tough for a little one,' Bo remarked once, in their early days, watching her lifting the corner of a sofa as if it were nothing. He often called her 'titch' back then, or 'little babe', which she loved because it made her feel feminine, though she knew she was no oil painting and, of course, anyone was 'little' compared to Bo.

No one watching her now, thankfully.

And there it is, Roz's coffin, already safely in the garden, shielded from view by the hedges and the darkness, and any minute now she'll have it through the glass doors and inside the conservatory, and after that she'll move the van into the garage. And then it'll be a matter of moving the armchair and the rug to get to the trapdoor, taking off the wrapping, turning the steel contraption on its side to superglue the set of casters (also from the DIY) to its base (because there's no way the pallet will fit through the trapdoor) and waiting for the glue to dry.

Dry now.

'Okay,' Frankie says, takes a deep breath, turns the coffin right way up.

Says a quick, catch-all *'help me'* prayer to anyone who may be listening who may not yet have given up on her entirely. She says things like 'Christ knows', or 'thank God', same as everyone, but never any of the mumbo-jumbo they tried to ram down her throat at St Agnes, and she thinks, vaguely, that there may have been a time in her childhood when she believed, but whatever that faith was it's long gone.

Now's when she'll find out how clever a poor cow she really is.

Another breath, and she slides the coffin on wheels over to the open trapdoor, then, without any more procrastination, begins easing it down through the square opening, hugging the terrible steel box with both arms as it starts to slip away from her, groaning with the effort, trying to keep a grip on it for as long as possible so it won't have too far to free-fall.

'Shit.'

It slides out of her arms, disappears into the dark, lands with a

35

deafening clang, and Frankie's ferociously glad it's steel, hopes the casters haven't come unstuck.

Lowers herself through after it, into the underfloor space, gets down on her knees, takes a torch from her pocket and has a look.

One of the casters is loose, but the others are solid.

More important, her measurements are spot on. Plenty of room for her to push the thing into the far corner, as far from the hot water pipe as possible.

Plenty of space to raise the lid.

It's the rest of the process that's been keeping her awake nights.

What comes next.

Climbing back up through the trapdoor, turning, finally, to the thing she has resolutely avoided looking at through all this.

Not a *thing*.

Roz is still in her chair, almost entirely covered with a blanket, only her slippers and the fingertips of one hand visible.

Moving Roz is what comes next.

Now.

Taking the plastic bag off first, because otherwise, when she thinks about Roz in the future, which she hopes she won't do too much, but if she *does*, she'll picture her with the bag still over her head and tied round her neck, and that's too ugly a thought, so, horrible as it is, that's got to be the first thing.

Then she'll move her.

Frankie's been saving her pills for weeks in preparation, cutting down on her regular dosage, and she knows that's bad for her, asking for trouble, but unless she takes precautions and ups her medication now, there's no knowing what kind of a panic attack might hit her, and God knows she can't afford to freak out all the way.

No doctors for her now, no shrinks, not for a long, long time.

Not till this is all finished and she's had a chance to recover, get over what she's done, start really taking root in her new home, new life.

But first, she has to move Roz.

Not really Roz any more.

Remember that.

Hold on to that.

And as she begins the worst part, the *very* worst part, whether it's the medication working, or perhaps an actual element of her

36

OCD, a compulsion to make it all perfect, or whether it's just pure luck, it isn't quite as terrible as she feared it would be. She doesn't feel too bad, she feels quite calm.

Strong enough to get the job done.

Finished, all except the return of the van, which will be done after she's cleansed herself and then, finally, rested.

Bo would be proud of you, she tells herself much later, after her fifth shower, when the hot water's run out and she's too spent to go on, when she stumbles into bed – Roz's bed, hers now, made earlier with new sheets, her own sheets, mattress vacuumed and vacuumed – and she's way beyond spent, she's wrecked, her back and shoulders in flames with pain, all of her body, all of her mind, exhausted

That's a bloody lie.

Mind still working sufficiently to tell her that.

Bo would be horrified by what she's done, would punish her for it.

But Bo's not here, Frankie reminds herself.

So it doesn't matter.

Chapter 9

Alex noticed him right away.

Standing by the lift on the ground floor of the Barry Building at the Royal Sussex County Hospital.

Something about him. Not just his looks, though that was part of it, undeniably, and she asked herself right away, quite sharply, if something other than his dark brown hair had simply reminded her of Matt.

No. This man, in jeans and an old brown leather jacket, was slim, too, but stronger-looking than Matt, too physically compact to call rugged, though his small but slightly crooked nose and uneven features brought a lightweight boxer to mind.

Not tough though, definitely not tough.

But there was something.

Special.

He turned, saw her looking at him.

Smiled at her. Nice smile, good lines around the brown eyes.

And suddenly, for just a second or two, Alex was eleven again, and she wanted to walk away, was sure he must see what she was feeling, but couldn't seem to move.

And then the lift doors opened and he stepped inside, and other people entered after him, layers of strangers filling the lift, making him disappear.

And Alex realised that she had been holding her breath.

Chapter 10

Frankie was made for this

Made for it.

There's so much to do. It's unending, it will never be done, never be finished. Roz is out of sight – though she doesn't want to think about that – and the van has been returned to Gloucester. But even when every trace, every invisible microbe, every speck of Roz and of Roz's leaving is eradicated, there will be dust and new germs and grease and crumbs and dirt from her own shoes when she's been outside, and it will go on and on.

And Frankie loves it.

She's conscious, now and again, of letting it fill her, fill every nook and cranny of her *self*; knows that there's a risk, a real danger, of it taking her over again. Her trouble.

It's never forgotten, just shoved into the back of her mind, stuffed in bin bags in spaces in her head, messily, muckily, the way Frankie would never dream of storing anything. But at times like this – not that there's ever been a time quite like this, as shockingly *wonderful* as this – when she knows she's taking big chances, the bags split and *it* leaks out, the memory of it all.

The shrinks and the shitty nurses and the unit itself, the *place*.

Bo.

Not now. Don't ruin this now.

She brings herself back from the brink, takes pains to balance her medication, tells herself she can be normal and still do what she loves.

Cleaning her place. Her very own, beautiful house. Keeping her lovely three-piece suite – grey with white piping, but a really soft kind of grey, not the cold, clinical kind you sometimes see – as

39

dust- and mite-free as humanly possible, using whichever of her various sets of bristle and extra-gentle brushes is appropriate to get into every crevice of every ornament and to tenderly care for each painting – including her favourite, the clever little miniature of the house that Roz commissioned a few years before, and which hangs in her bedroom – *my bedroom*. Generally cleaning and scrubbing and dusting and polishing and disinfecting and wiping and mopping, and cleaning and scrubbing and dusting and . . .

On and on. Spring-cleaning with a vengeance.

Thank you, Roz.

Chapter 11

It was a source of slight surprise to Jude that, even after Earl had been transferred from the Royal Sussex ICU to the Hove Neurological and Rehabilitation Centre, he had continued to spend so much time visiting him.

'I'm so grateful to you,' Ray Cobbins kept telling him. 'So glad my son has a good friend like you.'

It embarrassed Jude when he said things like that, though he had let the poor man know at the outset that he was just a workmate, but then again, Jude didn't want to rub in the fact that Earl didn't appear to have any real friends. According to one of the nurses at the Centre, no one except Ray and Jude and Ron Clark and two of the guys from the Luddesdown site had been to see Earl since his admission – and the two blokes only came once, out of pity and, Jude suspected, a kind of superstition. A *'there but for the grace'* kind of thing.

'Good job he's got you,' that nurse had said.

'I only look in now and then,' Jude said.

'Bit more than that,' the nurse said.

It had occurred to Jude then, suddenly, that if she thought that, maybe Ray might be thinking he was going to be there for Earl when, eventually, he got out of hospital, maybe even as some kind of carer.

'I really am just a workmate,' he told the ward manager next time he went to the Centre. 'Couple of beers after a long day and that's it, I'm afraid.'

'You a builder then?' The manager looked surprised.

People often appeared surprised when Jude told them what he did for a living, often said – unless he was in overalls or a hard

41

hat or covered in grime – that he didn't look like a builder. He knew what they meant, he supposed; that he didn't seem the 'kind' of man to be a labourer, but he also knew that was crap, knew there were as many reasons for people entering the building trade as there were for them becoming nurses or ward managers in neurological and rehabilitation centres.

In Jude's case, becoming a builder, he often thought, had saved him.

He had been twelve, living in Haywards Heath with his family, when Scott had died and their mum had hanged herself. Four-year-old Scott, his half-brother by Steve Ritchie, the man Carol Brown had married when Jude was six – Jude's own father, Billy Brown, having pissed off a week after Jude's birth because, according to Carol, they'd been having a row over his name.

Jude the Obscure was one of the few books Carol had really loved at school, and she'd carried the name somewhere inside her mind from then on, just waiting for the chance to give it to her own child. Billy hadn't heard of the book, and the name, so far as he was concerned, was short for Judas, and he was fed up with Carol's moods – Carol admitted she'd been moody through her pregnancy – and with marriage in general.

'He'd been looking for a way out for a long time,' she had told Jude when he was nine or ten, 'but he didn't think it was right to go while I was pregnant, but then the row about your name got out of hand, and that was that.'

'Couldn't you just have called me something else?' Jude had asked her then.

'Why?' Carol had looked upset. 'Don't you like it either?'

'Course I like it,' Jude had said, because he hated it when his mum got upset, though he couldn't help thinking that he might have liked having a father – his own real father – even more.

Then again, given that Billy Brown had never once got in touch with him, had never sent so much as a birthday card, and given that he knew how hard his mother had always tried to give him a happy life, maybe, he accepted, they were better off as they were. And even after she'd married Steve Ritchie, who Jude had never really much liked, but who had seemed to love Carol, life had stayed pretty good at home, especially after Scott was born, his very own baby brother.

*

42

Jude remembered half hoping that Billy Brown might show up for his mother's and Scott's double funeral, but not only did Billy not appear, but Steve Ritchie – who had scarcely said a word to his stepson since Scott's death – had chosen the morning of his last visit to the undertakers to take Jude along and to insist he bid Carol and Scott a final farewell on his own.

Alone, with the two open coffins, one larger than the other.

'Don't leave me,' Jude had said, dizzy with horror and grief.

'Why not?' Ritchie had asked. 'Too much for you, boy?'

Jude hadn't answered, had just stared at his stepfather.

'Just a bit –' Ritchie's blue eyes had been cold with hate '– just a tiny *bit* of what you deserve, you stupid little bastard.'

'What for?' Jude had been filled with utter confusion.

'What for?' Ritchie had echoed. 'For making this happen, that's what for.'

Jude had been mute again.

'Always jabbering on in the car, *always*, and I told you and told you to shut up, told you that drivers had to concentrate, and you knew your mum wasn't the greatest driver in the world, but you just can't help yourself, can you? You have to be the centre of attention, don't you?'

It wasn't true, Jude knew it wasn't true, *thought* it wasn't, prayed it wasn't, but maybe it was, and he had stood there in that terrible room, trying to think back, trying *not* to, hardly able to look at his stepfather's reddening eyes and white, angry, grief-shattered face, not knowing where else he could bear to look; but there wasn't anywhere or anything that was bearable, so he shut his eyes, covered them with his hands.

'And I hope you're well chuffed with yourself now –' Ritchie had gone on, unable to stop, letting the words spray out of his mouth like hot lava, not caring what effect they might be having on the boy before him '– now you've done *this* to my wife and my boy.'

He had grabbed at Jude's hands, wrenched them from his eyes.

'Look at them, boy. *Look* at what you've done to your mother and brother.'

Jude had looked towards the coffins.

'And just in case you've been hoping you still have a father after this,' Steve Ritchie had said, 'you'd better go and look for Billy Brown.'

43

And he had left him.

Jude had obeyed, had stood in the room, alone with Carol and Scott, trying, to begin with, not to look at them, but knowing that he had to.

And if he had thought he'd already experienced the two worst moments of his life, seeing Scott on the driveway straight after the accident and seeing his mother hanging in the garage, here was something even worse.

It's not them, he told himself. *Not really them.*

But it was, he knew that, it was all that was left of them. And soon the lids would be screwed onto those coffins, and he would always know for sure that they really were there in the boxes, really down in the earth, rotting away, and he didn't know how he would bear it, live with it.

Ritchie had said he'd made it happen.

'I didn't,' he said to his mother. 'Tell me I didn't.'

She looked like a life-sized doll in the box, her poor neck covered with the white frilly high collar of some kind of nightie that Jude didn't think she'd ever have chosen for herself, because Carol liked T-shirts and sometimes little short, really pretty nighties that showed off her arms and legs, and her . . .

'I'm sorry,' Jude told her.

He'd looked at Scott, but that had been even worse, because he was so much smaller, and because he looked so perfect, almost as if he were sleeping, but it wasn't real, he didn't *look* real, he looked like a ventriloquist's dummy, his little, sweet, dead face all waxen and . . .

'I wasn't talking,' he told his brother, and it was true, he hadn't been, but he had been in the car with their mother, and she had been talking to him, so in a way it was true, he supposed, because if he hadn't been there, she wouldn't have been talking, so maybe Steve was right.

'I'm sorry,' Jude whispered to Scott.

Who just lay there in his coffin, neither reproaching nor comforting, and Jude forced himself to look at the unnatural face, and then to look at his mother, and suddenly the unbearableness of it all roared up through his body, right through from his toes and fingertips up into his bowels and stomach and heart and throat and his head, and he gave a great cry of agony and ran to the door.

Tried to open it.

44

Found he could not.

And began to scream.

He'd slid downhill for a long time after that, had turned to drink early in his teens, and with no parental guidance to speak of – Ritchie having accepted he had no legal option but to provide his stepson with roof, food and education, but that was *it*, that was all, and that only till Jude was sixteen and he could sling him out – Jude had taken friendship where he could find it. He missed Carol and Scott more than he could say, missed family and normality and a clear, guilt-free heart and soul, and if the rougher tougher kids at school and in the arcades were willing to spend time with him, seemed even to like him, then that was some kind of balm for his appalling loneliness. And part of his mind – the part still surviving from *before*, the happy part, the free-and-easy part – warned him it was only a matter of time till he got into trouble, but the rest of it, the desperate, lost part, told him what the fuck would that matter, to him or anyone else? And he supposed, later, that the only thing that had stopped his situation getting even worse was that he would not, absolutely refused to, touch drugs, hated, instinctively, anything to do with them from the word go.

Still, bad enough with the boozing and nicking cars and joy-riding with his mates, all mindless stuff, no big deal; Jude telling himself he needed it to get over the anger and pain, not stopping, not back then at least, to register the fact that he was taking cars from people who'd worked hard for them. He refused to do any 'real' robbing, either from houses or shops or handbags, because that seemed wrong to him, but cars, he told himself, were just hunks of insured metal with no sentimental value or real individuality – and maybe, he reflected years later, whereas his stepfather, needing someone to blame for their tragedy, had chosen him, Jude had subconsciously pinned his own hatred on cars. But in the end, he and three of his pals crashed a stolen V8 Jag into the kitchen of a bungalow in Burgess Hill, and it was a miracle they didn't kill themselves let alone the toddler who'd been playing in the house just feet away; but Jude was the oldest member of his 'gang' and ought, therefore, to have known better, and though his plea to all charges was guilty and his attitude genuinely remorseful, he made the mistake of going to a pub for some Dutch courage on the way to court and overdid it; and it was not his first offence, and Steve

Ritchie had washed his hands of him, and so, all things considered, they made an example of him. And of course they were right to do so, Jude really believed that, and it came to him right there and then as he was being damned for all to hear, that he was letting his mum and baby brother down.

Letting himself down most of all.

Never again.

Really.

He stuck to that in the youth custody centre they sent him to, determined to find a way through his sentence and whatever came after, hoped to God he hadn't sunk so low that he couldn't manage it. It was a matter of getting on with it, one of the kinder officers had told him soon after his arrival, of keeping his head down, and making the most of the schemes on offer to give himself the best chance after release.

He'd always liked and been good at painting and sketching at school, used art in the custody centre to keep himself going in his darkest moments. But he knew he wasn't outstandingly talented, and even if he'd believed he was, he had too much commonsense to kid himself he could make a living by it.

'Maybe you could still paint,' his probation officer had suggested. 'Decorator by day, canvases or whatever by night.'

'Dunno,' Jude had said, not sure if he much fancied painting walls.

Building certainly had never appealed to him, and he'd picked gardening over construction inside, but then, one day in Lewes not long after his release, walking past a building site near his hostel, Jude had caught sight of a young man breaking up concrete with a sledgehammer. And maybe it was fanciful bollocks, or maybe it was his artist's eye, but there seemed a kind of actual joy in what the man was doing, in the sheer physical effort and power of it, and it looked like the kind of explosive release you experienced if you ran as fast as you could, too fast for too long, so that you had to stop or blow your heart and lungs.

Jude had stood for several minutes watching that man labouring, saw that there was a measured concentration about his work, that he'd probably practised long and hard to achieve that natural swing, to gauge what his body was capable of without collapse, and Jude found it enviable, found he wanted it for himself.

'Sounds like he was probably in demolition,' his probation

officer had remarked. 'I'd have you down as creating, not knocking down.'

'Yeah, whatever,' Jude had said, carelessly, but he'd gone back to the same site next day, had watched for a while longer, then gone to find the foreman and wangled his way into a hard hat and permission to observe at closer quarters and to chat to some of the blokes in their lunch hours.

Three years later, various apprenticeships and a clutch of City & Guilds qualifications under his belt, Jude had a job with a firm in Newhaven, and that in itself had thrilled him, the bonus of living and working near the sea. And it was all as he'd hoped, the blending of physical strength and skill and intelligence and steadiness and patience, and the comradeship, and the sense of achievement at a solid, visible job well done. And when it was over each evening, after a beer – two at the most, he'd learned his lesson – with the lads, he would go home to his bedsit and make himself a decent dinner and then paint or sketch till he was exhausted and ready for sleep.

All good things, brought to him via his new trade; even Paula, his wife, the daughter of Denis Lennon, the manager at the Newhaven firm. *All* good things, Jude had thought back then, content with his lot: love, a shared home life, work he enjoyed and a hobby he loved and from which he was beginning to derive extra income and a minor reputation.

He'd thought Paula felt the same way, at least about their marriage.

Fooled himself (he knew that now), sure that if she were unhappy or dissatisfied in any way she would have told him, been as honest with him as he always was with her. And she had told him, when it was too late, after she'd found her own personal satisfaction with Mike Norton, who ran his own company over in Seaford, and now Norton and Paula lived together there in the neat little detached job they'd been planning while she and Jude had still been married.

Paula the Obscure. Jude the Fool.

So here he was, alone again, though used to that by now, and pretty well-adjusted, he thought, hoped, with a good name in the trade he still enjoyed, living in his own small but wonderfully located Brighton flat, with just enough space to work at the rather delicate art he'd begun specializing in. He liked the town, liked the

47

sense of belonging in the buzzy place with its semi-gay, semi-conventional heart and its galleries and restaurants and cafés and myriad shops, and its overcrowded summers and emptier, almost but not quite desolate, wind-lashed winters. Like being at home in the district in general, liked sitting on the front at Hove, sketching the pale-green beach huts and passing the time of day with locals strolling by; liked going to the White Horse Hotel in Rottingdean for the Sunday carvery, or sometimes, on a Saturday, having a chat there in the bar with Johnnie Grey (who told good stories about when he used to play tenor sax for Ted Heath, and once did backing for The Beatles) and Mrs Sutton, who always came in with Gizmo, an elderly shih-tzu left to her, she said, by a local police inspector.

But if anyone understood about coping with loneliness, Jude did. Which was perhaps why he did keep going back to visit Earl, because he realized that nothing could be more isolating than the inability to communicate properly, and the Centre staff were great and Earl's dad's amazing, but Jude could see how tired poor Ray Cobbins was getting. And it wasn't that big a deal, just going to Hove when he had a little time to spare on a lovely spring evening or weekend afternoon, sitting and telling the guy stuff about the world waiting for him outside, after rehab, after he got his language skills and some kind of mobility back.

Least he could do.

Chapter 12

Her house is in order now, and will remain so, because Frankie will make sure of it.

She feels she has, in a sense, rescued it, the way people rescue cats and dogs that have been previously ill-treated. Before, in Roz's day, while Frankie was just the cleaner, allowed in twice a week to give it what Roz called the 'once-over', her role was painfully limited. Now that she's living here, the house is, at last, safe in her hands.

So Frankie can set about the next stage.

She's never much liked 'make-over' programmes on the telly, almost always thinks the victims look better before the so-called experts start interfering.

Frankie doesn't need anyone's help, she's always known how to dress, how to do her hair, to be 'chic'. Even Bo used to compliment her sometimes, and that was an achievement if anything was.

'Looking good, babe,' he'd say now and then, when she made a special effort, or even, more of a bloody miracle, when she didn't.

But then, after Bo, after her trouble, after she'd given up on everything, Frankie stopped caring about her appearance, and that was part of what her clients liked about her, she realized, her drabness. Just the cleaner, a nonentity, which was why, once she'd had the idea, she knew it would be easy enough to transform herself into a new woman, someone no one would recognise as plain old Frankie Barnes.

Not that anyone's even been to call at the house, not anyone who might remember, no one much at all, come to that. No one ever did call at Roz's front door when she was alive either except, in the early days of Frankie working for her, the milkman or

49

Deveson's, delivering fruit and veg, but Frankie took care of that by telling Roz it was more convenient for her to bring it all from Waitrose and M&S when she did the 'big' shopping runs for her in Western Road in Brighton.

'I never expected you to do my shopping,' Roz said, early on.

'I don't mind,' Frankie told her. 'I quite like it.'

Which was true, she did quite like it, so long as she went early, before it got crowded and too full of mothers of infectious children, and at least by going that bit further, sticking the Fiesta in the Churchill Square car park, she could be anonymous, keep to her rule of never going to the High Street in Rottingdean for anything unless it was absolutely vital, which, as it turned out, it never was.

So after that, it was only ever the postman who called at the house with an occasional package or packet too big to shove through the letter box, and meter readers, of course, and that was about it – apart from once, when Mrs Osborne from the house down the hill rang the bell because she'd received and opened one of Roz's letters by mistake and wanted to explain rather than just tape it up and push it in. Frankie was vacuuming and didn't hear the bell, so Roz went to answer it, and Frankie didn't realise, walked into the entrance hall with the Dyson, and Mrs Osborne saw her behind Roz; but that didn't worry Frankie too much because she saw the neighbour's face – all made-up as if she was off out somewhere special, too much powder blusher and mascara for delivering a letter – saw that she was wholly disinterested in her, and knew, with grateful bitterness, that the only time Mrs Osborne might show the slightest curiosity in her would be if her own daily abandoned her.

Plenty of time and space now for Frankie to get 'chic' again, the way she used to be. Only better, much, *much* better, because there's cash available now, and Roz doesn't need it any more.

Poor Roz.

Four feet under the conservatory, in her pricey coffin.

Don't think about that.

Frankie doesn't like thinking about it, she really doesn't.

She's pushed herself, sometimes – not often, it's not good for her to do it too often – to think not so much about *what* she's done, but about *why* she's done it. She's not too keen on thinking of herself as a bad person, and though there have been plenty of times

50

when she's been forced to recognise her psychiatric problems, she still doesn't think of herself as in any way mad either.

They write, sometimes, in the papers, about people being 'mad or bad'.

If she has to, she supposes, she'd rather settle for bad.

It wasn't jealousy, entirely, that made her do this, or even anger. It was, she feels, a great underlying and longstanding irritation about the uneven and unfair order of things that gave people like the Chigwell women and Roz Bailey – nice enough people in themselves – such beautiful houses, and Frankie Barnes the possibility of no more than a poxy council flat, and *that* only if she begged her way onto some housing list and gave a thousand details of her personal life and income.

It was that irritation that started her off, and the gradual awakening to the fact that, if she used all her energies, mental and physical – she could, perhaps, change that. That she could, she actually *could* shift the ground beneath Roz Bailey's world and her own just enough to tilt the balance, to slip Roz neatly underneath the house, and slip herself into it.

And once she knew she could, she had to do it. It became, like the other things she'd had to do in her life, had to have – *gottahavit* – a compulsion.

Simple, really. Before, it was all wrong. Now it's right.

Not for Roz, of course, but definitely right for Frankie.

Definitely.

Roz's clothes have never been on the agenda for Frankie. For one thing, Roz was bigger all over, for another, her colouring was totally different, and though Frankie never thought she had bad taste (no one with this house could be accused of that) and knew she spent money on her clothes, none of them were really Frankie's style – neither the old Frankie nor the new. And even if there were some she might have fancied, they'd all have to be cleaned again and again before Frankie could even consider putting them next to her skin, and *then* there's the risk – a tiny one, but a risk is a risk – that she might be out and about and bump into someone from the casino or maybe Roz's hairdresser in Brighton, who might just recognise a 'Roz outfit' and pause to take too good a look at Frankie.

So it's all new stuff now. No hardship there, except starting out,

51

because Frankie can't do her initial shopping locally because that would mean letting shop assistants see her as she is *now*, Frankie-the-cleaner, not Swanky-Frankie, as she's planning to be. Or maybe not exactly *swanky*, but classy. Definitely classy.

She starts off, in the end, going all the way to Bluewater in the first week of May for the basics: new knickers and bras and nighties and some decent T-shirts and jeans and loafers, just enough to get her going, plus a new haircut and highlights. No more nondescript mousy middle-of-the-road not-really-a-hairstyle; now Frankie has properly layered hair that glints in the light, the kind of style she used to admire when she worked in the salon, the kind that Jo-Jo, the best stylist there, did all the time, the kind that takes off years and turns her hazel eyes whisky-coloured.

'Wicked cut,' says the boy who takes her cash at the desk.

'Thank you,' says Frankie, amused by the word.

Wicked. Forget mad or bad, wicked's probably just right, and, apparently, a compliment these days.

Wicked.

The following week she goes even further, to London, leaves the Fiesta at home – *home*, she still can't get used to that word, the wonder of it – takes the train to Victoria and the tube to Oxford Circus, plumps for Debenhams first, then Selfridges, and walking in there out of the filth of Oxford Street is like escaping into a giant oasis, and she gets over feeling intimidated quite quickly, likes the sleekness of it, the way it at least *looks* clean, though she knows it's only surface-deep and the prices are enough to make her gasp.

You got it, Frankie, so spend it.

But coming back out is a nightmare, a horror of dirt and stink, and she can't face the tube again, that's too bad to even think about, it makes her shudder just to remember; so she takes a taxi back to Victoria, clutching her carrier bags, but all the same, by the time she gets back to the house on Winder Hill, she knows that even the brand-new clothes wrapped in fresh tissue inside the bags are going to have to be washed and dry-cleaned before she'll let them near her skin again. And she always wipes the soles of her shoes with Dettol when she enters the house and puts on her boil-washed cotton socks, but that's not enough after the West End, and it takes forty-eight solid hours of obsessive-compulsive overdrive

52

before she and the house feel clean enough, *safe* enough for her to pause for longer than a couple of hours' sleep.

All worthwhile though, in the end.

Old, mousy, invisible Frankie gone.

New Frankie here to stay.

Class act.

Worthy of the woman to whom Roz Bailey has entrusted the care of her home while she's away.

'Visiting her cousins,' Frankie says out loud in front of the mirror in Roz's bedroom – *her* bedroom – practising for when she has to say it for real. 'In Canada.'

Plausible.

'Oh, yes, didn't you know?'

Very calm and cool and more than plausible, especially coming from a stylish woman like her.

Swanky-Frankie.

Chapter 13

Alex was entering the day room at the Centre in the second week of May, about to meet Earl Cobbins, a new patient, when she saw the man again.

The one from the lift at the Royal Sussex. The one with the slightly beaten-up leather jacket and nice face. Wearing jeans again, with a navy guernsey, sitting chatting to Cobbins, who was in a wheelchair over by the windows.

The man looked up at her as she approached, then rose quickly, smiling.

'Small world,' he said.

His smile was warm – and *that* was it, Alex realised, that was what had taken her back last time, back to being eleven outside Croydon Grammar and getting her first glimpse of Matt. Instant warmth.

And he was attractive, too. Much less delicate than Matt, but . . .

Don't compare.

Alex reminded herself whom she had come to see.

'Mr Cobbins.' She put out her hand to shake his.

Left hand to his left, his working side for now, though Alex knew from his assessment reports that things were looking up for Earl Cobbins, that with effort and determination, there were real hopes for a good semi-recovery.

'I'm Alex Levin,' she said.

'Earl,' he responded.

The name emerged sounding more like 'Er', but it was a good start, and Alex was glad of it, accustomed by now to first encounters with patients too angry or miserable to want to even *try* with yet another stranger, who had, in some instances, already given up by the time she entered their lives.

'Glad to meet you, Earl,' she said. 'And please call me Alex.'

The man from the lift shifted awkwardly.

'I'd better go,' he said. 'Leave you to it.'

His accent was hard to place, London-ish, maybe, but his voice was pleasant and warm-toned.

Warm. That word again.

'Sorry,' Alex apologized for excluding him. 'But Earl and I are going to be a while getting to know each other, so it might be best.'

'Earl's very determined,' he said.

'Good,' Alex said. 'That makes two of us.'

He put out his right hand.

'I'm Jude Brown,' he said.

'Hello,' she said.

And Earl sang out, quite passably. 'Hey, Jude.'

'All the time,' Jude said with a grimace. 'Do me a favour and add a few more songs to his repertoire.'

'I'll do my best,' Alex said.

And that was that.

Except that later on that afternoon, something Suzy had said to her a few months back, when she was nagging at her to find someone new, came back to Alex, and then, after that, kept on coming back.

'Someone wonderful,' Suzy said.

And every time the phrase repeated itself in Alex's head for the rest of that day, and in the days that followed, she remembered Jude Brown.

And every time that happened, she told herself to get a grip.

Chapter 14

There's something wrong with the hot water.

Not with the boiler, which seems to be turning on and off at the preset times (so it's not the clock either), and heating up and making the right noises.

But the water isn't passing through Roz's pipe system – Frankie's system – as swiftly or smoothly as it ought to. As it was doing.

It could, Frankie supposes, be the pump, but she's looked at it, listened to it, felt it, and she thinks it's working, though then again she's no more an electrician than she is a plumber.

Of all the things to go wrong in her new house, this is the worst by far. Being the middle of May, it doesn't matter if she has heating or not, but without a plentiful supply of hot water, all her work will be ruined.

One germ becomes a thousand.

She doesn't want a plumber, doesn't want anyone coming in, so she goes to Roz's computer – her computer – and downloads all kinds of articles and advice pages on plumbing, pipework and heating systems. But even as she reads and stresses and goes on reading, she knows she's being foolish, knows it's pointless, because not only is plumbing dirty, unhygienic work, if she tries to tackle it herself she might make things worse, and then she'll really be lost.

A thousand germs become a million.

She needs a plumber.

There's a *Yellow Pages* in the hall cupboard which Frankie just stopped herself from throwing out in the big clean-up and which,

56

instead, she wiped and sprayed with disinfectant, then dried and wrapped in clear plastic.

So many plumbers in Brighton and Hove and beyond.

Everyone talks about the preciousness of good plumbers, don't they? How a trustworthy, competent plumber's even rarer than a decent, honest cleaner, but most people are only worrying about whether some cowboy's going to bugger up their system or charge an arm and a leg for doing not a lot.

Frankie's got bigger things to worry about.

But still, she *needs* a plumber.

Chapter 15

Jude was at the checkout in the cafeteria at the Centre paying for three coffees and two blueberry muffins when he saw her coming in.

Alex Levin.

Neat dark hair, boyishly cut and all the more feminine for it. Long-legged in narrow blue jeans, cornflower blue cotton sweater, pale blue tennis shoes. Small feet, dainty, like the rest of her.

Her eyes were blue.

Jude was stupidly but intensely glad they weren't grey.

Just because Paula's eyes were a quite beautiful grey, didn't mean he had to be prejudiced against all women with grey eyes, yet still he did feel glad.

Alex Levin smiled at him, and something dipped in his stomach. Excitement.

He took a breath and stepped out in front of her, not bothering to pretend that his interception was anything other than deliberate.

'Time for a coffee?'

Alex Levin glanced swiftly at her wristwatch, then smiled at him.

'I can grab a few minutes,' she said.

Jude looked down at his own tray, at the extra coffees and muffins.

'These are actually for Earl and his dad,' he said. 'So I can't be long either.'

Not that Ray, who regularly urged Jude to find a 'nice young woman', would mind. On the contrary.

Jude found a table while Alex bought herself an orange juice and joined him, and it was another brief encounter, yet by the end of it they were no longer strangers. Jude knew that Alex had lost her husband almost five years ago, but that Matt's sister, Suzy, was still her closest friend even though she lived in London, and that Suzy – or rather Suzy's speech therapist – was the reason Alex had chosen her career. And Alex knew that Jude was a divorced builder who had done time in his late teens for joy-riding.

'Do you always tell people that right away?' she asked.

'Not unless they're interviewing me for work,' Jude replied, 'and then only because I worry they'll find out anyway.'

'Why tell me?' Alex asked.

'Figured I'd get the bad stuff out of the way,' Jude said.

'Is that it?' she asked. 'All the bad stuff, I mean.'

'In a nutshell, yus,' Jude said. 'There's some sad stuff too, from way back, but yeah, that's the bad.' He paused. 'Any chance you'd consider having dinner with me sometime?'

Alex thought for a second, remembered what he'd done time for.

'So long as you let me drive,' she said.

'Quite respectable now,' he said. 'Second-hand Honda CR-V four-wheel drive, payments up to date.'

'Even so,' she said.

Chapter 16

Andy Swann, the plumber from Hove she found in the *Yellow Pages*, seems like a nice enough chap, Frankie thinks.

For a plumber.

For a man whose work is so essentially dirty.

He's small, shorter than her, in blue, well-pressed overalls, hair slicked down with gel, she supposes, though it looks to her more like that slimy Brilliantine actors used to put on their hair to make it shiny in old films, and the greasy look of it makes her feel uncomfortable, but still, she tells herself, he seems nice enough.

Not that *nice* matters.

Plumbing matters.

Hot water matters.

'Probably a blockage,' he says in a fussy, slightly high-pitched voice, standing beside her near the sink in the kitchen. 'Where, of course, is the big question?'

'Not too big, I hope,' Frankie says.

'Can't say, can I?' Swann says. 'Not till I've found it.' He smiles. 'Vicious circle, like so many things, Mrs Barnes.' He pauses. 'At least your floors aren't concrete. Should help a bit.'

'Good,' Frankie says.

She thinks he's waiting for her to offer him tea, but all she really wants to offer him, already, is the door, and she wanted to tell him to take off his shoes when he arrived, but the thought of his feet was even worse, and she's bloody certain that Swann's socks don't get boil-washed every day like hers do; and maybe she should have put down plastic on her floors, except that would spoil her lovely carpet, and anyway, she wasn't planning on visitors.

'So how,' she asks, 'exactly, would you go about finding it?'

'Pick a starting point,' Swann says, 'and hope for the best.'

'Not exactly scientific,' Frankie says.

'If it's the cost you're worrying about, I can assure you I'll do what I can to keep it down. I'm very good like that, Mrs Barnes, you can ask any of my other clients.'

'No need for that,' Frankie says.

'Some of these houses,' the plumber says, 'have trapdoor access to the pipes under the floorboards.'

Frankie's stomach turns over.

'I noticed,' Swann goes on, 'your conservatory.'

It's like a bad dream.

Should have known.

She supposes she did know, really, just didn't know what else to do.

'Very nice, if I may say so,' Swann says ingratiatingly, 'and an add-on, if I'm not mistaken. With one of those suspended floors?'

'I'm not sure,' Frankie says.

Wanting him out.

Needing him out.

'Only that means that part would be easiest to get to. And you never know, we might even get lucky, if the trouble's near there.'

'That would be good,' Frankie says. 'But you can't start now.'

'Why not?' Swann enquires.

'Because I have to go out. A relative's been taken ill.'

'I'm sorry to hear that.'

'Yes.' Frankie moves towards the kitchen door. 'So if you don't mind—'

'It's up to you, of course –' Swann follows reluctantly '– but while I'm here—'

'I have your call-out charge, obviously.' She prepared two plastic bags earlier, one with the minimum, the other with a hundred pounds, and now she removes the smaller one from her jeans back pocket, holds it out.

'Thank you, Mrs Barnes.' Swann takes it.

'Thirty-five pounds,' Frankie says. 'Count it if you like.'

'I'm sure it's fine, thank you,' the plumber says. 'But it's not just the money.' He glances back in the direction of the conservatory. 'Your problem might get worse if it's not dealt with.'

'It will be,' Frankie says. 'Dealt with.'

Her need to get him out is growing intense now.

'Only I can't always be available, obviously.'

'I wouldn't expect you to be.' She opens the front door.

'Though you can depend on my trying to come back, when it's more convenient for you, Mrs Barnes. I take a pride in my work.'

'Good,' Frankie says.

Stands back, watches as, given no further choice, he steps over the threshold.

Out of her house.

First thing, afterwards, Frankie has to clean.

Everything he's touched. *Everything*.

Several times.

No pleasure in it, just desperation.

Which makes her angry.

Which makes her clean more thoroughly.

Filthy, smarmy man.

Filthy.

And now she's perspiring, which means she has to shower again.

And again.

And again.

She's angry about the pipes too, about the blockage.

Angry with Roz for letting them get that way.

She goes into the conservatory, moves the chair and rug and opens the trapdoor – and oh, how she *hates* opening it, has been trying so hard to forget it – but she has to open it now, *has* to, just so she can tell Roz how angry she is with her.

'I'm glad now that you're dead,' she tells her.

She wasn't glad before, but now she is.

'You deserve to be dead for being so fucking careless.'

And now what? *Now* what's she meant to do? Go to fucking night school and learn plumbing?

And she's sweating again, which means another shower. Practically cold now, because the hot water's still fucking about, isn't it, but she has to have it, has to.

And another.

And another.

Chapter 17

Dinner at Quod in North Street in Brighton the Thursday after their meeting in the cafeteria, the effervescence of Festival time bubbling around them inside the restaurant as it had out on the streets, and Alex and Jude went on sharing with such uncommon ease that they both felt a similar sense of surprise and pleasure.

Sharing a Pizza Diavola and more of their histories, happy and sad, over a couple of glasses of red, talking and listening in equal parts, giving and receiving.

Liking each other.

Jude didn't linger over his tragedies but, knowing they were an essential part of him, finding he wanted Alex Levin to know all about him, he had to talk about Scott and Carol and his non-relationship with his stepfather. Even harder, he had to try to explain a little more about the personal inadequacies that had led him into youth custody.

What seemed remarkable, Alex said, was that he appeared to have emerged so intact.

'Are you?' she asked. 'As intact as you seem?'

'I think so,' Jude answered. 'So far as I can tell.'

'That which doesn't kill you makes you stronger,' Alex quoted wryly.

'I've heard that,' Jude said, 'but I don't know who said it.'

'Nietzche.'

'I'm impressed,' Jude said.

'Don't be.' Alex grinned. 'It was on a TV quiz show last week.'

'Do you believe it?' Jude asked. 'About suffering and strength?'

'Not really,' she answered. 'It's probably true in some cases, but on balance I'd say that people get on just fine without too much suffering.'

'People like Earl, you mean,' Jude said.

'And most of my patients,' Alex agreed.

'You've had your share, too.' Jude spoke quietly. 'Losing Matt, supporting his sister through all that horror.' He looked around the still busy place, realised he'd hardly been aware, for the past half hour or so, of their surroundings. 'Losing your restaurant must have been hard too.'

'It was,' she said. 'Change of life. Literally.'

'You never considered keeping it going?'

'Matt was Café Jardin.'

Her tone, as she spoke those simple words, was measured, but Alex knew from bitter experience that the jarring desolation of that period, long since tightly scrunched up and pushed to a dark corner of her mind, could still unfold without a second's notice, spring out and poleaxe her.

She waited now for that to happen, to destroy this new ease, but it did not.

'Are you all right?' Jude asked.

Alex heard his gentleness, looked into his eyes, knew the kindness was real.

Which made her happy.

They ordered desserts, vanilla panna cotta for her, tiramisu for him, shared those too, and Jude told her about the other part of his working life, as an artist.

'It helps balance me, I think,' he said. 'I suppose I became a builder originally because I thought it might help if I found a way to channel my emotions into something physically demanding but useful.'

'What are your paintings like?' Alex was intrigued.

Jude smiled. 'Always a hard one for me to answer.'

'Perhaps I could see for myself one day,' she said. 'If you wouldn't mind.'

'They're nothing special.'

'Special enough for people to want to buy,' Alex pointed out.

'A few. Occasionally.' Jude shrugged. 'They do seem to come from a totally different part of me; they're softer, a bit fragile. That's what I meant by balance: hard labour by day, sketching or painting by night.'

'Do you really think they're nothing special?'

He grinned. 'I think they're bloody fantastic.' He paused.

'Sometimes.'

'I really would like to see them,' Alex said.

'Tonight?' Jude asked.

Alex saw intensity in his eyes, found that she wanted, urgently, to say yes.

'Not tonight,' she said.

Chapter 18

Four days and two hours after his first visit, Andy Swann comes back.

Rings the bell.

Frankie, upstairs in Roz's – *her*, damn it – *her* bedroom, looks out of the window, sees the little white van with its blue sign on the side:

ANDY SWANN
Plumbing & Heating
No Job Too Small

She sees him get out, starts to back away, but it's too late because Swann has seen her, is waving at her.

Bloody little man. Bloody, *dirty* little man.

He waves again, mouthing something.

No choice now but to go down and open the door.

No damned *choice*.

'I've been worrying about your problem,' Swann tells her.

He's on the doorstep because Frankie hasn't invited him in.

'I'm like that,' he says. 'Can't help myself.'

'There's no need,' Frankie tells him, trying not to clench her fists.

'But there is, Mrs Barnes.' Swann flashes his ingratiating smile. 'More at stake than your blocked pipe, too, there's the question of the bad name some plumbers have given the whole trade. And as I think I already told you, I'm the type of chap who likes to see a job through to the end.'

Stupid, fucking, dirty, *conceited* little man.

'It's not convenient,' Frankie says.

'I don't need to do the job now,' Swann says. 'Just another quick look, just so we can see how bad things are.'

'There's no *need* –' Frankie stresses the word, suddenly inspired '– because I've had another plumber in.'

Disappointment turns Andy Swann's cheeks pink, but he stands his ground.

'Who?' he asks.

'Another firm,' Frankie answers, getting really pissed off now.

'Only I'd be interested to know,' Swann persists with something approaching stroppiness, 'because I was at one of our association functions just yesterday, and it so happens I was talking about your little difficulty, as we do. And I've been in the game for a long time, Mrs Barnes, so I know all the reputable people in the district, and if any of them had been called in by you, they'd have told me.'

Really pissed off now.

Pissed off enough to let him in.

Because she can tell he's the type of man who won't just go away. And if he really has already started talking about her and her 'difficulty', then if she's too unpleasant there's no knowing what he'll tell his mates next, and the last thing Frankie wants, the last thing Frankie can tolerate now, after all her work, all her planning, all her pain, is people *talking* . . .

'You'd better come in,' she says.

Chapter 19

As soon as Health and Safety had given the go-ahead for work to continue at the site in Luddesdown Terrace, Ron Clark had taken on a new roofer, who'd promptly come down with flu, and then one of the brickies and a painter had come down with the same bug, so now Clark had found another man, an all-rounder called Mike Bolin; a tall, broad, tough man in his thirties with curly dark hair and a handsome face, but with something behind his almost black eyes that was making a couple of the other blokes a bit edgy around him.

Jude liked, wherever possible, to refrain from making snap judgments.

'Nice tattoo,' he said, the first time he saw the small black rabbit on Bolin's right shoulder. He said it easily, genuinely, appreciative of the design, which seemed to him better than average, remembering some of the sickeningly careless tattoos that had branded some of his fellow inmates back in his teens.

'Know what it means?' Bolin barely glanced at Jude.

Jude shook his head.

'It's like a symbol,' Bolin said. 'Lot of tats mean something.'

Jude tried to think what rabbits might be symbolic of, could only think of fertility, thought better of saying so.

'Think of the March Hare,' the other man said, and walked away.

Chapter 20

Andy Swann claims that he can tell, right away, just turning on the hot tap in the kitchen, that Frankie hasn't called in another plumber.

'I'd know,' he says, 'if you had.'

'So can you fix this or not?' Frankie asks, trying to keep down her anger with this meek, crawly little plumber now turning into a real smartypants, a real nuisance.

A risk.

'Not without taking a proper look,' Swann says, with exaggerated patience.

More than a risk.

'Okay,' Frankie says. 'But not in the conservatory.'

Giving him another chance. To leave. Walk away.

'Why not?' Swann asks.

'Because like you said the other day –' now she's the one putting on the patient act '– it's all nice and new in there, and I don't want it messed with.'

'But you see,' Swann says, 'that's exactly *why* I want to start there, Mrs Barnes. Because I'll bet you that if we find any of those trapdoors I was talking about in the rest of the house, they'll be stuck fast – they usually are. And then you got to lever them open, and that does make a mess. But there'll be no need to force a nice new one, will there?'

Frankie can't think of an argument to that. Knows he's right, anyway, knows very well how easy the one in the conservatory is.

One more chance.

She takes a breath.

'Mr Swann,' she says, 'the fact is I've decided the problem isn't

69

that bad, after all, and I'm sorry you've had a wasted journey, but then again, I didn't ask you to come back, did I?'

'I couldn't help myself,' Swann says, smiling. 'It's in my nature to worry at things. I'm like a dog with a bone, worrying at it.'

Smarmy dog, Frankie thinks, with that slimy smile, as if what he's said is clever or even halfway original.

'So, Mrs Barnes, what's it to be?' he cajoles. 'Are you going to let me look, or are you going to wait till the problem's out of hand? Because if you do that, there's no guarantee you'll be able to get hold of me or anyone else when that happens.'

He sounds like a fucking dentist now.

Frankie hates dentists. *Hates* them.

'That's another thing about me, you see,' Swann goes on. 'I'll never walk out on a client once I've started a job, not even if the Queen herself were to call me to Buck House.'

Frankie would like to punch him in the mouth.

'All right,' she says instead. 'You win.'

She waits while he goes out to his van to get his tools, watches him, knows she could just shut the front door now, not let him in again, tell him she's changed her mind and he's to leave her alone, except then he'll whinge on about her to his mates.

Can't have that.

Can't.

So she keeps the door open, waits for him to get his bag and come back. And she takes a step back as he passes, and she knew, the other day, the first time he came, that he was dirty; it took her hours and hours to eradicate him, didn't it, and if she stops to think about where he's been, where he puts his hands, arms, what he crawls about in . . .

Not now, Frankie.

She pushes the dirt-thoughts away, reminds herself of how he's pissed her off with his pushiness and slimy manner.

He shouldn't have come back.

Shouldn't have told her that he talked about her to other people.

Shouldn't be walking through her house again now as if he owned it, tramping his dirt, his germs, over her beautiful grey hall carpet – and she should have put down plastic, *should* have – and now he's touching her door handle.

Asking for it.

70

'Let's take a look-see then,' he says.

Asking for it.

Frankie goes ahead of him into the conservatory, passing her lovely, tasteful furniture, the couch with its pretty cushions, shows him where the trapdoor is.

'You just need to move the chair and it's under the rug,' she says.

'Rightie-ho.' He looks round. 'Very nice.'

'Thank you,' Frankie says. 'I hope your hands are clean, Mr Swann.'

He holds them up for inspection. 'Do you, will they?'

Frankie nods, though it's hard for her, knowing that what a man like this thinks is clean is a million miles from . . .

Not now, Frankie.

She sees, suddenly, exactly how it's going to be.

Remembers the itch in her hand the day Roz died.

Her own restraint then.

The miniature scythe she was holding that morning – the blade she still uses regularly to whip off even the tiniest whisker of weed that dares protrude from between her Spanish tiles – is over in the corner beyond the orchids, close to the glass doors. In its stand beside the matching baby trowel, next to the watering can and Baby Bio spray.

Frankie remembers Roz looking at the scythe and frowning, saying she hoped Frankie hadn't scratched the stone.

That was when her hand itched.

Andy Swann has moved the cane chair, setting it well out of the way, handling it with care and respect, she'll say that for him.

'Don't you worry, Mrs Barnes,' he says.

'No,' she says. 'I won't.'

She moves past him as he's lifting the rug.

Goes to pick up the scythe.

Her hand's itching again.

There'll be blood.

Something inside her recoils, a great part of her, her stomach and her gut and all those other organs and messy things she can't bear to think about, sending awful, spreading, sick disgust through to her arms and legs, and for a moment she's jelly, weak and appalled.

71

But Andy Swann is already on his knees, looking at the trap-door.

Head bent.

Neck exposed.

Frankie thinks of a film she once saw, years ago, about Henry VIII and one of the wives he knocked off, she can't remember which one, never can, though she does remember the old 'divorced, beheaded, died' rhyme they all learned as kids.

There'll be blood, Frankie, you can't take blood.

Which is true, Christ help her, it's true.

But the coffin is down there, Roz is down there, and it's not just that Andy Swann will see it, it's that *she* might have to see it again, and Frankie doesn't want to even think about what's happened to Roz since *then*, let alone see it for herself.

Get ready.

The other part of Frankie Barnes strengthens, the tough part, the part that got her out of the unit, the *place*, after her trouble; the part that helped her survive after Bo, the part that gave her the idea and helped her organize it.

That helped her put Roz down there where no one would ever see her again.

Down *there*.

Andy Swann's neck is still exposed.

Frankie's always had a thing about visible veins and arteries, hates it when they stick out of people's necks and hands and temples or even foreheads, has to look away when they're too prominent.

The veins or arteries in Andy Swann's neck are not especially unsightly. But they are visible, are there.

Here and now.

And Frankie knows she has to do it.

Wants to do it.

'All right then,' Swann says.

Takes hold of the handle on the trapdoor, starts to open it.

Frankie has a memory flash, abruptly, of a school PE teacher telling her years and years ago during some kind of ball game that she had good hand-eye co-ordination.

The trapdoor's open.

Frankie feels dizzy, sick, feels pounding in her head.

'What have we here?' says Andy Swann.

72

Frankie grips the scythe tightly, gulps in a breath.

Swings it.

Swann gives a yell, claps his right hand to his neck, then pulls it away and stares, first at his palm, ruby wet, then up at Frankie.

The blade has sliced right into the side of his neck, right into whatever that most external bluish vein or artery is called, and Frankie's aim and the velocity and angling of her blow were all as unerring as if she'd been practising the move for months, as if she'd been trained by a fucking commando or something.

She's looking down at Swann now, but not really seeing the man, only seeing the blood, and oh, God, there's so *much* of it, pumping at first, like when they struck oil in Dallas, but this is red and warm and it *smells*, and there's so *much*, and oh, dear Jesus.

Andy Swann falls forward, topples from his already folded position, makes one more sound, a kind of gasp of pain and outrage and shock.

And becomes silent.

But even now, as he's lying there, his forehead jutting over the open hatch leading to Roz's burial place, the blood is still pouring out of his neck, spreading into a red pool around him, seeping down into the cracks between the tiles.

Frankie stands over him, the scythe still in her hand, trying not to scream or to be sick or faint or just go out of her mind, because the blood is on her too, on her *too*, on *her*.

While Andy Swann dies.

Messily, but quietly.

Chapter 21

Alex knew she'd fallen, was, at the very least, falling.

Jude was intruding on her thoughts many times each day. A welcome intrusion, yet still a little disconcerting because it had been so long.

No one since Matt. No one significant.

Five years.

'Long enough,' Suzy said when Alex told her, on the phone, about Jude, and asked her opinion. 'And it shouldn't matter what I think about him.'

'Probably not,' Alex agreed. 'Yet it does.'

'Okay.' Suzy paused. 'An ex-con builder.'

'And artist,' Alex added.

'Except you haven't seen his paintings.'

'Not yet.'

'Is he exhibited anywhere?' Suzy asked.

'Not at the moment,' Alex replied. 'Though he has been.'

'So you can't see his work without going to his place.'

'Correct.'

'Are you sure he was inside for joy-riding, nothing worse?'

'That's what he says.'

'Would you like me to ask David to check him out?'

'Absolutely not,' Alex said.

'So you do believe him?' Suzy asked.

'Yes,' Alex said. 'I do.'

'Then go for it,' Suzy told her. 'And if he tries anything on . . .'

'Yes?'

'Go for that too, kiddo,' Suzy said.

Chapter 22

Standing there, watching Swann die, the part of Frankie's brain
that's still in working order throws up the painting she's often
thought of when she's in the middle of a really big, major freak-
out. It's a picture of a bald, weird-looking person screaming, and
she thinks she saw it once, maybe on a poster, she can't remember where, but she felt like she was looking right inside her own
head, right at the ugliest, most messed up, most frightening part of
her mind. It's very famous, one of the shrinks at the unit told her
when she talked about it, a symbol of anguish, according to her,
and she's seen it on the news since then, the painting, because
someone nicked it, but it's been a long time since Frankie thought
about it, probably because her OCD was more under control. And
even when Roz died (that's how she chooses to think of it now, as
'Roz dying'), Frankie wasn't too bad, not *really* freaking out, just
cleaning and cleaning.

This is different.

This is very, very bad.

There's a pain, an actual pain, in her head, and she's never
known a headache like it, she doesn't often get headaches. But then
this isn't just a headache, this is much worse, and for a few
minutes it's so scary that it almost stops the rest of the freaking
out; almost, but not quite.

Then it recedes, becomes part of the rest of the horror.

She wants, needs, to rip off her clothes, everything down to her
panties, and run to the shower, scrub and scrub until *she* bleeds,
but she knows she can't do anything until Andy Swann has finished
dying, is entirely, completely gone.

She thought, a few minutes ago, that he was dead, but then she

75

saw a flicker of something under the skin on his left temple, and realised it was a pulse, and then *true* horror hit her, because what if he didn't die, what if she had to do something more, what if he suddenly moved, or got up, the way they do in horror films?

But he didn't.

And now, now, he is gone, really, truly.

Dead.

She tries reminding herself of how well she managed after Roz, but this is so different because Roz's dying was so clean and this is so terrible, so obscenely filthy, and what to do first, what to *do*? And the panic rises again, the painting in her head, and she is in the painting, and she may not be screaming out loud, but she is screaming inside, which is worse, much worse.

You first.

Still a bit of clarity left, a fragment of control.

Well done, Frankie.

She strips off her skirt and sweater, takes off her socks, and she can hardly bear to look at herself, but she manages to lift one foot at a time, forces herself to inspect the soles of her feet, and she knows the blood must be there, hiding under the skin, knows she'll have to scrub them raw later, but for now they *look* clean enough, so she can at least move, start to take care of things, do what she has to.

She walks on jelly legs to the kitchen, starts assembling what she needs, taking it through the hall into the conservatory. But it takes numerous journeys back and forth, because she's feeling very weak and keeps forgetting things, and she knows that will mean more cleaning later, because each journey is more footprints to eradicate, but she has to have everything: all the bin liners she can find, gloves, J-cloths, paper towels, disinfectant and detergents and buckets, two at a time, of hot, soapy water, and there is hot water for now, and when it stops again, becomes blocked again, she'll start boiling cold.

Looking down at Andy Swann, at the mess of his neck, the mess around him, Lady Macbeth slips into her mind, the bit everyone knows about the dead man having so much blood in him.

She wonders if any of Swann's blood has dripped down through the hatch, and just the idea of that, of having to cope with going down there again makes her feel so sick, but she knows she mustn't be sick, because that's even worse than blood to her . . .

Deep breaths.

There's blood on the grout between the tiles.

'No,' Frankie says out loud. 'No, no, no.'

If she doesn't clean that first, before anything, it'll get ingrained, and then she'll have to redo the grouting or even replace the tiles, and she'll never find the right ones, not exactly the same colour even if she can find the right shape. And that'll always show, always be there to remind her, and other people might notice, too, if she ever lets anyone else in again, that is. Because after this, after *this*, she'll be damned if she'll ever let anyone in again, doesn't matter who they are, doesn't matter if the plumbing clogs up completely or the electrics go or the ceilings fall down, no one's coming into her house again, no one . . .

Tiles first.

Then Swann's van, into the garage, worry about it later.

Then the rest.

Chapter 23

Jude couldn't recall when he'd last cleaned his flat this thoroughly, or last taken this long over deciding what to wear or which cologne, if any, was the right one, or what to cook for dinner.

Moussaka. Smelling pretty great, if he said so himself.

He'd almost backed off from cooking for her because there were so many great little places all around where they could eat far better, and certainly – especially during the Festival – more interesting food than he could provide; and because Alex's late husband had been such a terrific chef, which had started Jude worrying that she might think he was trying to compete or replace, neither of which was true because Jude knew there could be no future in that. Alex Levin and Jude Brown had to like each other just as they were, no frills.

She'd told him on the phone, when they'd arranged this evening, that she was looking forward to seeing his work.

'If you're sure you don't mind showing it to me,' she'd added.

'I'll only mind,' he said, 'if you hate it.'

'I can't imagine I will,' Alex said.

'You might,' Jude said. 'But you don't have to worry about telling me the truth. I'm tough enough to take it.'

Though, as a matter of fact, he could not remember ever caring this much about what any woman (not counting Eva Hauser, of course, when she and Ed were debating whether or not to include two of his paintings in their first exhibition at the E Gallery) thought of his work. Paula used to comment freely and frequently, whether he asked her to or not, and Jude never minded too much when she disliked a piece unless she was just pissed off with him and being a bitch, which didn't happen often, though then again he

78

never used to realise how much of the time Paula was pissed off with him during their marriage.

He did, however, feel as if he was going to care a good deal about whether or not Alex Levin liked his work.

She said that she couldn't wait till after dinner, though she did accept a glass of wine.

The flat was, essentially, one room plus a tiny kitchen area and bathroom, but the sleeping area was on a platform two steps up from the living section, and Jude had created a studio space at the window end, semi-partitioned from the rest by self-made white cotton, pine-framed screens.

Alex was very quiet for several minutes as she looked at the works on Jude's walls and those that he removed for her, one at a time, from racks and shelves; some canvases, some sketches in books, some carefully wrapped, rendered on fine linen.

Jude felt tension fill him till he was fit to burst.

'Well?' he asked finally.

She turned to him. 'How do you *do* that? How do you make them so fragile?'

The watercolours were ethereal, the acrylics looked to her as if they'd been embroidered in colourful silks, the pen and ink drawings spider's web-fine.

'I don't know exactly,' Jude said. 'I don't like to analyse it too much.' He paused. 'But it calms me when I need it, and excites me, too, sometimes.'

'I can understand that,' Alex said. 'I think.'

She remembered suddenly Matt saying that kneading dough often made him horny, and that making spun sugar desserts sometimes made him want to abandon the kitchen and make love to her.

And then she looked back at the paintings and drawings.

Back at Jude.

Saw the way he was looking at her, saw a tiny pulse in his right temple throb, betraying his tension, the fact that she mattered to him.

Put those older memories aside.

Their ease continued, became a strong, almost palpable source of elation to them both. While sounds of music and raised voices and laughter flowed up from Union Street and Meeting House Lane and

79

they sat at Jude's small table and shared his moussaka and more stories and their thoughts about news, politics, the world, while they offered their opinions and spoke about their work.

While they made love.

Alex had been afraid that she might, when the time came, find herself drawing comparisons with Matt, because on the few occasions she had slept with anyone since, she had done exactly that, even though there never had been any real comparison because the experiences had not really touched her, not where it mattered.

She had been afraid, too, that no man would ever touch her in that way again, never really move her again.

But Jude already had touched her, and now, this evening, lying with him in his little platform bedroom as they made love, Matt never entered her mind. He did creep in, briefly, poignantly, after the first time, while she was lying in Jude's arms, but that was only, Alex thought, because of the profound sense of relief she was experiencing at being able to feel again, care again.

'Don't you think, maybe,' Alex asked, a moment of caution urging her to hold back, 'we ought to take things slowly?'

'Bit late for that, isn't it?' Jude said.

'I'm talking about feelings,' she said, with an effort. 'Not just sex.'

'So am I,' Jude said.

Chapter 24

All done.

Andy Swann is resting beside Roz.

His van in the locked up garage, sprayed blue now, almost the same colour as the sign.

Words obliterated.

Like Swann.

No handsome, expensive steel coffin for him, just layers of heavy plastic bought together with the blue spray paint from a DIY near Lewes.

Unimaginable horror for Frankie, all of it, the worst ever.

Ever.

She upped the dosage again, right after Swann was dead, as soon as she felt clean enough to get to her stash, and it got her through, she supposes, though there's a long period of time she can't account for now, total blanks, dark pits of nothingness for which she is grateful.

She's lucky to have got away with playing such desperate juggling games with her anti-depressant, anti-obsessional tablets, she knows that. She remembers the soberness of the lecture when they released her from the unit, warning her about sticking to the prescribed dosage, about the perils of sudden, unmonitored withdrawal and of simply taking more than usual – all kinds of risks, from arrhythmias to full-blown heart attacks or stroke, about the more obvious life-threatening dangers of overdose.

But here Frankie still is, in her house.

Hanging on.

She suffered pain, of course, same as after Roz, physical pain from struggling to wrap the body, then heaving the monstrous dead weight down into the underfloor space, though Frankie's blocking the actual memory of that because it's too much, too *much*. There was pain, too, from the effort of cleaning, even more complicated than last time, because of the blood and because of having to boil water, over and over again, and all that must have gone on for at least five days and nights, because she knows Swann came back on a Monday, and turning on the TV for the first time since it happened, she sees it's Monday again, and she's not sure how long she spent in bed, recovering, but it was at least twenty-four hours, *must* have been.

Not that it matters.

What matters is that it's been a week, and no one has come looking for the plumber, and could she really be that lucky a second time? Could Andy Swann really have no one to miss him, no wife or mother or lover or colleague or friend?

The worst of the pain in her back and arms has receded, but Frankie's skin still hurts from scrubbing, her hands are red and rough and chapped, her nails are ragged and ugly. *She* is ugly, she sees that each time she passes a mirror, and she never realised before how many mirrors there are in Roz's house.

Her house.

Though even that is spoiled now.

Especially that.

The house, so hard won, will never be the same for Frankie again, will never feel right. And it isn't just that van, skulking bright blue in her garage, though she doesn't, she really *doesn't*, know what she's going to do with that. And it isn't even the memory of the blood, though that does still fill her head, splashes behind her eyes every time she closes them. But it isn't just that.

It's Andy Swann down there under the floor.

It was all right so long as Roz was alone, because it was all so planned and perfect, so clean and nice, such a respectful, expensive, guaranteed *sealed* coffin. The right thing, for both of them. Roz able to rest in peace, Frankie to sleep in peace.

Not any more.

All ruined now.

It's not just the filth of the man down there wrapped in those sheets of plastic, not *just* the decay, the corruption – though that is, of course, the very worst, the most unthinkable thing of all. But ever since Frankie came out of her dark blank pit, she has felt as if she were being watched.

82

As if Swann might not be dead after all, might be *watching* her.

She knows that's impossible, knows how very, very dead he is, but that knowledge doesn't seem to be good enough, and Frankie knows, too, that if she doesn't do something about it, find a solution, she'll lose it again, big time, *big* time.

There is only one solution.

Another house.

She'll have to keep this one, of course, have to keep it nice and clean, come to check up on it all the time, make sure everything's under control. But she'll have to find somewhere else for her real *home*, for her to sleep in, live in.

Only one way she knows how to do that.

Same way as before.

Frankie Barnes is going to have to go drab again.

Go cleaning again.

Start looking again.

Chapter 25

'Room for two not so little ones for a weekend soon?' Suzy asked Alex on the phone on the last Tuesday of May.

'Suzy, yes, please!' Pure gladness shot through Alex like a warming shot of brandy. 'When? Just give me a few days to make the place presentable, but please make it longer than a weekend, I want you to stay for a week or two at least.'

Suzy laughed. 'I don't think David could quite manage that.'

'Dump David,' Alex said.

'I'll think about it,' Suzy said.

'When pink elephants fly over Trafalgar Square,' Alex said.

They agreed that the Maynards would come the weekend after next, and Suzy was adamant that she wanted to sleep upstairs in Alex's spare room rather than on the sofa bed in the living room. Still in a wheelchair much of the time, she was adept, for relatively short distances, on crutches, and loathed stairlifts with a passion.

'Stairs are what bums were really made for,' she said.

It was only when Alex went to take a closer look at the spare room that she began to realise how badly she'd been letting things slide on the household front. The cottage was, not to put too fine a point on it, grubby, and with Suzy always a little more at risk than most from opportunistic infections, something drastic needed to be done.

Not enough hours in the day was generally her personal justification for not taking care of domestic chores. More important things to take care of: the patients, first and foremost, in-patients at the Centre for now, though she would, quite soon, be undertaking domiciliary work, visiting patients at home; but wherever the patients were, there was still a constant flood of paperwork and meetings.

And now there was Jude, too.

He said that, amongst other things, he liked her sense of priorities.

If she was honest, housework always had been pretty low down that list. Alex recalled Matt once saying it was a mercy they could afford staff to clean and organize the kitchen at Café Jardin, and she recalls, too, pointing out that it was his kitchen to clean, not hers, and that she was meticulous about other important things like keeping them in profit – and that anyway, when it came to tidying and cleaning up in the flat, Matt wasn't that much better than her.

Jude was a tidy man.

'Not deep down,' he'd said a while back, when she complimented him on the neatness of his home. 'My instinct is usually to let it all go hang, but living and working in a small space makes that a really bad idea.'

'I could live in a box or a castle,' Alex had said, without pride, 'and still be untidy.'

'I remember being a mucky kid,' Jude had told her. 'But then my stepfather used to get on my case when I left anything lying around, and then when I went inside, I really had no choice. And if things don't get put in the right places on building sites, it can cause all kinds of chaos.'

'It's okay.' Alex had smiled. 'No need to apologize for being tidy.'

'I don't know,' he had said. 'I rather like your mess.'

'Why?'

'Because it's relaxed,' Jude had said. 'And it's your clutter, so it tells me stuff about you.'

'It's not so much the clutter that's worrying me,' Alex had said, ruefully. 'It's the fact it's all getting a bit dirty.'

He offered, when Alex told him on the phone about Suzy's and David's impending visit, to help her clean up the cottage, but Alex wouldn't hear of it.

'You have little enough time as it is,' she said, 'between the site and painting and visiting Earl and boosting his dad.'

'Except there's nothing I like better than spending time with you, and if we spend some of it doing housework, that's fine with me.'

85

Alex said she could think of things she'd rather do with Jude.

'Anyway, I've already decided I'm just going to have to get someone in.'

'Good idea,' Jude agreed, 'if you won't let me help.'

'I've never done it before. It's never seemed quite right.'

'Paying someone else to clean up your dirt, you mean.'

'God,' Alex said. 'It sounds awful.'

'So long as you pay the going rate,' Jude teased, 'you can always hope the cleaner won't mind too much.'

'I'll have a good tidy before they come,' Alex said.

'Of course, Alex,' Jude said.

Chapter 26

The cottage in Woodingdean is far and away the winner, Frankie decides, at least on appearance. White-painted stone with low flint walls surrounding the small, slightly overgrown front garden, two rose bushes and an apple tree to the left of the pathway leading to the oak front door.

Much too near Rottingdean, of course.

Much.

But Frankie likes it, and though the address itself is Falmer Road, which leads all the way down through Ovingdean into Rottingdean, Melton Cottage is set well back off the road, fields to either side, and its nearest neighbour even further away than Mrs Osborne's house is from Roz's.

It's nowhere near as elegant as the house on Winder Hill, mind. Not remotely in the same league.

Yet, at least from the outside, Frankie really likes it.

It's got something special.

It looks cosy. Like a real home.

So, less than an hour after first seeing the card in the newsagent's window up in Downs Parade, Frankie's ringing the doorbell of Melton Cottage, and it's a real bell, which is nice, not one of those nasty fake chimes, and the woman opening the door looks nice enough too, quite young and attractive, though a bit scruffy, in need of a bit of a make-over, in Frankie's judgment.

'Mrs Levin?' Frankie says. 'I'm the cleaner.'

'Great,' Alex says and puts out her hand.

'At least –' Frankie shakes it, then slips her own hand into her jacket pocket, wipes it over the antiseptic wipe that's in there, ready and waiting '– I will be if you want me.'

Alex smiles, steps back to let her in.

'I'm afraid,' she says apologetically, 'you may decide it's a bit of a tall order.'

'Nothing I like more than a challenge,' Frankie tells her.

There's something really restful about Melton Cottage.

This woman's cottage.

Alex Levin.

Frankie thinks – as she's shown around the small, untidy, dirty home, and the other woman offers her tea or coffee and she says no thanks because she never lets an unclean cup touch her lips – that Levin is a Jewish name, and though she doesn't think Mrs Levin looks particularly Jewish, it wouldn't bother her if she did or if she was. She's never been like that, never been racist like Bo.

She prides herself on being good at interviews, has learned from experience how to get the upper hand, knowing that she has what most potential clients want from a cleaner. But still, there is one bad moment today when, after they sit down together in the sitting room (timber beams in here, same as in the pretty little kitchen, and a real fireplace too – extra work keeping those clean, Frankie knows that from experience, but well worth it when it's your *own*), Alex Levin mentions what she does for a living.

Some kind of therapist.

No, Frankie says in her head. *No, no, no.*

'Are you okay?' Alex Levin looks concerned.

Frankie pulls herself together, says that she's fine, makes herself ask:

'What kind of therapist did you say?'

'Speech and language,' Alex tells her.

Okay.

Frankie relaxes again.

'That must be interesting,' she says.

'It keeps me very busy,' Alex says. 'Which is my excuse for the place being such a tip.'

Full of germs.

'That's all right.' Frankie fingers the wipe in her pocket again, trying to remember if she's touched anything with her hands since they sat down.

'I was thinking,' Alex suggests, 'perhaps a real blitz, however long you think you'll need, and then after that, maybe one day a week?'

'Two,' Frankie says, 'would be better.'

She sees the other woman's doubtful expression.

'One day a week, you never really win,' she explains. 'All you end up doing, even if you're thorough, is moving dust from one bit to another.' She refrains from mentioning germs, knows people don't want to be reminded of the nasty things lurking in their homes. 'If it helps,' she adds, 'I could cut my hourly rate a bit.'

'I wouldn't want you to do that.'

Frankie sees from her expression that Alex Levin means that, and warms towards her.

And towards her house.

Frankie's dream cottage.

Gannahavh

Chapter 27

The following Saturday afternoon, as Alex and Jude were taking a stroll, hand-in-hand, along King's Road near the desolate-looking wreck that was all that now remained of the West Pier, a funeral procession passed by. Five black cars following the hearse, which gleamed in the sunlight, the pink and white rose wreaths on the mahogany coffin suggesting the departed as female.

Alex felt Jude's tension instantly, almost as sharp as the salt wind in her face, felt the sudden clenching of his hand before he pulled it away from hers.

'Jude?'

He'd gone quite pale, his jaw taut, and then, abruptly, he turned away, and it was another second or two before Alex realised that it wasn't her, but the hearse, on which he'd turned his back.

She gave him a moment, then tentatively took his hand again.

'Sorry,' Jude said.

'Don't be.' Alex looked around. 'Let's find somewhere to sit, get a coffee.'

'I'm okay,' he said.

'No, you're not.'

She encouraged him over the road and into the creamily graceful Grand Hotel.

'It's lovely inside, too,' she told him when he resisted out on the pavement. 'Calming, not stuffy or pompous at all.' They entered, walked up the steps and into the hall, passing the dark-grey marble pillars, two of which, Alex's mother had noticed when they'd come for tea, had been faked to match the two originals that had survived the infamous bomb of 1984.

90

By the time they were settled in two comfortable old armchairs in the Victoria Lounge and Alex had ordered coffee for herself and a Jamesons for Jude, his colour had returned to normal.

'I want to explain,' he said. 'But this seems too nice a place for an ugly story.'

'The place doesn't matter,' Alex said. 'Though it's up to you whether you explain or not.'

He waited for the coffee in her cafetiere to be ready for pouring before taking a swallow of his whisky and then telling her about being left alone by his stepfather with his mother's and brother's open coffins.

'Been a bit phobic ever since about coffins in general.'

'Hardly surprising,' Alex said, dismayed by Steve Adenic's cruelty.

'You'd be amazed just how many films and TV shows have coffins in them.' Jude was over it again now, his grin shamefaced. 'My reflexes are pretty good, though. Shutting my eyes is usually enough – I don't have to leap out of my seat.'

'But seeing the real thing's a bit much.'

He nodded. 'Extraordinary, really. Such power after so long.'

They sat in silence for a moment.

'What about you?' Jude asked. 'Any phobias? Or are you totally balanced?'

Alex smiled. 'I hope not.' She considered. 'I'm not great with enclosed spaces. Not a full-blown phobia, thankfully, but I have to push myself to get into crowded lifts, and I never use the tube in London if I can help it, and I still haven't been able to bring myself to use Eurostar, though I'd like to in a way.' She paused, then added: 'And you've probably noticed I leave doors open and I'm always opening windows whatever the weather.'

'I hadn't noticed,' Jude said. 'Or maybe I have, but I just assumed you like fresh air, and it suits me that you keep doors open because I'm not too keen on them being closed either.'

'The room at the undertakers,' Alex said.

Jude nodded, then picked up his glass, drained his whisky.

'You were right about this place,' he said. 'I'd like to come back here again, bring you for one of those big cream teas.' He looked around. 'Maybe even stay a night sometime, if you don't mind.'

'It's very expensive, I think,' Alex pointed out.

'Next time I sell a painting,' Jude said.

'I don't need that kind of thing,' Alex said, softly.

'Maybe not,' Jude said. 'But I like the idea of doing it for you.'

'We could do it,' Alex said. 'For us.'

Chapter 28

By three days prior to Suzy's and David's arrival, Melton Cottage, thanks to Frankie, was spotless; the little kitchen itself, the Aga, fridge and every pot, pan, coffee mug and visible piece of cutlery and crockery gleaming; the living room looking as much like a photograph in *House & Garden* as it ever could, and both bedrooms looking fit, Alex told Frankie, for royalty.

'Too good for that lot, if you ask me,' Frankie said. 'It's a lovely little house for real people. Shame to let it go to pot.'

'No chance of that,' Alex said, 'if you're prepared to carry on.'

'Twice a week?' Frankie asked.

Alex looked around. 'Can't imagine it's going to need that much time, not now.'

'Skin deep,' Frankie said. 'Dirt back in a flash if you open the door.'

'All right then.' Alex smiled. 'Twice a week.'

She had noted the signs of what she suspected was obsessive-compulsive disorder from Frankie's first day at the cottage. The cleaner's exaggerated meticulousness; the way she lined up, perfectly, the tools of her trade, from the bright-red Henry vacuum cleaner down to the cans of polish and bottles of disinfectant, each item returned to its position after every single use; the repetition of jobs, sometimes several times after the work had, to Alex's eyes, already been perfectly accomplished. More significantly and concerning, from Alex's point-of-view, was that hint of something passionate, even desperate, in Frankie's eyes as she scrubbed and swept and mopped and polished.

'Poor woman,' she'd said to Jude one evening, early on.

93

'OCD – if it is that – can be a real curse.'

'I know,' he said. 'I worked with a brickie for a while who had something like it, was totally obsessed with straight lines – and I'm not talking about the actual bricklaying, but everything, you name it. Used to count things, too, over and over again. Got the boot for wasting time and materials. Some of the blokes took the piss, but I could see how much it hurt.' He paused. 'Have you asked Frankie about it?'

'It's not really my place,' Alex said. 'I hardly know her, after all. And, I suppose, if she does have OCD, then at least she has it well enough under control to be able to do her job brilliantly and get some kind of satisfaction out of it.'

'But isn't that a bit like asking an alcoholic to do wine tasting?'

Alex winced at that. 'I might be wrong about this. I'm a speech and language therapist, not a psychiatrist.'

'Either way,' Jude said wryly, 'at least you've got a bloody good cleaner.'

Chapter 29

'I love it,' Alex said, first warm greetings over, about Suzy's hair, which was blonder than ever, shorter than her own, and spiked with some sort of gel.

'All part of her new girl racer image,' David said.

'Girl racer notwithstanding –' Alex turned straight to the subject still concerning her '– are you really sure about these stairs, Suzy? They're so narrow and quite steep.'

'She said you'd start as soon as we got here.' David grinned. 'She was laying odds you'd have bedding out for the sofa as well as upstairs, just in case.'

'Then she's lost her bet,' Alex said. 'But it only takes two minutes to make up if you change your mind,' she added to Suzy.

'I won't.' Suzy returned her attention to the ground floor of the cottage, wheeling herself first into the kitchen, then back out into the entrance hall, into the oak-beamed living room and out again. 'So where's the man?'

'If you mean Jude,' Alex said, 'he's at work.'

'Of course I mean Jude.' Suzy put the brakes on and started the process of getting out of her wheelchair.

'He couldn't get the time off.' Alex watched David, still slim and fit from daily gym sessions, ready with her crutches, giving her just the right amount of help, thinking, for at least the hundredth time, what a great team they were. 'He'll be here for dinner.'

'I should hope so.' Suzy, out of the chair, manoeuvred ahead of them back into the living room. 'We've only come down to meet him.'

'Speak for yourself,' David said.

Suzy wandered around the room, then got herself down onto the

95

blue Habitat sofa. 'This is all seriously gorgeous, Alex.'

'I like it,' Alex said, pleased.

'And don't think I haven't noticed you've had the doorways widened for me.'

'Of course I have,' Alex said. 'And the shower's wheel-in. I told you I'd never live anywhere you couldn't spend time. The staircase is bad enough.'

'Shut up about the stupid stairs,' Suzy said, 'and make us some tea.'

'On the other hand, bossy boots,' Alex said, 'you could always go to a hotel.'

'Now then, children,' David said. 'Play nicely.'

'You look happy, darling,' Suzy said to Alex.

'I am,' Alex agreed.

'Jude's a lucky man,' David remarked.

'Better believe it,' said Suzy.

The dinner, of homemade mushroom soup and fresh lobster – Suzy's favourite – was prepared and enjoyed, but Jude did not show. Nor, even after Alex had left two messages on both his home phone and mobile, had he returned her call.

'Not impressed,' said Suzy.

'I'm sure Jude has a good reason,' David said.

'Better be a bloody good one,' Suzy said. 'It's not as if he lives far away.'

'It's not a bit like him,' Alex said.

Seeing car crashes in her mind.

He telephoned, finally, at two in the morning, not long after she'd gone to bed.

'Alex, I'm so sorry.'

'Jude, what happened?' Still wide awake, she fumbled for the light switch, far too relieved at the sound of his voice to think of being annoyed.

'It's Earl,' Jude said. 'He collapsed late this afternoon.'

'Oh, God.'

'They took him back to the Royal Sussex, but he died just before nine.'

'Oh, Jude, no.' Alex wished she could put her arms around him. 'I'm so sorry.'

'He had a massive heart attack. I was with him at the Centre, dropping in a book he'd asked for, when it happened.' He paused. 'When Ray got to the hospital, he asked me to stay, and to be honest, Alex, to begin with I forgot all about Suzy and David and your dinner, and then, when I did remember, the payphone wasn't working, and I didn't like to switch on my mobile and I didn't want to walk out on Ray.'

'Jude, of course not.'

'And then later, Ray was in such a bad way I forgot just about everything – not you, I didn't forget about you for a moment, but—'

'Stop beating yourself up.' Her tone was firmer. 'You have absolutely nothing to apologize for. I'm just so terribly sorry, it's such a tragedy.'

'Ray really lost it,' Jude said. 'For a while, they were talking about giving him something to knock him out, but he wouldn't hear of it.'

'Is there something I can do?' Alex got out of bed, went to her open window, gazed into the dark June night. 'Where are you now? Would you like me to come?'

'I'm back at the flat, waiting for Ray. He was talking about driving back to London, but the state he was in, I told him it was a bad idea.'

'Lethal, potentially,' Alex agreed. 'So he's going to stay with you?'

'For tonight, yes. Maybe longer, I'm not sure. He made me go ahead, said he needed to stay a while, sit with Earl, I suppose.'

'Poor man.'

'Yes.' Jude paused. 'Alex, I'm so sorry to let you down.'

'Don't be daft.'

'And obviously I'd love it if you could be here, but you know how small the flat is, and I have a feeling Ray might find anyone else, even you, too much to take. And anyway, you can't walk out on Suzy and David.'

'I could,' Alex said, 'but in the circumstances, I won't.'

In the distance, at the other end, she heard the sound of Jude's buzzer.

'He's here,' he said.

'Go and take care of him,' Alex told him. 'Tell him how sorry I am.'

'I hope Suzy and David understand,' Jude said.

'Of course they will,' she said.

David certainly seemed to understand when Alex explained over breakfast pancakes, but Suzy was less convinced.

'Couldn't he leave the guy for an hour now and come and say hi?'

'I wouldn't want him to,' Alex said. 'Ray won't be in any shape to be left.'

'I'm sure you're right,' David agreed.

'He and Jude have got very close since the accident,' Alex explained.

'How come, if Earl was just a workmate?' Suzy frowned. 'Jude doesn't blame himself for what happened, does he?'

'Why should he?' Alex asked, surprised.

Suzy shrugged. 'Just wondering.'

'Come on, Suzy.' David was mildly reproachful.

'If you're looking for guilty secrets, for reasons I can't imagine –' Alex was bristling '– Jude was halfway up a ladder when Earl fell off the roof.'

'I wasn't suggesting he pushed the guy, Ally.'

'I should hope not.' Alex paused. 'Earl hadn't made any friends in the area.'

'Right,' Suzy said.

'Don't you remember how it was for you?' Alex said, a little more gently. 'How much support you needed.'

'Yeah,' Suzy said. 'I suppose you're right.'

Preparing to go down into Brighton on Saturday morning for some tacky fun on the pier and a little shopping in the Lanes, Suzy suggested they might take the opportunity to drop in on Jude.

'Just for a minute, to be friendly, since we're going to be on his doorstep.'

'It's a top-floor flat,' Alex pointed out. 'But if he's there, I'm sure he'll want to come down and say hi.'

'Maybe we should just leave him,' David said. 'His friend obviously won't be up to meeting strangers.'

'I'll phone before we leave, see how things are,' Alex said. 'But I'm not going to push.'

'Perish the thought,' said Suzy.

Alex threw her a look of exasperation. 'What is with you today, Suzy?'

'Nothing.' Suzy saw David looking at her. 'Sorry.'

Getting no reply to her phone call, Alex left the Maynards sitting in Food for Friends and, carrying the bunch of purple lysianthus she'd picked up for Ray in Woodingdean, walked quickly round to Union Street, tried the buzzer and then, after a few minutes, left the flowers with a young man on the ground floor.

They had 'done' the pier – had thrown balls at baskets and tin cans, David had shot his way to a cuddly toy for Suzy, and she had insisted on buying them all sticks of rock – and had gone back to a shop in Dukes Lane for a black Miu Miu sweater Suzy had been tempted by earlier, and were all back at Melton Cottage, a little after four, when Jude phoned, full of regret at having missed her and very touched by the flowers, as was Ray, who came, very briefly, to the phone.

'I feel so bad,' he told her, 'about keeping Jude from you all.'

'Ray, don't even think of that,' Alex said. 'I'm just so very, very sorry about Earl. I liked him so much, and he was so brave and so determined.'

'He thought a lot of you, too,' Ray told her.

And then his voice choked up, and Jude took the phone from him.

'We were at the Centre this morning,' he explained quietly, 'picking up Earl's belongings, and it was all a bit much for him.'

'I could have done that for him,' Alex said.

'I think he wanted to do it himself, you know?'

'Of course.' Alex paused. 'Any idea how long Ray's going to be with you?'

'Olivia, his sister, is flying in to Heathrow on Monday, and I know he wants to be there to meet her, but I'm not sure if he plans to go from here straight to the airport or go home first.'

'Then until he does leave, Jude, you stay close to him, and don't stress about not getting over here, right?'

'I don't want Suzy and David thinking I don't want to see them.'

'They won't think that.'

'They might,' Jude said. 'My being so geographically close and not—'

'Jude, stop,' Alex said. 'You can't leave Ray and that's that.'

'Let me see how things are tomorrow,' Jude said.

'Stop worrying about us.'

99

'Okay,' he said. 'Thanks.' He paused. 'I miss you.'

Alex heard his strain. 'Jude, are you all right? You, I mean, not Ray?'

'Better for talking to you,' he said.

He called again next morning, reported quietly to Alex that Ray was still in bad shape, then spent a few minutes on the phone speaking to both Suzy and David; but by Sunday evening the slightly dubious air was still around Suzy whenever the conversation came back to Jude.

'She's worried,' David explained quietly to Alex while Suzy was in the downstairs loo before going out for dinner, 'that she pushed you into a relationship—'

'She didn't,' Alex said. 'She knows that.'

'And that Jude may not be good enough for you.'

'I'd have thought,' Alex said, 'this proves just how good he is.'

'Good to a relative stranger,' David said. 'Not quite so good, perhaps, to you.'

'Kindness is kindness, surely,' Alex said.

Chapter 30

Frankie has been procrastinating about whether or not to come to
work at Melton Cottage this Monday morning, because Mrs Levin
was hazy last week as to when her London guests would be
leaving, and as in Roz's case, the fewer people she meets as
Frankie-the-Cleaner, the better.

On the other hand, there's no point pissing off her new client
and maybe-target.

So she comes.

The Maynards are still there, as sod's law would have it, both
standing in the narrow entrance hall with their weekend bags and
folded up wheelchair at the ready, on the verge of leaving.

Could have left five minutes earlier.

Wouldn't have been sod's sodding law then, would it?

'Frankie, I'm so glad,' Alex Levin says warmly. 'Just in time to
meet my two very dearest friends.'

'Not much of a meeting, I'm afraid.' The blonde, Suzy the
sister-in-law, leans on her left crutch and puts out her right hand
to shake Frankie's.

'Longer next time, I hope,' her husband, David the lawyer,
says.

And of course, being polite, he has to shake her hand too, and
Frankie, no antiseptic wipe in her pocket, tells him she looks
forward to it; and the encounter isn't really all that bad because,
like most people being introduced to the cleaner, the Maynards
don't actually *look* at her properly – though there is just one
slightly curious look from the crippled woman as Frankie stands
back to allow her more room to pass.

And then they're outside on the path, and it's hugs all round and

101

getting the woman into the front seat, and Alex Levin walks out onto Falmer Road and stands there waving till the Maynards' car has disappeared, and then she turns, with a sigh, to come back inside the cottage.

'Nice weekend?' Frankie asks.

'Lovely, thanks,' Alex says.

'Cuppa?' Frankie offers.

'Good idea,' Alex says. 'Thank you.'

And Frankie goes to put the kettle on, and after that it's more or less business as usual, though Mrs Levin seems a bit down, not quite her usual self.

Not that Frankie knows yet what her usual self really is.

She doesn't know anything very much, anything *private*, at least, about her yet.

But she will.

Chapter 31

Jude phoned while Alex was at the kitchen table, catching up with some overdue filing, and Frankie was hard at work up in the spare room removing all traces of the visitors, to say that Ray had just left for London.

'And I don't have to go back to work till tomorrow, so if you're still speaking to me, I'd love nothing better than to see you.'

'I'm still speaking to you,' Alex said.

'Are you very busy?'

She looked down at the mess of paper spread over the table. 'Beach, between the piers, about an hour?'

'Near the Fishing Museum?'

'I'll be there,' Jude said. 'Thank you.'

She did a little more filing, then shoved it back in the old box labelled *Filing*, filled a flask with hot vegetable soup, gave Frankie her money and left her to it, then jumped in the Mini she'd invested in when she'd landed the job at the Centre, and headed down towards Marine Drive. If she found a parking spot easily near the piers, she knew she would be early, but the fact was she'd found she simply did not want to wait a minute longer than necessary to see Jude; and perhaps he might be early, too, and even if he wasn't, she never tired of strolling on the beach, especially when it was quiet, loved the unique, constantly changing sounds of the pebbles under her shoes, liked all the sounds, the wind and the voice of the sea and the gulls and the other human visitors walking their dogs or just taking the air.

He was already there, waiting for her, sitting on the pebbles, back propped against an old boat, stood up quickly as he saw her coming down the slope from the street above. He wore his navy guernsey and jeans, had brought a red and blue checked rug which was slung over one shoulder.

'You look wonderful,' he said.

She held back from saying that he did too, showed him the thermos instead. 'I brought soup,' she said, 'since it doesn't exactly feel like June.'

'Lovely,' he said. 'Thanks.'

They were inches apart now, but had not yet touched, and Alex wondered if he felt what she did: a new invisible barrier between them, created, perhaps, by their very different and separate weekends. His had been infinitely worse, of course, must have been dreadful, caring for poor Ray, yet her own time with Suzy and David had been unexpectedly strained, partly, she supposed, because of Jude's absence and the reason for it, but also because of Suzy's uncharacteristic, prickly mood swings.

'Are you okay?' Jude's eyes were on her, intent.

'Absolutely,' Alex said.

'Would a hug be out of the question?' he asked.

'A hug,' she answered, 'is exactly what I've been hoping for.'

She put the flask and her shoulder bag down on the pebbles and they wrapped their arms around each other, leaned into each other, both finding that the closeness, the warmth, the physical touching, was, in fact, everything they needed.

'God, I've missed you,' Jude said softly, after several moments.

'Me, too,' Alex said.

'Really?'

'I wouldn't say it if it weren't true,' she said.

They walked for a while, arm in arm, enjoying the wind in their faces, talking as they went, speaking mostly about Earl and his father, and about the shock of sudden death that they both had personal experience of, and, most sobering of all, about Jude's real fear over the past few days that Ray Cobbins had been contemplating taking his own life.

'How was he when he left?' Alex asked as they paused from their walk, and Jude laid the rug down for them to sit on. They sat half facing the charred framework of the West Pier, ghostly in the low cloud, looking like the partially submerged, blackened skeleton of some vast sea beast.

'He seemed as okay as he could be,' Jude answered her question.

'And you?' She was particularly gentle, knew he had to have been thinking of his brother and their mother's suicide and all the rest.

'Better now,' Jude said, and gripped her hand.

She opened the flask and they shared the soup and gazed, for a while, away from the pier, out onto the Channel which looked grey, choppy and uninviting.

'What about the funeral?' she asked, at last.

'Ray said that Olivia, his sister, will help him with that. He said that in a strange way, he's looking forward to dealing with it.'

An enormous flock of gulls, dense as a cloud, circled the pier and then swooped and became invisible, a part of the structure.

'The last thing he can do for his son, maybe?' Alex said.

Jude nodded, squeezed her hand tighter. 'More or less what he said.'

'When you know where and when,' Alex said, 'I'd like to be there, if that's okay, with Ray and with you.'

Jude knew she was remembering the old fears he'd shared with her.

'More than okay with me,' he said.

They telephoned the Maynards from the living room at Melton Cottage that evening, Jude reiterating his regret at not having met them, telling Suzy how important he knew she was to Alex and how much he was looking forward to the next opportunity.

'Very charming,' Suzy said to Alex after Jude had passed her the phone.

Alex gritted her teeth and ignored the irony, said instead how gorgeous it had been to spend a little time with them.

'Your Frankie's a bit odd,' Suzy said.

'In what way?' Alex asked.

'I'm not sure,' Suzy said. 'I just felt there was something weird about her.'

'You only saw her for about a minute.' No chance, Alex thought, for her to have noticed Frankie's obsessive-compulsive habits.

'I know, but I still had a feeling about her.'

'She's getting paranoid,' David called out for Alex to hear.

105

'I think he's right,' Alex said.

'Maybe I am,' Suzy agreed, but suddenly her voice sounded flatter.

'You okay, darling?' Alex asked.

'Peachy.'

'Sure?'

'Course,' Suzy said. 'Get back to your Jude.'

They waited a while and then tried Ray's number in London, and his sister, Olivia, came to the telephone and spoke first to Jude, and then to Alex, and they spoke for a few minutes, about Ray and about Earl, and the other woman's warmth transmitted clearly across the phone line.

'My brother's told me how kind your Jude has been,' she said, 'and of course we haven't met yet, though I expect we will soon.'

'We'll certainly be coming to the funeral,' Alex said.

'I'm glad of that,' Olivia said, 'but I just wanted to urge you, both of you, to hold on tightly to each other, because life can be very cruel and much too short.'

'Yes,' Alex said, trying not to cry. 'Thank you, Olivia.'

'Hold on tightly, don't forget, Alex.'

Alex said she would not forget.

And later, in bed, they did as Olivia had said.

Chapter 32

On the whole, Frankie decides, she's feeling better.

Maybe it's because she's cleaning again professionally – for Alex Levin in Woodingdean and for a widow named Valerie Leigh who lives in a detached mock-Tudor house just outside Newhaven, a nice house, sheltered from the main road and the sea (though Melton Cottage is still winning hands down, still feels like Frankie's dream cottage). And maybe *that's* it, maybe she's feeling better because she has the cottage to dream about.

Or maybe it's because the *things* under the conservatory have stopped invading her mind quite so regularly.

Whatever the reason, she is coping better from day to day, no longer has that awful, creepy sense of being watched.

And then, one Thursday afternoon, almost a month after the plumber's last visit, the front doorbell of the house on Winder Hill rings.

Leave it.

Her first instinct.

Except she only came in from shopping a little while ago, and maybe this is someone who saw her come in, and maybe if she doesn't answer . . .

She puts on the security chain and opens the door, just a crack.

It's a woman of about forty, with red hair and a pudding face.

'Mrs Barnes?'

'Yes.'

Should have left it.

'My name is Meg Harris.'

Welsh, Frankie thinks, though with her whole body alive with fear, who the fuck cares where this pudding comes from?

'I'm sorry to trouble you.'

'No trouble,' Frankie says.

Politeness costs nothing, she remembers her dad saying once, which she knew even then was a bit rich coming from him, always effing and blinding all over the place, especially about her.

'Only I'm looking for someone,' Meg Harris says. 'A plumber.'

She feels a searing kind of sensation, from her head to her toes, remembers the van in the garage, thinks of this woman bringing the police, scraping the blue paint off the side of the van, coming inside the house, into the conservatory.

'Aren't we all?' she says, somehow managing wryness despite her panic.

'Oh.' Meg Harris's disappointment is plain. 'Only I think this man might have come to look at a job for you some time ago.'

And Frankie's fear lifts and flies away, the searing with it, already healed, because she sees, suddenly, that it's she who has the upper hand, that this woman has come on the off-chance, that she can tell her anything within reason, that there's nothing suspicious in her calling.

'Just a sec,' she says, leans the door to, removes the chain and opens it again.

Does not invite her in.

Never again.

'His name's Swann,' Meg Harris says. 'Andy Swann.'

'Yes.' Frankie nods. 'He did come here, about five weeks ago now, I think. He came to take a look at a problem, but that was all. He went away and never came back again.'

'Oh,' the other woman says. 'I see.'

Frankie wonders if she's his lover.

Hard to imagine Mr Brilliantine with the fussy, high voice having a lover.

Frankie prefers not to imagine, not to *think*, about him at all.

'Do you need a plumber too then?' she asks.

Meg Harris shakes her head, and her expression too is wry now.

'What I need is paying,' she says, and explains. 'I do his books, you see, once in a while.'

'Has he done a runner then?' Frankie asks.

The round-faced woman pulls a face. 'Looks like it.'

'I'm sorry.' Frankie starts to shut the door, then opens it wider again. 'If you see Mr Swann,' she says, 'remind him I'm still waiting.'

Meg Harris says that she will.

Frankie shuts the door, goes through the hall, through the kitchen and into the utility room, where she picks up a pair of disposable gloves, the long brush, some plastic and a bottle of Jeyes fluid, and then she returns to the front door, opens it again, checks to make sure no one's around, then pours fluid onto the step and brushes it carefully, thoroughly, making sure the disinfectant has covered every inch.

Since Swann, the doorstep has become Frankie's battlefront. If she could, she would dig a moat, but she knows she can't, and anyway, if things go well with Alex Levin or the Newhaven widow (though she still can't quite imagine herself in Valerie Leigh's house, smart as it is; it just doesn't *speak* to her the way Melton Cottage does, doesn't say 'this is for *you*, Frankie Barnes', let alone *gottahavit*) – but whichever and however, if things go well, she'll be able to leave this place behind.

In the meantime, the Jeyes is still her first line of defence.

She wishes she hadn't said that last thing to Meg Harris. What if the woman gets it into her head to send her someone else, another plumber? It wasn't necessary to say it, was it, she didn't have to get cocky at the last minute.

Stupid was what it was, just plain stupid.

And Frankie Barnes is cleverer than that, better than that.

She closes the front door again, wraps the head of the brush in plastic, turns back to the kitchen and, passing the mirror in the hall, glances at herself.

She's looking better again, too, on the whole.

Still Swanky-Frankie inside the house, not 'going out' swanky, but 'at home' swanky. Not the same person who arrives in Woodingdean and Newhaven to clean those other women's homes.

But looking closer, at her eyes – more hazel again than whisky now that the highlights have retreated well away from her roots – she sees that *it* is still there.

Not that she needs to look to know that. Her thought processes are enough of a warning. Like the moat idea. She had that same idea once in the bad old days, in the Bo days, and she told him about it and saw the disgust in his face, and just after that he

109

started deliberately missing the toilet bowl when he peed, and oh God, oh God, she can't even bear to think about that.

Her headache is back, the bad, bad pain that she got after Swann died, and she blames pudding-faced Meg Harris for that, and she knows it won't stop hurting now till after she's showered. And she didn't touch the plumber's bookkeeper, but the woman has touched the plumber's books, hasn't she, and she remembers Swann's filth, and Frankie knows all about airborne germs, so she'd better shower quickly, quickly and thoroughly, and then maybe the pain will go

Chapter 33

Alex had been anticipating domiciliary sessions with mixed feelings. There was real pleasure in seeing patients back in their own environments, surrounded by families or, at least, by their own possessions. There was also, in many cases, sadness attached to seeing institutionalized patients still fearful of their ability to cope, finding it hard to adjust to life outside the hospital or rehabilitation centre in which they had spent so long, depressed about seeing themselves as burdens, and angry, in some cases, at what they saw as abandonment by the private hospitals from which some had been discharged.

'Seeing patients in hospitals or at the Centre,' she told Jude over supper one evening towards the end of June, 'where you're surrounded by health care professionals and resources, there's always someone to turn to if something unexpected happens.'

They were in the Bath Arms near Jude's flat, glad of the chance to relax, had, a few days before, attended Earl's funeral in London, Alex conscious of being there as much to support Jude as Ray; and though the service had been beautiful as well as moving, they were both relieved it was behind them.

'But on the outside you're on your own,' Jude said now. 'And if you're conscientious, like you, and empathetic, like you, you're likely to end up needing some kind of care yourself if you're not careful.'

He had been listening to Alex's occasional tales of anonymous patients with sympathy, occasional amusement and mounting concern. Though well-trained for her new role, Alex was finding it hard to ignore her patients' other needs, not to mention those of their all-too-often over-stretched, over-strained carers. In the last fortnight she'd been late for a number of appointments for all kinds of reasons: once because she'd tried to help the depressed husband of a stroke patient make contact with his son; another time because she'd assisted a woman with washing because her carer had not turned up to give her a bath – frustrated by the health and safety regulations that prohibited her from going so far as to help the poor woman actually bathe. Finding one patient adamant that she could not concentrate on speech therapy because her daughter had bought her the wrong chocolate biscuits, Alex had dashed out to a shop to buy Hobnobs, more for the daughter's than the mother's sake; and on two other occasions she'd run to local chemists' to fill urgent prescriptions it seemed no one else was likely to find the time to do.

'If you're going to run yourself ragged on a daily basis,' Jude told her, as she finished her chocolate puddle pudding and turned to her coffee, all too clearly needing it to stay awake, 'then you're just going to have to let me help you with more stuff.'

'What kind of stuff?'

'I don't know – shopping, boring stuff.'

'Your life's not exactly empty,' Alex pointed out, mindful that the Luddesdown Terrace deadline was looming close, which meant longer hours for the builders.

'Can't compare my strain with yours,' Jude said.

'Mine's only a matter of getting used to. Better discipline.' She grimaced. 'All home health visitors have to learn to balance compassion with common sense, we're told.'

Jude looked at her for a long moment.

'There is one big thing you could do for me,' he said, 'that would actually force you to slow right down for just a little time most days – like yoga, but easier.' He grinned at her puzzled face. 'Let me paint you.'

'Do you paint people?' Alex was surprised, having seen landscapes, abstracts and painstakingly fine miniatures of houses, but no portraits.

'Rarely,' Jude said. 'Would you mind?'

'Do you really want to paint me?' She was pleased, unable to mask it. 'Or are you just thinking of ways to slow me down?'

'What do you think?'

'I'm not much good at sitting still.'

'I've noticed,' Jude said. 'All you have to do is relax.'

'Not much good at that either,' Alex said.

'So learn,' he said.

112

Chapter 34

Frankie has just felt really irritated with Mrs Levin for the first time.

'I thought you were going to be out,' she said, arriving on the first Wednesday morning of July to find her client in the kitchen, surrounded by even more clutter than usual.

'More paperwork,' Alex explained. 'Sorry.'

Frankie shrugged. 'I'll work around you.'

'Would you rather leave it for another day?'

'I'm here now,' Frankie said. 'I'll manage.'

Alex looked around the kitchen, the general cleanness of which, Frankie noted, still regularly appeared to astonish her.

'I've been thinking, anyway,' she said, 'that maybe one day a week might be enough. Now you've got it all so beautiful,' she added quickly.

'We've already talked about that.' Frankie felt a frown pucker between her eyebrows. 'It wouldn't be enough.'

'I think,' Alex said, 'that maybe I still can't seem to get used to asking someone else to clean up my mess.'

That was what really irritated Frankie.

Two can play that do-good game.

'I don't think it's right for someone to work so hard to help other people,' she says, almost, but not quite, smoothly, 'and then have to come home to more work.'

Mrs Levin still looks doubtful.

'Anyway,' Frankie adds, 'I need the money, don't I? So you're doing me a favour, too.'

And Alex gives way.

Frankie knew she would.

*

113

She isn't quite sure yet that this is going to work out for her.

A man's been in Melton Cottage.

Mrs Levin never leaves unwashed dishes or glasses from the night before – at least not when Frankie's coming next morning – but Frankie can tell from the extra towels in the bathroom and from the bed. And she *hates* that, because men are so much dirtier, and she can't bring herself to actually think about what might be on the sheets, but she's been going through even more packets of disposable gloves than usual, and she'd wear a mask if she could – one of the things she can only do when Alex is out, since she can't afford, doesn't really want, to offend her. And she may not be *that* sort of therapist, but still, Frankie has a feeling she may suspect about her OCD, which is one of the reasons she's still not sure about Alex Levin or her cottage.

Except that she really does love it so very much, knows she would be happy living in it.

Has dreams about it often.

About being here alone.

All traces of the Levin woman eradicated.

Frankie already knows it's not going to be nearly as easy as it was with Roz, that even if this as yet invisible man does not turn out to be specially close to the speech therapist, there's still the couple from London, the sister-in-law and her husband. And okay, Suzy Maynard's a cripple, so she's not exactly ever going to be rushing back and forth to the seaside, and the man defends crims for a living, which means he won't have time to drive his wife to and fro. But it's going to take some time till Frankie can be sure how regularly they communicate, and even if they don't speak all that often, there's no question that there are a lot of other people – patients and colleagues at the Centre – who would definitely miss Alex Levin if she were to vanish.

Not impossible though.

Things happen, don't they? Shit happens. Accidents.

Mrs Levin wouldn't have to vanish, she could just have an *accident*.

Except then everyone would *know* about it, about the tragedy, so Frankie wouldn't be able to just take over Melton Cottage, and that's the whole *point*, isn't it?

How could she have forgotten that, for God's sake? Is she losing it, is her OCD taking over again, or is it this bloody headache that keeps coming back?

If she had this cottage, her headache would go.

In the dreams she has about living here, there is no headache, everything is calm and peaceful and she's home, really home, sitting in her pretty kitchen with the beams overhead and the white tiles and pretty blue Aga and the blue-and-white blind that Alex Levin told her she had made to help make the cooker fit in; something to do with her dead husband, Frankie remembers her saying, though she wasn't really listening at the time, was too busy thinking about the white-and-navy tiles and rug in the conservatory on Winder Hill and the white van she painted blue in the garage, about all the *blues* going on in her life. But she *ought* to have been listening, it's one of the things she does best, after all, and bloody crucial in a case like this.

In the dreams, she doesn't have to listen to anyone, and there's no headache, and this is her home, and everything's okay.

If she had this cottage, it *would* all be okay.

Chapter 35

'Ron says you're a bit of an artist,' Mike Bolin said, while he and Jude were both shovelling cement into the mixer at Luddesdown Terrace.

'A bit,' Jude said, surprised, since Bolin had barely spoken to him since those few early words about his tattoo.

'You a faggot then?' Bolin asked.

Jude answered with no more than a look.

'You look like a faggot,' Bolin said.

Jude smiled.

Bolin stared, his dark eyes openly hostile.

'Shift your arses,' Ron Clark bawled.

And Jude went back to shovelling.

Chapter 36

Frankie's working hard at what she does best aside from cleaning.

Making herself indispensable to Alex and getting her to talk to her, which is not all that hard because, although the other woman knows how to mind her own business, she's also naturally friendly.

Frankie knows that, in the circumstances, which aren't as great as they should be, she ought to be spending more time working on Valerie Leigh, the Newhaven widow, but she can't seem to get herself going the way she should over there.

She knows why, what the problem is.

The problem is that Mrs Leigh smells, and worse, so does her house. Even now, despite all Frankie's ministrations – and face it, no one, but *no* one, cleans better than Frankie.

'Nobody does it better,' she sings sometimes, when she's alone, vacuuming or scrubbing, and she's always had a crap voice – Bo told her often enough, so she knows, but Bo isn't here, is he, so she can sing as much as she bloody well likes.

If it weren't for the smell situation, she supposes she might really like, if not quite fall in love with, the Newhaven house, but it's a stale kind of odour that seems to follow Mrs Leigh around, growing worse as July progresses, even though the weather hasn't really been particularly warm yet. Frankie's already taken charge of washing her clothes and underwear, and she almost wishes she could bath the widow herself, give her a good scrubbing – though the thought of that is positively repulsive to her, of course, and the only way she could ever actually do it would be with a mask and gloves and overalls and by upping her medication, too, and what a stupid bloody waste that would be.

117

Especially when there's bound to be something much more worthwhile she'll need the tablets for, ultimately.

Either Newhaven or Woodingdean.

Melton Cottage, preferably.

So she's still concentrating on getting to know all about friendly Alex.

Though as a matter of fact, she's beginning to think there might be a bit more to that friendliness than, say, Roz Bailey's, because, after all, with Alex being a therapist – and whatever kind, she is still that, a *therapist* – Frankie's almost certain that she's been trying to get stuff out of her. Stuff out of her head, and whether that's out of professional snoopiness, or whether she wants to *help her* – fucking therapists all the same, all the bloody *same* – it doesn't matter, because Frankie's guard is up, so she might as well be wearing a steel helmet, and Alex Levin can ask all the casual, polite questions she wants, and make Frankie a million cups of tea, she still won't get anything out of her.

Nothing real.

Chapter 37

Jude and Bolin were passing each other up on the scaffolding on the rear wall of the house at the eastern end of the terrace, when Bolin stumbled and knocked into Jude, who grabbed at a hand rail and swore.

'All right?' Bolin asked.

'Fine,' Jude said, the image of Earl falling still too vivid in his mind.

'Got to be careful up here,' Bolin said.

'Yeah,' Jude said. 'You do.'

'Good job you know how to handle yourself,' Bolin said, and smirked.

'Nasty piece of work,' Jude told Alex next morning over breakfast at the cottage.

He seldom stayed over on weekdays, but her first appointment this morning wasn't till ten, and he'd had toothache for days now, and the only slot his dentist had been able to offer him was nine-thirty, so Ron had told him not to come in till after.

'I mean seriously nasty,' he added.

Alex looked alarmed. 'You don't think he pushed you deliberately?'

'Course not.' Jude shrugged. 'But he enjoyed scaring me.'

'You could always tell him you're straight.'

'I don't believe in pandering to homophobic bullies.'

'Nor do I,' Alex agreed. 'At least, not safely on ground level.'

Her tone was light, but the notion of Jude in danger had touched an old weak spot inside her, and several times lately she had found herself having to curb an urge to nag him to be careful.

119

The doorbell rang.

'Frankie.' Alex stood up. 'She has a key, but she always rings if my car's outside.'

Jude saw the woman's expression change as she entered the kitchen behind Alex and saw him. Smaller than he'd expected her to be, though with a wiry kind of strength, and a bit mousy to look at, but with something tough and wary behind her eyes.

'Time you two met,' Alex said. 'Frankie Barnes, this is Jude Brown.'

'Good to meet you.' Jude stood up and put out his hand.

Frankie didn't take it, just nodded, her smile tense.

'You, too.' She turned to Alex. 'We can give today a miss if you're busy.'

'We'll both be off out in a bit,' Alex told her.

'I'll make a start then,' Frankie said.

'Coffee first?' Jude looked at the pot on the table.

'No,' Frankie said. 'Thanks just the same.'

'Not too keen to see me, was she?' Jude said softly just outside the front door.

'I think she wouldn't take your hand because of the OCD.' Alex was quiet, too, though they'd left Frankie working in the kitchen, at the back of the cottage.

'I should have thought,' Jude said, wincing.

'You can't help being polite.'

'The coffee too, do you think?'

'She brings her own cup,' Alex said.

Jude shook his head. 'Poor woman.'

120

Chapter 38

Frankie isn't sure how she got by this morning.

By cleaning like a demon, that's how.

It wasn't just that he was there – she already knows he stays over, doesn't she? But it was the *way* he was there. Offering her coffee, like it was his place.

At home.

'Shit, shit, shit,' Frankie says now, back in the safety of her own living room.

Her own, but not right any more.

She sits down in one of the armchairs and starts to cry.

Not for long. She seldom cries for long, hates the way it makes her feel, the way it stuffs up her nose, and she never feels clean when she's blocked up, it's too much like having a cold, reminds her of germs, so now she runs the shower till it's hot and gets under the sharp needles of water and turns her face up into it to get the full power. And it's strange about the shower, about the hot water in the house, really weird, because ever since Andy Swann came back, it's been fine again, no real problems at all. Which means she never really needed a *plumber* at all, and she wishes she'd known that, wishes it badly, because then he wouldn't be down there in plastic—

Don't think about that.

– and she wouldn't be having to find somewhere else, like Alex's cottage.

Only that's out of the bloody question now, isn't it? Because Mr Jude Brown has got his feet well under Alex Levin's table, and he looked at her, *right* at her, properly, like he was seeing her as a person, not just someone's cleaner, and that's bad news too. And

121

even if their romance doesn't last, there's still the sister-in-law and her husband, and Frankie knows now that Alex and Suzy talk at least once a week, and they wouldn't buy Alex just disappearing, *certainly* wouldn't buy her taking over Melton Cottage.

So that's that.

That's bloody, sodding well *that*.

She lies awake right through this long night, wretched in her own body, and she's sweating now, and sweating's much worse than crying, and she's used all the hot water and the boiler's off, so she has to shower in cold; but at least she's clean for a while until the sweating starts again, and what's she going to do without the cottage to dream about, what's she going to *do*?

There's always Newhaven and the widow – most of her friends gone the way of her late husband, her only son living up in Manchester and hardly ever in touch with her, though no son at all would be better, and anyway, Frankie still hasn't found a way to conquer that *smell*, and she doubts now that she ever will, which is why she was planning to tell Mrs Leigh this week that she won't be coming any more, and she really doesn't *want* to go anywhere other than the cottage.

'You'll have to go on looking,' she tells herself out loud, just after four in the morning. 'Find somewhere else, some*one* else.'

But in the meantime, she reasons, she may as well keep her hand in at Melton Cottage, and in a way just cleaning there with no ulterior motive may be less of a strain on her. Just cleaning is still, after all, what she does best, and maybe a miracle will happen, maybe Alex will give up work and Jude Brown will fall out of love with her, and the cripple and the lawyer will emigrate to Australia.

'And maybe shit won't stink,' Frankie says.

That was one of Bo's sayings, and she always hated it, wishes she hadn't said it now, because even *saying* it makes her want to shower again.

Find something nice to think about.

The cottage.

Not that.

New clothes.

She thinks about Roz's stash of cash, dirty as it is. About spending a little more of it, maybe getting herself up as Swanky-Frankie again and going into some really nice, really expensive (pricey

always feels that bit cleaner) boutique and getting herself something new. And even if she does have to come home and put the
new things in the washing machine and take five showers, it's still
better than lying here thinking about Swann and how bad, how
wrong, this house still feels to her too much of the time.

She gets up again, even though it's only four-fifteen.

Showers again.

Starts getting ready to go out.

Chapter 39

Alex had just emerged from HMV in the Churchill Square shopping centre on the last Saturday afternoon of July and was tucking the small plastic bag containing the Norah Jones CD she'd bought for Jude into her shoulder bag, when she looked up and thought, for just a moment, that she had seen Frankie walking into Debenhams, then realised it couldn't have been.

Not just because of the obviously expensive clothes that the woman was wearing, or the carefully done hair or make-up – it was stupid and offensive to assume that Frankie might not get herself up like that in her free time, just because she came to work looking so – *ordinary* – she couldn't think of another word.

The point was that this woman's walk was totally unlike Frankie's, her whole attitude was different.

That was exactly what she looked like, Alex thought, moving on, smiling to herself. Frankie with *attitude*.

But probably not her at all.

Chapter 40

'Not me,' Frankie says two mornings later after Alex – dropping home for a quick sandwich lunch – asked if it was, by chance, her she saw out shopping in Churchill Square the other day.

'You've got a double then,' Alex says. 'Or almost.'

'They say everyone does, don't they?' Frankie says.

Feeling sick.

The headache's troubling her again, and she isn't feeling as physically strong as usual, and she's been getting really jumpy. And on the subject of seeing people at the shopping centre, it so happens she actually thought for a second or two that day that she saw Bo there, coming out of Clarks. And she didn't, of course, it wasn't him at all. But still, it ruined the shopping for her, made her feel nervier, dirtier than ever, so it was home again, quick as possible, to the shower.

That's not the worst of it though.

The worst is that she thinks – only *thinks*, she isn't sure, thank Christ – but she thinks there's a smell in the house, and it's not the kind of smell that's put her off Valerie Leigh's house, not that kind of smell at all, and this might be the pipes, or—

Don't.

Or it might—

Don't!

That's why she's still coming out to work, to clean, to be Frankie-the-cleaner, to be *here*, especially, in this calm cottage, her dream cottage; impossible dream now, of course, she knows that, but still, she can keep on coming, can't she?

'All right?' Alex asks.

'Fine,' Frankie answers, reining in her thoughts. 'Bit of a headache.'

'Would you like some paracetamol?'

'No, thank you,' Frankie says, because she never takes other people's tablets.

And that's another thing, her own stash of medication's beginning to run low, and that's Swann's doing, isn't it, bloody Swann—

Don't think about him.

So she goes on cleaning.

Chapter 41

A fortnight later, with Luddesdown Terrace complete, Alex too busy at work to find time to sit for her portrait, and two weeks clear for Jude before he was scheduled to begin his next job (a retirement complex in Church Road, Hove, close to the Centre and with much, so far as Jude could tell, to commend it), he had gone on the road, as he periodically did, offering to paint miniatures of people's houses in the area.

Driving up Winder Hill in Rottingdean on a decidedly brisk for August afternoon, remembering that he had painted a house at the top of that hill two or three years ago, and wondering if any of the owner's neighbours might like to follow suit, Jude observed that the house in question had a new conservatory. He recalled the owner, Mrs Bailey, quite clearly, recalled liking her, remembered how delighted she had been with his work, and so he parked his Honda jeep outside, picked up his album of photos of past commissions – in case she'd given away his painting or forgotten him – and went to ring the bell.

The door was opened, after several moments, on the security chain.

'Yes?'

Jude peered through the narrow opening. 'Frankie?' he said, surprised.

She began to close the door.

'Frankie, it's Jude,' he said quickly, put out his hand on impulse, laid it lightly against the door. 'Alex's friend.'

'Don't do that,' Frankie said, faintly.

Jude removed his hand. 'Sorry.'

Frankie took another moment, then leaned the door to a little and slid off the chain. 'What do you want?'

'I've come to see Mrs Bailey.' Jude smiled. 'Small world.'

'She's not here,' Frankie told him.

'What a pity.' Jude opened his album, found the photograph, held it up, page open, for her to see. 'I did that for her before the conservatory extension. Thought she might be interested in an update.'

'She's gone away,' Frankie said. 'To Canada, to stay with cousins.'

'Where in Canada?' Jude asked.

'Toronto,' Frankie said.

'Nice,' Jude said. 'When's she due back?'

'She isn't.' Frankie paused. 'And I don't want the house painted. It's not my kind of thing.'

'That's fine,' Jude said, easily, and shut the album. 'If you change your mind, you can—'

'I won't, Frankie said, and shut the door.

Jude walked back along the path to the jeep and, glancing back at the house, at the conservatory, noticed some cracking in one of the walls and made a mental note to tell Alex, in case she felt it appropriate to mention it to Frankie.

Chapter 42

Frankie is shaking as she shuts the door.

Waits, listening to the sound of Jude Brown getting back in his car, starting the engine, driving away.

Bastard, she thinks.

'Bloody nosy bastard,' she says out loud.

Hasn't he done enough damage already by just being Alex Levin's lover, without coming round here smarming with his poxy little book of paintings?

'*Bastard*,' she says again.

She wonders why she said Toronto, knows she had to say something, but it probably would have been better to say nothing. Safer. But Toronto was the first place that came into her head, and God knows it must be a big enough city, and it's not as if Mr Jude – *poncy* name – Brown's going to be looking for Roz there or anywhere, since all he was after was selling her another painting.

She remembers the miniature hanging in Roz's – *her* – bedroom.

She liked it till he came, but now she's got a good mind to take it off the wall and stick it in the bin or burn it, except then there'll be a patch on the wallpaper, and then she'll have to do the whole room and she's got it all so nice.

'I don't want the house painted.'

She shouldn't have said that either. He would have assumed she was the cleaner, wouldn't he, and gone off just thinking that it was, as he'd said, a small world. But now he's going to be wondering about how a cleaner could either own or rent a big house like this, because even a full-time housekeeper wouldn't have said something like that.

'I don't want the house painted.'

129

Stupid.
Frankie's head gives a violent stab of pain.
She remembers his hand on the door.
Shudders.
Goes to get the Jeyes.

Chapter 43

'She was definitely at home,' Jude told Alex later, as he chopped onions for the vegetable lasagne he was making for them in his tiny kitchen space. 'I mean, she wasn't there working, I'm sure she was living there.'

'Probably just staying there,' Alex said. 'Looking after the house for this woman while she's in Canada.'

'Except Frankie said Mrs Bailey wasn't coming back.'

'Maybe it's on the market and Frankie's staying there meantime.' Alex smiled. 'Nice arrangement for her.'

Jude washed an aubergine, set it on the board and began slicing.

'She said *she* didn't want the house painted again, as if it was her decision to make. "Not my thing," she said.'

Alex shrugged. 'Maybe she's paying rent.'

'Maybe.'

'Jude, give me something to do.'

'Nothing,' he said. 'My turn.'

'You know I hate doing nothing,' Alex said.

'Pour us both a glass of wine and sit down,' Jude told her.

'That's really hard work,' she said, fishing in a drawer for the corkscrew.

'Frankie said that Mrs Bailey had gone to stay with cousins in Toronto.'

'And?' Alex asked patiently.

'And I spent quite a bit of time with Roz Bailey while I was working on her miniature,' Jude said, 'and I specifically remember her telling me she had no family.'

'Maybe these are distant cousins,' Alex said.

'Maybe,' Jude said again.

131

'But?' Alex pulled the cork out of the bottle. 'I hear a definite but.'

'Only that I remember a few other things she told me. That she hated flying, for one, wasn't keen on the hassle of travelling at all, which was one of the reasons she said she'd chosen to live close to the sea.' He tipped the aubergines and onions into a large saucepan. 'She said it made her feel she had freedom on her doorstep.' He paused again. 'Toronto's not on the ocean.'

'Lake Ontario's a Great Lake,' Alex pointed out, pouring Merlot into two glasses. 'And there's no reason she shouldn't have changed her mind about travel. Any number of reasons why she might have.'

'Sure,' Jude said. 'You're right.' He opened the fridge, took out two large mushrooms. 'That reminds me.'

'Now what?' Alex laughed.

'Nothing to do with Mrs Bailey going to Canada.' Jude began washing the mushrooms. 'Though it's something she might want to know about.'

He told Alex about the cracking he'd noticed.

'Whoever's house it is now, there might be a problem.'

'Subsidence?' Alex asked.

'Could be,' Jude said. 'I'd have told Frankie myself if she hadn't given me such a bum's rush.' He grinned. 'And then she might have thought I was touting for art *and* building commissions.'

Chapter 44

'Frankie never showed up this morning,' Alex told Jude on the phone early the following evening.

'Hope it's nothing to do with me,' Jude said. 'Maybe I embarrassed her.'

He was sketching, almost absently, charcoal on a paper pad, another drawing of Alex, a whole litter of partial sketches around him on the couch.

'Not your fault if you did,' Alex said.

She was in her kitchen, wondering what to make for dinner, knowing there wasn't much in her fridge, momentarily regretting turning down Frankie's offer to take over her food and grocery shopping.

'Though I really did get the feeling something wasn't right with her,' Jude added.

'You sound like Suzy.'

'I know.' Jude recalled Alex telling him that Suzy had thought Frankie 'weird'. 'Maybe Suzy wasn't being that paranoid after all.'

'I hope she was,' Alex said. 'Since she wasn't all that sure about you either.'

'True enough,' Jude said.

'Frankie might be ill,' Alex said.

'Phone her,' Jude said. 'In fact, why haven't you?'

'I only have her mobile, and I've left a message.'

'Can't do more then, can you?'

'Suppose not,' Alex said.

'Instead of worrying about Frankie –' Jude rubbed gently at a fine charcoal line with his middle finger, smudged it a little '– why

133

not come here and let me get started on this portrait?'

'Paperwork,' Alex said.

'You just did your paperwork.'

'Bills,' she said, looking at the litter of still unopened envelopes waiting for her attention on the table. 'Lots of them.'

'You'd rather pay bills than sit for me.'

'I certainly wouldn't rather pay bills than *be* with you,' Alex said. 'It's the sitting I'm not too sure about.'

'You wouldn't need to sit,' Jude said. 'You could lie.'

'Lie where?'

'On my bed,' Jude said. 'Or anywhere else that takes your fancy.'

'Is this for you to paint me or—'

'Or *anything* else that takes your fancy,' Jude said. 'Or mine.'

Alex felt, suddenly, horny as hell.

'Sod the bills,' she said.

Chapter 45

Her head's been worse today.

Not up to work this morning or afternoon, and she imagines Alex will be trying to call her on her mobile (Roz's mobile, still being paid monthly by direct debit via her bank account, and the Internet's working well enough, except Frankie's got a bit slack lately about paying cash in at the hole-in-the-wall, so she needs to be more careful).

She's been beginning to think she might need a doctor for her head, but obviously she isn't registered anywhere in the area, and she could have looked in the *Yellow Pages*, but that's where she found Andy Swann, and even just the thought of picking the book up makes her feel queasy, so the other day, when the pain got really bad, she looked on the Web to see if there might be one of those walk-in places in the Brighton and Hove district; but then she got too stressed and couldn't find anything – and the Web's like that, she's found, there are days when it works really well, really smoothly, and others when it drives you barmy.

Not hard now, in her case.

That bastard coming here really freaked her out.

And then there's the smell.

She doesn't know what to do if it's that.

Him.

Them.

She has a feeling it's unravelling.

She's unravelling.

Chapter 46

With a home visit in Ovingdean on Thursday afternoon, and concerned about Frankie having missed a second morning's work at Melton Cottage, still without a word, Alex decided, after her own appointment, to see if she could find the Rottingdean house where Jude had accidentally happened upon her.

Even on this wet, humid, slightly misty afternoon, the grey house at the top of Winder Hill was easy to spot, the conservatory that Jude had spoken about clearly visible from the road through the privet hedges surrounding the back garden.

Alex parked the Mini, she walked up the front path and rang the bell.

If Frankie was unwell, she realised as she waited, she might take some time to reach the front door.

A minute or two passed, and she rang again.

If Frankie was feeling really rough, she might not want to bother answering.

Or might not be able to.

Alex rang one last time.

Might not be here at all.

She heard a soft sound, and then the door opened a little way, on the chain.

'Frankie?' Alex said. 'It's Alex. I'm sorry to—'

'I was resting,' Frankie said.

Alex peered through the gap, saw, in the shaft of daylight striking the older woman's face that she looked pale and quite alarmingly gaunt, considering it was only a week since she'd last seen her.

'Frankie, you look awful.' The words were out before she could stop them.

136

'I've not been well.' Frankie gripped the edge of the door with one hand.

'I can see that,' Alex said. 'I've been worrying about you.'

'No need.'

'Not so sure about that.' Alex noticed that the fingers clutching the door were raw. 'That looks painful.'

'It's fine.' Frankie removed her hand. 'What is it you want? Only I'm really tired, and—'

'Maybe I could come in for a moment? See if I can help you, for a change?'

'I don't need any help,' Frankie said.

Ordinarily, Alex disliked pushiness, found it went against the grain when, on occasions, it was necessary to persuade a patient to accept help. Frankie was, of course, wholly entitled to her privacy, especially when she was unwell, and Alex was unsure exactly why she felt such an uncharacteristic need to persist.

'Couldn't we just have a cuppa together?' she said. 'Bit of a catch-up, and then after that, if you want, I promise I'll leave you in peace.'

For an instant, she had the sense that the woman on the other side of the door was on the verge of tears, but then, instead, she seemed almost to sag, as if the effort of resisting had been too much.

Frankie slid off the chain and stepped back.

'Better come in then,' she said.

Chapter 47

Frankie isn't certain exactly why she's let Alex Levin in.

No one was going to be allowed through that door ever again, were they? She swore that, didn't she, after the plumber, and no one *has* since then, have they, no one, not even Mr Jude Brown, has got any further than the doorstep.

Till now.

It's her head.

That's why.

She needs help, and, finally, she accepts that. Even though she knows this woman can't really help her, because Frankie can't *let* her help, can't give in to being ill, can't have a doctor coming in, can't tell them she's been screwing around with her tablets, can't risk someone saying she needs to go to hospital, can't risk leaving the house open to do-gooders. And she knows what Alex would do if she was really ill; she'd ask for the key and want to come in here and keep the place nice for her, *clean* for her, would know that was important to her, would insist on doing it.

Shouldn't have let her in.

Cup of tea and then out, that's the only hope.

Except her head is so *bad*.

Her head is on *fire*.

Chapter 48

'I didn't know you lived so close,' Alex said.

'No,' Frankie said.

They were in the lovely grey and white kitchen, and there was no longer the tiniest doubt in Alex's mind about Frankie's obsessive-compulsive disorder, because the room was clinically clean and tidy, anything in view – not that there was much not put away – standing in militarily perfect lines and sparkling, and the smell of disinfectant was strong enough to make her eyes water.

'Why don't you let me make the tea?' she asked casually, not wanting to push.

'No, thank you,' Frankie said and filled the kettle, even though her hands were trembling and she bit her lower lip when she bent her head because of the pain.

'Maybe you might feel a bit better if you open a window?' Alex suggested. 'Bit of fresh air, specially if you haven't been out.'

'No.'

It might just have been because of the rain, but the 'no' came swiftly and harshly, and Alex wondered suddenly if Frankie's condition might have worsened to the point where she feared germs floating in through open windows.

She said nothing more about it, sat down at the table, rested her right hand on the surface, noticed the other woman's anguished glance as she did so, removed it quickly, guessed that the instant she left, Frankie would clean that part of the table, maybe even clean the chair she was sitting on, or the floor where her feet had trodden.

It was, she knew, not her place to help with this; she was qualified neither professionally nor as Frankie's real friend, but there

139

seemed such a sense of isolation about the woman, and her wish to at least try to help was so intense that she gave way to the impulse.

'Would you like to talk about it?' she asked gently.

'About what?'

In the process of moving the used tea bags from mugs to the bin, a few drops of brown liquid sprinkled on the floor tiles, and Frankie bent to wipe the drops away with paper towel, wincing with pain, but Alex could see from her expression that merely wiping the tea away was not enough for her.

'Let me help with that,' she said.

'*No.*' Sharp again.

'All right.' Alex sat still, finding it hard to watch Frankie's compulsion battling with her physical pain, suspecting that even after three scrubs with Dettox, the other woman might still feel the need to return to the spots after she had gone.

She managed to wait till Frankie joined her at the table.

'How long have you suffered from OCD?' she asked, finally.

Frankie said nothing, stared down at her tea.

'It is OCD, isn't it?' Alex asked gently. 'Your need to clean, so beautifully, over and over again?' She paused. 'I do know how hard it can be.'

'Do you?'

Alex heard and saw the pure hostility, had expected nothing else. 'Not personally, no,' she answered. 'But I know a bit about it.'

'You would,' Frankie said. 'Being a therapist.'

'I'm not that kind of therapist,' Alex said, 'and I'm just speaking as a friend.'

'You're not my friend,' Frankie said. 'You're my client – my employer, you probably think.'

'Client, definitely,' Alex said. 'You do a service for me, which I pay for.'

'Whatever,' Frankie said. 'I don't want to talk about anything.'

'Okay.' Alex paused. 'You really don't look well though, Frankie.'

'I'm not. I told you that.'

'Do you have a temperature?' Safer ground, Alex thought.

'No.'

'Seen a doctor?'

'No,' Frankie said. 'If you're not going to drink your tea, I'd really like to go and lie down for a bit.'

'Why don't you do that now?' Alex suggested. 'I could make you a little something to eat.'

'I'm not hungry.' Frankie stood up.

'Right.' Alex got up too.

'I'm sorry,' Frankie said abruptly, and put a hand to her head.

'Don't apologize,' Alex told her. 'I invited myself, and anyway, you're ill.'

'It's just a headache. It'll pass.' Frankie walked towards the door.

'Do you get them often?' Alex asked, following her into the hall.

'Sometimes. Not often.'

Alex looked around. The entrance hall was spacious, carpeted in spotless grey, with a number of doors leading off it, every inch of wall and mirror and framed print gleaming, unsurprisingly.

'This is a beautiful house,' she said.

'Thank you,' Frankie said. 'I like yours better.'

'Do you?' Alex was surprised. 'Thank you.'

She was almost at the front door when she remembered.

'I almost forgot,' she said, 'about Jude coming here.'

'What about him?' The hostility was back.

'Just that it was such a coincidence,' Alex said lightly. 'He was telling me about having painted the house before, and how much he liked it.'

'He told me,' Frankie said wearily.

'There was something he wanted me to mention to you.'

'Not now,' Frankie said. 'My head's really bad, Alex.'

'I know, it's all right, I am going,' Alex said quickly. 'But Jude said this might be important.' She looked back through the hall at the door that led, she guessed, to the conservatory. 'He noticed some cracking, on one of the extension walls.'

Frankie didn't speak.

'It's a conservatory, isn't it?' Alex took a couple of steps back towards it. 'Jude said he thought it might be an idea to check if the cracks had gone through.'

'They haven't.' Frankie's voice was harsh again.

'So you've had it checked?'

'Alex, I don't want to be rude, but—'

'You're not being. It's my fault.' Alex looked at her white face again. 'Frankie, are you sure you don't want me to stay? I could call a doctor, stay a while.'

141

'No.' Frankie opened the front door.

'Right.' Alex took a step forward. 'I only mentioned the wall in case I forget next time I see you, and Jude said it might be sensible to—'

'Oh, *God*.' Frankie clapped both hands up to her head. 'Oh, God, it *hurts*!'

'Frankie, it's all—'

Frankie began to sway.

Alex caught her as she fell.

Chapter 49

'A stroke,' she told Jude later on the phone from the Royal Sussex.

'Poor Frankie,' he said. 'How bad?'

'Not good,' Alex said. 'Though it's a little too soon to tell.'

She was in a colleague's office, using her mobile, had already called the Centre to ask for back-up in reallocating or rescheduling her last two appointments of the day.

'In case Frankie needs me,' she explained to Jude now. 'So far as I know, she has no one.'

'No family at all?' Jude asked.

'She's never mentioned anyone. I found her driving licence in her handbag when the ambulance came, but there's no one listed for emergencies.'

She had already, she told Jude, alerted hospital personnel to her entirely unconfirmed suspicion that Frankie might have obsessive-compulsive disorder, partly in case it affected her treatment in some way, partly in case they became aware that hands-on care was causing her exceptional distress.

'I can't help feeling responsible,' she said.

'For her having a stroke?' Jude said. 'That's ridiculous.'

'She wanted me to leave, asked me more than once, but instead of just going, I banged on about those stupid cracks.'

'If that were enough to cause a stroke,' Jude said, 'then I'd be the one responsible, not you. But since you've already said that Frankie had a terrible headache, you know perfectly well that it could have happened any time.'

'It happened when I was there.'

'And if you hadn't been, she probably wouldn't have been able

143

to call for help, might even still be lying on the floor somewhere in that house.'

'I know,' Alex said.

'Do you?'

'I suppose so.'

'Alex, come on.'

'Yes, all right,' she gave in. 'Of course I know, I'm just being self-indulgent.'

'Would you like some company?' Jude offered.

'I'd love it,' Alex said, 'except I'm going back to check on her, and she's in ICU, and they probably won't let me in, let alone you, so there's not much point.'

'Later, maybe?'

'If I can get away,' Alex said.

'Whether you can or not,' Jude said, 'please stop beating yourself up.'

The stroke having occurred in the left hemisphere of Frankie's brain, it swiftly became apparent that her right side and speech had both been affected.

'Fairly badly,' Alex told Jude when they finally got together at Union Street the following evening. 'Though it could all be much worse, I'm told. She's up in Solomon Ward now, and she's not incontinent, thank God, and she was having some trouble swallowing, but that's already almost back to normal.'

'And the rest?' Jude asked. 'Is she paralysed?'

'It's not exactly paralysis,' Alex explained. 'They call it hemiplegia, which means her right side's very weak and floppy, and her facial muscles are drooping a little, but these things sometimes improve fairly quickly.'

'What about speech?'

'I've had patients all day, so I only popped in to see Frankie briefly this morning, and she didn't speak, but the senior sister says she has spoken a few words, and she is slurring, but clearly that could be much worse too.'

'Is she very distressed?' Jude asked.

'I couldn't tell,' Alex said. 'She's mildly sedated, and she was pretty closed off while I was there, but on the face of it, she didn't seem too bad.'

'But she knew you?'

144

Alex shook her head. 'Couldn't be sure.'

'One more question,' Jude said.

She smiled tiredly. 'Go on.'

'Are you hungry?'

'Ravenous.' Alex sniffed the air. 'Lamb?'

'You have an excellent nose,' Jude said, and kissed it.

'One piece of very good news,' Alex remembered a little later, sitting at Jude's table. 'I don't know how I could have forgotten, except I was tired and hungry.' She finished the remains of her first helping. 'This is absolutely wonderful, Jude, you're so good to me.'

'No more than you deserve.' Jude poured her a second glass of red wine. 'So what's this good news?'

'More about Frankie,' Alex said. 'According to the sister, just after I left this morning, another visitor arrived. A man who said he was her ex.'

'Ex what?' Jude asked. 'Husband?'

Alex shrugged. 'Husband or boyfriend – that's not really the point. The point is he just went in to Frankie's room and sat down next to her bed and took her hand.'

'No objections from Frankie?'

'Evidently not. Apparently she didn't say a word or even try to, but her expression clearly said she was glad to have him there.'

'So how did he know, whoever he is, that she was there?' Jude asked. 'Since no one knew who to phone.'

'No idea.' Alex smiled. 'I'm just happy for Frankie's sake that he did.'

Chapter 50

Frankie isn't sure how long he's been sitting there.

She was lying here, in this same, unfamiliar bed, surrounded by contraptions, feeling very odd, not like herself at all, yet not especially *minding* that, not even minding the tubes coming in and out of her body – knowing at the same time, in a rather vague, muddled way, that it wasn't like her *not* to mind such things – when he first came in.

She remembered him right away. *Thought* she did.

Someone she used to know.

He came to her bed and looked down at her, and though everything was a bit blurry, she could still tell that he was someone special.

Remembered his dark, almost black eyes.

'Hello, Frankie,' he said, and then he sat down on a chair next to the bed and took hold of her left hand.

Wrapped it in his own much bigger hand.

'How you doing?' he asked.

She tried to answer, but felt too tired to manage the words.

'It's all right, babe,' he said.

And she knew it was.

He's still here now, still holding her hand.

Making her feel safe.

146

Chapter 51

'Do we know yet who he is?' Alex asked one of the nurses on Solomon Ward next time she visited.

Frankie's mystery visitor was not currently at her bedside, but word was he had been there in the two-bed room for several hours, sitting quietly, holding her hand.

'His name's Michael Bolin,' the nurse said, and saw the startled expression on Alex's face. 'Ring a bell?'

'Yes,' Alex said. 'Maybe.'

'Problem?'

'I don't think so,' Alex said.

'So does this sound like your Michael Bolin?' she asked Jude that evening.

It was milder, more seasonal, and they were walking to the Cinemateque in the Media Centre in Middle Street to see a low-budget Canadian film someone had recommended to Alex.

'"Tall, dark and quite dishy," was the description,' Alex went on.

'Could be him, I suppose.' Jude thought back. 'The one from Luddesdown Terrace had a tattoo on one shoulder, though I don't suppose anyone at the hospital will have seen that.'

'Little black rabbit tattoo?'

'Exactly,' Jude said, surprised.

'Frankie has one too,' Alex said. 'I saw it once when she was changing her T-shirt after she spilled something on it.'

'Proof of some kind of relationship,' Jude said, as they entered the Media Centre. 'If not of her good taste.' He grinned. 'And I'm not talking about the tattoo.'

147

'They seem to think,' Alex said, over a glass of wine in the bar after the film, 'that having Bolin there might make a difference to Frankie's recovery.'

'That's good,' Jude said, dubiously. 'If they think so.'

'It's obviously far better than her being alone and afraid.'

'You said she didn't seem too distressed,' Jude said.

'On the face of it,' Alex said. 'Underneath, you can bet she's terrified.'

'Poor woman.' Jude was silent for a few moments, before he said: 'If Frankie isn't speaking, how can they be sure she's really okay with Bolin being there? If he's an ex, that must mean there was a split of some kind.'

'I don't suppose anyone can be completely sure,' Alex admitted. 'Frankie's definitely confused, but apparently she's being quite expressive, especially about things she doesn't want or like. Bolin's been holding her good hand for long periods, and if Frankie wanted to pull away, she could have.'

'Okay,' Jude said. 'That's good, I suppose.'

'In the circumstances,' Alex said, 'I'd say it's better than good.'

'You're right, of course,' Jude said, reluctantly. 'If Frankie likes him.'

Alex smiled. 'Takes all kinds, Jude.'

Chapter 52

'The doc says you can go home soon, babe.'

Frankie nods at Bo, her smile crooked but sincere.

'He says it's okay cos I'm going to be there too,' Bo says.

'Good,' Frankie says, though the slurred word sounds like 'ood'.

'You do want me there, don't you?' asks Bo.

She nods, because that's easier than speaking, and because she's aware that her voice sounds funny, like she's drunk. Alex tells her off sometimes when she comes for being lazy about talking. Not unkindly – Alex is never unkind, always patient – but she keeps telling Frankie that the more she practises speaking, the quicker she'll get back to normal.

Nothing's normal in here, least of all herself, with her heavy, weak right side, and sometimes, usually when she wakes up, she has a panicky feeling, can't think where she is or what's happened to her, and then she remembers she's had a stroke, and for a moment that shocks her, upsets her, but then she comes to a bit more and settles down, and feels that maybe it's not so bad after all.

Specially when Bo's here.

Half the time, in here, there's someone on at her, nagging at her to do things, like making her fucked-up hand and arm and leg work, or Alex is on at her to do the pain-in-the-arse speech exercises that the therapist wants her to do, and Alex says that once she goes home to the house, if Frankie wants, she'll be able to come and do her speech therapy officially. And though Frankie didn't really remember how she knew Alex till the other woman told her, she can't imagine why she wouldn't want that.

Alex is a nice woman. They're all nice to her in here, but Alex, especially, behaves like a mate, like they've known each other for years, and Alex has helped with all sorts of things, like filling in a few of the gaps. Like telling her that she helps people keep their homes clean and tidy. Like telling her she lives in a lovely house in Rottingdean.

Home.

Home's a bit of a blur.

One of the many things Frankie can't seem to get her head around.

Like not really minding being unable to do things for herself. She doesn't know why she doesn't mind more, but she really does not.

'Don't upset yourself,' people are always saying to her when she can't manage things. 'It will get better.'

Bo doesn't say things like that to her.

Bo is just quiet and gentle, holding her hand.

She likes that. Big, handsome man with dark gypsy looks holding her hand.

Loves that.

She has remembered now, not just because he's told her, but remembered herself that she used to love him – that's one of the things she's fairly clear about. Clear enough, anyway, to be grateful to him for being here.

'I'll take care of you, babe,' Bo says now, and his eyes are kind. 'They're showing me stuff, and I can help you same as anyone.'

Frankie smiles again.

'When we get you home,' he says.

She tries once again to think about home, shuts her eyes and tries to conjure it up, but there's just a jumble in her head, and it's too tiring to worry about.

So she doesn't.

150

Chapter 53

The commencement of Jude's new building job in Hove in the first week of September, and the final plans for Frankie's homecoming from the Royal Sussex – directly home, rather than via rehab, mostly due to Mike Bolin's assurances that he would be Frankie's full-time primary carer – coincided with real summer at last in the shape of a heatwave dragged up over the coast by southerly winds from Africa.

In Brighton, the hotels grew more packed, as did the beaches.

On the new site in Hove, the men stripped off and tipped cans of cold drinks down their throats, most of them thriving on warmth and sunshine; but Jude, never a lover of heat, found himself drained by each successive nightfall.

'Not much good in this,' he apologized to Alex one night in bed.

'Good enough,' she told him, and kissed him.

His portrait of her – barely begun – was already on hold; most things non-work-related were on hold, and Jude, in common with many of the other locals, was happy to shun the beaches and jammed restaurants and stay home either at his flat or in the cottage.

Alex liked warmth, would have been happy to have ventured out into the crowded streets, but then again, with her own workload heavier than ever, she was tired too, and, more importantly and satisfyingly, she was, she found, content to be anywhere with Jude.

'Come on down,' she said to Suzy on the phone one day. 'Or wait till the worst of the heat's gone, if you like, and then come.'

'Come up,' Suzy said. 'It's been forever since you came to London.'

'Too much on down here,' Alex said. 'For us both.'

'You could come without Jude,' Suzy said.

'Of course I could,' Alex agreed. 'Except the truth is I don't much want to go without him just at present.'

'That's been a long time coming,' said Suzy.

And then she added that Matt would have been glad.

Chapter 54

It hits Frankie for the first time when she sees the house.

Not panic, exactly, but a hard, unwelcome sensation in her stomach, violent as a blow from a man-sized fist.

'Here we are,' says Bo, lifting her out of the taxi, easily, almost effortlessly, for he is a strong, muscular man and Frankie has lost weight since the stroke.

Bo drives a dark-green Toyota four-wheel drive pick-up truck, with ample space in the back for tools and materials and, if needed, for a wheelchair, and it's already parked outside the house on Winder Hill, and he's told Frankie he looks forward to taking her for drives in it when she's ready, but for today he decided that a taxi was more suitable.

'There we go,' he says now, setting her down in her wheelchair.

Frankie stares up at him, at his dark curly hair blowing in the breeze. Then she stares back at the house.

'Home sweet home,' he says.

And wheels her up the path.

'I've done all the stuff they said you needed,' Bo says.

Frankie sees the wooden ramp ahead.

Then the front door.

That's when it hits.

'No,' she says, though she doesn't know exactly why, can't remember why.

'It's all right,' Bo tells her, pushes her up the ramp.

'No,' Frankie says again, more urgently, gripping the left arm of her chair.

'Don't be silly,' Bo says, unlocking the door.

Opening it.

'*No!*' she cries out.
But she's already inside.
The door shutting behind her.
'Be all right now, babe,' Bo says.
Frankie doesn't answer.
'Just the two of us again,' he says. 'Like old times.'
She looks up at him, into his eyes, sees reassurance there.
And the bad feeling melts away and disappears.

Chapter 55

The first time Alex visited Frankie back at the house on the hill, she found, to her great pleasure, a sense of something close to serenity in the air.

Mike Bolin very much in charge. Frankie almost entirely compliant, calm and, so far as Alex could tell, happy. All of which was a particular relief to her, in view of Jude's continuing doubts about Bolin.

'Will he get anything out of it, do you know?' he'd asked when he'd first heard that the other man was going to be living with and looking after Frankie. 'Do carers get paid?'

Alex had replied that it wasn't her province, but she expected there might be some kind of benefit available, though whether that was for him or for Frankie to claim, she didn't know.

'I'm not sure if Frankie's big on taxes or that kind of thing,' she added. 'So she might not be keen.'

'Same might apply to Bolin,' Jude had said.

'I know they've turned down home help,' Alex said.

'So Bolin's turning cleaner as well as nurse,' Jude said. 'Blimey.'

'He won't be nursing,' Alex had told him a little crisply, though she, too, had been surprised by the refusal of help, since many men thrust into caring roles were glad to accept every scrap of assistance offered.

'Still,' Jude said.

'Couldn't you at least try to be a bit less suspicious? This is a man doing a very good thing.'

'Let's say sceptical, rather than suspicious,' Jude had said. 'Sounds nicer.'

*

'You look very well, Frankie,' Alex told her now, moments after her arrival, finding her at the kitchen table in her wheelchair.

Frankie pulled a wry face and made a sound to go with it.

'She's doing great,' Bolin said, and ruffled Frankie's hair, longer now, in need of cutting, the last remnants of her highlights grown out, bits of grey taking their place amid the mousy brown.

Alex smiled at him before looking down at Frankie again. 'How do you feel? I gather the physio's been going quite well.'

Another sound.

'Come on, Frankie,' Alex encouraged. 'Tell me.'

'Good,' Frankie said.

'Glad to hear it,' Alex said.

All things considered, she thought that Frankie was quite happy. The question was how much of that contentment was genuinely rooted, brought about, perhaps, by Bolin's presence, and how much had been fabricated by blocking.

She had spoken about this to a psychologist at the Centre named Marian Taub, who had told Alex that she had come across this kind of about-turn before; previously highly stressed or difficult individuals seeming suddenly calmer after the massive blow of major stroke, strangely more content in themselves, as if, perhaps, their new disabilities had provided them with a kind of escape.

'Not such a bad thing,' Marian Taub had said, 'where there's no hope of significant recovery. But for a patient like Frankie, with potential for considerable further improvement, there's a risk she could become too placid.'

'Stop fighting, you mean?' Alex had said.

'Which would be quite tragic,' the psychologist said.

They had talked for a while about obsessive-compulsive disorder, and the fact that Frankie appeared to have, temporarily, at least, forgotten its domination of her life.

'Could she genuinely have forgotten, do you think?' Alex asked.

'It's a possibility,' Marian Taub replied, 'given that she has had other memory difficulties, but I suspect she may be blocking. Too much to bear for now.'

'So she's pushed the OCD into storage till she's stronger?'

'Perhaps,' the psychologist said.

'But it will come back, won't it?' Alex had asked. 'Whether or not she's ready for it, the OCD won't just disappear forever?'

The psychologist had said she would be surprised if it did.

'What if it's even worse than before?' Alex asked.

'One step at a time,' Marian Taub had told her, gently.

Seeing Frankie now on home territory, Alex became more certain than ever that the other woman's brain had managed, at least for the time being, to blot out her OCD. The kitchen, clean enough for the average person, came nowhere close to Frankie's fanatical hygiene standards, with no stench of bleach or disinfectant, unwashed mugs and several dishes standing on the granite work-tops and white draining board, and a stain of something that might have been wine on the table.

'How are you managing, Mr Bolin?' She followed him as he pushed Frankie's chair out through the hall, where a pair of his trainers stood, crookedly, by the wall, and on into the living room, where Bolin had made up a bed for the disabled woman.

The single bed itself had been neatly covered with a blue spread, but several issues of the *Sun* and *Argus* were strewn on the sofa – on which the previously immaculate white piping looked distinctly grubby – an empty videotape box lay on the carpet near the TV and an ashtray full of roll-up stubs stood on the coffee table.

No bad thing in itself, a bit of a mess, if it genuinely was not causing Frankie distress, though that, Alex thought, was hard to be sure of. And certainly the absence of a commode anywhere in sight was good news, she felt, since it presumably meant she was managing to get to the lavatory with help, and Frankie's acceptance of that kind of help surely had to mean that Michael Bolin's reappearance in her life had, whatever Jude thought of him, been a true godsend.

'We're managing fine.' Bolin had parked Frankie by the sofa, seen Alex looking around the room. 'Aren't we, babe?'

Alex thought about raising the subject of home help again, maybe just a gentle reminder that it was still on offer, but decided to leave well alone.

'Place looks all right, doesn't it?' Bolin asked testily.

'Of course.' Alex looked back towards the bed, at the small table beside it, currently bearing a small torch – good idea, since there was no lamp in easy reach, and trailing flexes were dangerous – and a glass of stale-looking water. 'Except, perhaps—'

'What?' he said.

157

'Just a small thing,' she said. 'That little table might be better placed on the other side of the bed.'

'But that's her bad side,' Bolin said.

'I know it seems odd –' Alex was certain someone, perhaps the physiotherapist, must have advised him of this before, but he might easily have forgotten, with so much to take in '– and I'm sure you prefer it this way, Frankie –' she smiled at the other woman's scowl '– but the more you have to use your right side, the better your chances of a full recovery.'

'She likes having water at night,' Bolin said. 'She'll end up knocking it over.'

'Even if you only lean over that way,' Alex said to Frankie, 'so you can cheat and use your left hand, that'll still exercise your muscles.'

'What do you think, babe?' Bolin asked.

'No,' Frankie said, bolshily.

Bolin grinned. 'Didn't think so.'

Alex smiled, too. 'Up to you both, obviously.'

She had realised, in the past few moments, what else was different about the place. The windows were open, which was extremely welcome in view of the heat, and a few flies were darting around the living room, though Frankie seemed not to be noticing them, the dirtiest of insects, any more than the general clutter.

Marian Taub was right about blocking, had to be.

'Want some tea?' Bolin offered.

'Not yet for me, thanks.' Alex looked at Frankie. 'When we've done a bit of work, don't you think, Frankie?'

'Yeah,' Frankie said.

'Want me to stay?' Bolin addressed the question to Alex.

'I think we can manage alone.' Alex checked with Frankie again. 'That all right with you?'

Frankie didn't answer. Instead she cast a look up at Bolin of disproportionate uncertainty, almost, Alex felt, of yearning, as if she could hardly bear for him to be out of her sight.

'You'll be fine, babe.'

He bent, kissed her forehead quite tenderly, and left the room.

Frankie's eyes followed him all the way, her expression, as the door shut behind him, quite bereft.

'He seems very nice,' Alex said, touched.

Frankie nodded.

'So lucky he was around.' Alex knew she was fishing, partly because she hoped the questions might make Frankie more communicative, partly because she was intrigued by the relationship.

'Yeah,' Frankie agreed.

'You certainly seem happy to have him,' Alex persevered.

'Yeah,' Frankie said again.

Alex suppressed a sigh, smiled instead, reached down to open her case and withdrew a book filled with pictures of household objects, ready to graduate to something more sophisticated if Frankie coped too easily or became insulted.

'Right,' she said. 'Time we got down to some real work.'

Chapter 56

After Alex has gone, Frankie sits alone in the living room, waiting for Bo to come back inside, and watches a fly as it lands on the right arm of her wheelchair.

She has some sense of not liking flies, but finds that she cannot, for now, remember exactly why not.

'Get it, girl,' Bo says, coming in, lighting a roll-up and watching her.

Frankie doesn't move.

'Go on,' he urges. 'Use your good hand.'

She lifts her left hand half-heartedly, and the insect takes off.

'Wouldn't kill a fly,' Bo says.

And smiles at her.

The smile – that *particular* smile – brings back the bad feeling for just a moment or two; like the one she experienced when he first brought her back from hospital, except that felt like a punch, and this feels more like something flashing through her mind, sharp as a sword blade, though once again, she isn't at all sure why.

She remembers waking up two nights ago thinking she was having a heart attack because her heart was pounding like a tom-tom and she was sweating, and she knew that something had terrified her, something to do with Bo, she thought, something awful, but she didn't know what it was. And she must have made a sound, maybe even cried out, because suddenly he was there with her in the living room, crouching beside the single bed.

'You had a bad dream, babe,' he told her. 'That's all.'

And it was gone again, and she was glad it was gone, bloody glad.

Yet she knows now that it's still there, lurking in the back of her mind, that dark, bad *something*, and Frankie still doesn't know what it is, only that it's an effort to think about it and that she doesn't *want* to think about it. And there are many things she chooses not to think about these days, like still not being able to use her right hand or walk or talk properly. And if she doesn't think about them, she finds they don't trouble her too much ...

'Not like you,' Bo says now, 'to put up with them.'

For a second, she doesn't know what he's talking about.

'Dirty little fuckers,' he says, and swats another fly away.

That one word stays with her for a bit, bothering her.

Dirty.

And then she pushes that away, too, and it's gone again, like the fly.

Chapter 57

'It does still worry me, a little,' Alex told Jude that evening as they strolled on the beach at Rottingdean below the White Horse Hotel. 'I know that what Marian Taub said about taking things a step at a time makes perfect sense, and I know I should be relieved that Frankie doesn't seem to be stressing out over the mess.'

'It does sound more like your place than hers,' Jude said.

Alex laughed and hit him. 'My place pre-Frankie, maybe, but that's the point I'm trying to make, isn't it?'

'But you said Bolin's keeping it reasonably clean.'

'Reasonably oughtn't to be anywhere near enough for Frankie.' Alex tucked her arm through Jude's. 'And I'm still surprised about neither of them wanting to accept a home help.'

'Maybe having to watch another person cleaning her home might be worse for Frankie than seeing it dirty?' Jude suggested. 'Maybe Bolin knows that, or maybe he just doesn't give a stuff about hygiene.'

'Or about Frankie's feelings?'

'I didn't say that.'

'Thought it, though, didn't you?'

Jude shrugged.

They strolled on, enjoying the sunset and the tide's roll against the rocks, regular as a slow, insistent pulse. The high temperatures were still holding, but the wind direction had changed, and the air this evening smelled fresher than it had for some time.

'Bolin is very gentle with Frankie,' Alex said.

'Comforting to think of a bigot bully having a soft side,' Jude said dryly.

'Do you think perhaps you might have been wrong about him?'

162

'Maybe.'

Alex looked sideways at him. 'But you don't really think so, do you?'

'I'd like to,' Jude said. 'Really. For Frankie's sake.'

They arrived back at Melton Cottage with a takeaway pizza to find that though the front door was locked as normal, the house had been broken into.

'Back door,' Alex whispered. 'Bloody hell, Jude.'

They went into the kitchen hand in hand, saw that the back door was open, glass smashed, then moved together into the sitting room, staring in dismay at the mess.

'Phone the police.' Jude handed her the pizza box. 'and stay on the line to them while I check upstairs.'

'Be careful,' she said. 'Please.'

'Don't worry.' He grimaced slightly. 'I'm not hero potential.'

'Good.'

Trying to stop her hands from shaking, she went to pick up the phone.

She had already hung up by the time he got back downstairs into the sitting room, was on her knees in the corner near the windows, looking at something on the floor.

'Long gone,' he said. 'Didn't you phone?'

'On their way.'

Her voice was low, but her distress was clear.

Not distressed, Jude swiftly saw, because of the spaces where her TV and VCR and computer and printer had been, nor even because the place had been horribly messed up, files of paper strewn everywhere, cushions ripped and stuffing scattered like lousy fake snow, wine bottles emptied and broken on the carpet.

But because her old photograph album had been pulled out of a cupboard, pages torn in half, pictures ruined, red wine poured over them.

'Oh, no.'

He picked his way over the wreckage till he was beside her, got down on the floor, saw that she was trying, in vain, not to cry. Saw that the photographs were almost all of her with Matt, some of her with him and Suzy in the old days.

'Do you have any of the negatives?' he asked, softly.

163

'Don't think so.' She tilted her face towards him, real pain in her eyes. 'I had a look in the kitchen,' she said. 'They even vandalized the Aga – carved it with a key, the way they do with cars.'

Knowing what the Aga had meant to her, Jude's anger, already intense, rose even higher.

'Bastards,' he said. 'Stinking bastards.'

The police having asked if anyone, other than Alex, had a set of keys, Jude said that he did. Alex asked how that was relevant, since the burglars had gained entry by smashing the glass in the back door.

'Having a key doesn't stop them doing damage,' one of them said, and looked back at Jude. 'And insiders sometimes do that kind of thing to cover up.'

'He's been with me,' Alex said, quickly and indignantly.

Jude grinned, despite himself.

'Something funny, sir?'

'Not at all,' Jude said. 'But she's right. I was with her.'

He waited until after they'd gone.

'You didn't tell them that Frankie has keys.'

'Obviously not,' Alex said. 'Waste of everyone's time.'

'Because of the stroke,' Jude said.

'Even without it,' Alex said. 'I trust her.'

'What about Bolin? If Frankie still has your keys ...'

'He's a builder, not a burglar,' Alex said. 'And anyway, even if I thought it might be him, which I certainly don't, I wouldn't tell the police because of what it would do to Frankie.'

Jude smiled.

'What?' Alex asked.

'Just thinking what a lovely person you are.'

'Thank you.' She was silent for a moment. 'You don't think there was anything personal about this, do you?'

'Because of the photos, you mean?' Jude shook his head. 'Just another scumbag who likes messing people's things up.'

'I didn't know you'd given Jude a key,' Suzy said on the phone next day.

'He's given me his, too.' Alex's hackles were already up.

'But you don't think ...' Suzy let her words trail off.

'No, I don't think.'

164

'It's just, with Jude's past.'

'Enough,' Alex told her. 'Okay?'

'Sure,' Suzy said. 'Sorry.'

'I should think so.'

'At least –' Suzy couldn't help herself '– now the locks have been changed—'

Alex put the phone down.

She asked herself, a little later, after Suzy had phoned back to apologize again, and after she had said she was sorry, too, for hanging up, if there had been any part of her, any fragment, that had thought for even one second that it might have been anything to do with Jude.

Knew there had not.

Was deeply ashamed for even asking herself the question.

Chapter 58

It went off in Frankie's head last night, at about three a.m.

Not like the last time when she woke up with her heart pounding. This was much stronger, like a kind of explosion. That's what it felt like, fireworks going off in her mind, lighting things up – not a pain thing, nothing to scare her that way, make her think she was getting ill again, having another stroke. Nothing like that.

It did scare her though, was a bad, seriously bad, feeling.

From the past again.

Except that the other times, when those jagged, frightening slivers of memory have flashed into her mind, they've gone again just as fast, and she feels as if, in some way, she's been stopping them coming back, as if she's managed to stuff them into a bottle and plug up the opening with a cork.

But this time they're not just flashes, and though they are still bits and pieces, fragments of her past still not quite connecting, still with blanks between them, now they're no longer going away. And all the peculiar comfort of her stroke seems to be disappearing, all these memories being gradually released from the bottle in her head, and she knows they're with her now to stay.

Memories.

Which she was happier without.

Like the memory, or rather the awareness, of her OCD, her disorder. That's been coming back to her, in stages; that and the fact that she's here right now, surrounded by dirt and germs and mess, and there's nothing she can do about it, and if nothing else kills her, *that* will. Being here, in her house, that woman's house, Roz Bailey's house – and she's remembered that, that it's her house or, at least, *was* her house, because letters come addressed

166

to her, and Bo has asked her about them, asked who Roz Bailey
is.

'Don't know,' Frankie says when he asks.

Which is true, more or less, except that she knows there's more
to remember, a lot more, but whatever it is seems to be shut into
one of those blanks, and she does know, somehow, that there's
something bad connected with Roz Bailey, something very bad, but
she can't remember what it is.

Doesn't want to remember.

And then there's Bo.

A lot of the memories coming back are about Bo.

Michael Bolin. Mike. Bo. Caring, gentle ex-lover, come back to
look after her.

Except there's no kindness in him in the memories.

Something else entirely.

Something ugly and frightening.

The real Bo.

Chapter 59

'I feel,' Suzy said on the phone to Alex less than a week after their previous conversation about the burglary, 'like a complete idiot and total bitch, in whichever order you prefer.'

'How come?' Alex enquired.

'You don't know?' Suzy asked. 'Obviously not.'

'What don't I know?'

'Can't tell you,' Suzy said. 'But you'll find out soon.'

'I'm not in the mood for games,' Alex said.

'Can't be helped,' Suzy told her.

Jude came to the cottage the following evening with an Indian take-away and a gift-wrapped box containing a handsome leather album.

Filled with old photographs of Alex and Matt and Suzy, many of them copies of the ones ruined by the burglars.

Alex could hardly speak.

'It wasn't difficult.' Jude made light of it. 'It was all Suzy really, digging out her own pics. Not all the same as yours, obviously, but she thought you'd like them anyway.'

'How did you get them?' Alex asked. 'You've been working flat out.'

'Suzy had the copies made, I bought the album, DHL brought them to Brighton, and I stuck them in.'

'And this?' Alex held the album open at the inside cover.

'It's a kind of pen-and-ink frontispiece,' Jude said. 'I hope you don't mind.'

'Mind?' She was incredulous. 'It's so beautiful.'

'I'm glad you like it,' he said.

'More than that,' Alex said. 'Much more.'

168

He explained that he had based his design on a Celtic love knot, with neither beginning nor end, that if she looked closely, she'd see that she and Matt and Suzy were all part of the twisted knot.

'The Celts believe the soul never dies,' Jude said.

'You're not in it,' Alex said, quietly.

'Not this one,' Jude said. 'But I'd like to think I'll be part of the next knot.'

Chapter 60

He wasn't sure why, but the house on Winder Hill kept coming back into Jude's thoughts at odd times of day and even night. Not, he felt, because of the cracks he'd noticed, since he had neither built the house nor added the conservatory, and no one had asked him to deal with the problem – on the contrary – and, of course, though he felt for Frankie in a general sense, and liked to feel he was a diligent builder, there had to be limits to his concerns.

Nor did he think that this niggle had anything especially to do with his having previously painted the house in miniature. Nor was it an outstandingly handsome or even particularly interesting house; good-looking, certainly, but of no real importance.

Just another house, when all was said and done.

Yet still, he kept getting this urge to go back and take another look at it.

'I shouldn't bother,' Alex said when he mentioned it to her.

'I wouldn't want to go inside,' Jude said. 'Wouldn't want to bother Frankie.'

'Or see Bolin.'

'There is that,' Jude agreed.

'If it's the cracks,' Alex suggested, 'I could mention them to him. He is a builder, too, after all. Though then again, it isn't really Frankie's house, and maybe Mrs Bailey has a builder she'd rather use.'

'I'd be surprised if she hadn't left instructions with Frankie.'

'I'm still not sure how much Frankie can remember.'

'Cracks on an outside wall not exactly high on her list right now,' Jude said.

'Definitely not,' Alex agreed.

Chapter 61

Frankie has been remembering more and more, during the hot, clammy night-time hours when the lights are out and Bo's asleep in his room upstairs (she isn't sure which room he's using, hasn't been up the stairs since the stroke, and he hasn't told her, and she doesn't want him to feel she's hassling him, and if he is using her room, maybe she's better off not knowing) and it's easier to think when he can't see her face, can't look into her eyes and know that it's coming back to her.

The bad times.

With him. With Bo.

What he was to her.

Did to her.

Before her trouble, before her *real* trouble.

Before the *place*.

She has remembered, too, how much she loved him. That he was the first, the only man she ever gave herself to. The only one she ever let take her over.

Though it wasn't easy, not even with him.

Letting him into her body.

Oh, God, that was bad, so bad it was always hard for her not to scream, not to push him away, but she loved him, couldn't bear to think of life without him, so she let him, had to let him, had no real choice.

That wasn't the worst of it, though, not for her. Plenty of women like her about that, about sex, about not wanting it, not wanting *it* put inside her.

Not many women like her though about the other thing.

Not many women as strange as her. As mad as her.

171

'You're off your head,' Bo used to tell her, and she knew he was right, but that didn't make it easier.

She never liked it, she remembers, not even when she was little, not even when it was just her mum and dad doing it to her.

Kissing her.

Putting their mouths on her.

Innocent kisses, theirs, always, *always*. No explanation for her trouble there, nothing low, nothing like that, and sometimes it was okay, when their lips were dry and they hadn't been eating and didn't smell of anything, but often they did, and she never liked that.

She learned about real kisses early on, like most kids. Told one of the girls at school it sounded 'yucky'. And the other girl agreed that it did, but she grinned at the same time, and Frankie knew that meant she didn't feel the same way about it because if she had, she could not have smiled.

Open mouths and tongues and teeth.

She remembers shuddering at the thought.

Remembers she went on shuddering about it into her teens and on into adulthood. Remembers trying to date boys, even liking one or two, but the minute they wanted to kiss her, she couldn't, she just *couldn't*, and sometimes, feeling guilty about that, she let them know that she didn't mind other things so much, and *that* took their minds off her mouth; pawing at her was much more worthwhile, grabbing at her tits, pushing their hands up her skirt and into her knickers. She hated that, too, but anything was better than the other.

Until Bo came along, and then anything was better than losing him.

He was working on a site in Chigwell, a road away from one of her clients, when he whistled at her one morning while she was on her way to the shops, and she never used to look at the building site because of the dirt, but she heard the sound, and it was a real wolf-whistle, and no one had ever whistled at her that way before, not *ever*, but there was no one else walking along, no one else it could have been directed at, so she had to look, didn't she? And there was Bo, this big, dark-eyed, handsome, incredibly masculine man, smiling at her, and she presumed, at first, that he was taking the piss, teasing her, but the smile was warm.

For her.

And she was lost. In love for the first, the only time. And the amazing part of it was, the miracle of it, really, was that he seemed to love her back.

Until he found out what she was like, underneath.

About her OCD.

'I don't believe you,' he said, laughing, after she confessed to him.

She remembers, even now, what it cost her to tell him about it. Remembers his face, the disbelief, the grin.

Then, when he knew she really meant it, the mockery.

And worse.

Much worse.

Oh, Christ, the things he did to her.

The things he *did*.

She thought he was out of her life forever. Prayed sometimes that he was, as much as she ever prayed for anything.

She remembers now thinking she saw him at Churchill Square that day, the day Alex Levin saw her going into Debenhams. Knows now that it was him, after all.

He must have known about her, must have been watching her, *must* have.

He must know about Swanky-Frankie, and . . .

The other things. The bad, bad things that started coming back to her in the firework moment. Things she's done – she knows that much now, because it keeps trying to surface, like sewage rising out of a dark, stinking pool, and if she had two good hands, Frankie would use them both to push those memories away, but she can't, and she knows they're coming back, all of them, will soon be complete, and she won't be able to stop them.

Concentrate on him.

On Bo. Back in her life, here and now, in this house.

Her carer.

'Oh, Christ, help me,' Frankie says in the dark, inside her head.

Knowing already that if there is a Christ, or God, He won't.

Chapter 62

'Too hot now, don't you think?' Alex said to Bolin as he saw her to the front door after her next session with Frankie. 'I'll be glad when it breaks.'

'Bloody awful,' he agreed. 'I left some milk out of the fridge this morning, and an hour later it was stinking.'

'We're not used to it, are we?' Alex said.

She had been wondering about the smell, wondering mostly at the fact that Frankie appeared not to have noticed it, realised now that it meant that though Bolin had presumably thrown the milk away, he might not have rinsed the carton out properly, had maybe chucked it in the bin in the kitchen and left it there, and *surely* that had to be driving Frankie almost mad?

'How's she doing?' Bolin asked, taking a backhand swat at a passing fly.

'Better,' Alex answered.

The walking frame that the physiotherapist had brought Frankie a while ago, and which Frankie had, by all accounts, so far refused to use, stood against the wall, where it was unlikely, Alex thought, ever to do much good.

'But still not great,' Bolin said.

'She needs motivation,' Alex said carefully.

'Lacks motivation,' he said. 'Like a bloody school report.'

'Not at all,' Alex said. 'But it's hard work for her, in many ways.'

'Bit of a kick up the backside needed, you mean,' Bolin said.

She looked at him.

'Only the very gentlest kind,' she said.

'Obviously,' Bolin said, opening the door.

Alex glanced down, saw some post on the mat, remembered seeing a stack of letters on the hall table on her way in earlier, the top one, at least, addressed to Mrs R Bailey.

'I couldn't help noticing those letters to the owner,' she said now.

'Couldn't you?' Bolin said.

She heard the sarky note in his voice, thought of Jude's dislike of the man, reminded herself that many people disliked outsiders interfering.

'I just thought,' she said quickly, 'knowing how busy you are –' she took a step outside to reassure Bolin that she wasn't planning to hang about '– if you had Mrs Bailey's forwarding address, I'd be glad to mark them up and send them on, take one job off your hands.'

'That's very kind,' Bolin said. 'But I can manage.'

'Of course you—'

He shut the door.

Chapter 63

Frankie doesn't think Bo knows that she's remembered about them.

About him. How it was.

She doesn't *think* he knows, but she can't be sure, because Bo always liked playing games at her expense, didn't he?

So far though, he's still being kind.

Loving.

It occurred to her earlier, while she and Alex were alone, that maybe it might have been okay for her to say something about Bo, use her still slurry, but improving speech to let Alex know that their past has been coming back to her, that things aren't quite the way they probably seem; not exactly asking for help or anything, but just letting her *know*. She'd never think of trusting the physio, but there's something about Alex that Frankie really likes.

But still, in the end, she didn't say anything, partly because Bo was just next door in the kitchen, partly, she supposes, because her mind's still playing its own games with her, making her remember right back to *before* the bad times, to when she still really loved Bo, to when he loved her too.

The way he's been since her stroke reminds her of those days.

Their days in the poky Barkingside flat.

The nearest to good times she's ever known with any man.

And maybe, if she can go on pretending to have forgotten the bad times, maybe Bo will go on pretending he cares.

And maybe he really *does* care. Maybe he's missed her. Maybe he's sorry.

And maybe he isn't.

176

Maybe he's waiting.
Biding his time.

She's started exercising when she's alone, when Bo isn't with her.
Not her useless right side, not the exercises the physio wants her
to do, because Frankie has no faith left in that side, can't imagine
her right arm or hand or leg ever becoming really strong again.
But she can bloody well try strengthening her left side, that makes
sense to her, anything to make her feel just a bit less helpless, less
like a victim.

Just simple exercises, all she can manage, especially in this
weather, things she can easily stop doing the instant Bo reappears:
fist clenches, wrist circles, imaginary pint-pulling to improve her
upper arm muscles. And if nothing else, so long as she counts to
herself while she's doing them – *and one, and two, and three* – at
least they push the other thoughts out of her mind.

The bad memories.
The fear.

Chapter 64

'So maybe you are right, after all, about Bolin,' Alex said to Jude that night.

They were in bed, in the cottage, lying in each other's arms on the under-sheet, the covers pushed back because it had grown even warmer again, the air that was flowing through the open windows very still, only a night bird calling, sporadically, without enthusiasm, as if it, too, was trying to conserve its strength.

'I'm sure I'm right about his not being a nice guy,' Jude said. 'But you do still think, on the whole, don't you, that he's taking good care of Frankie?'

'I think he is.' Alex leaned towards him, stroked the short, soft hairs on his chest with the palm of her hand. 'Though she didn't seem quite the same to me.'

'In what way?'

'Not quite as calm.'

'Isn't that part of her getting better?' Jude picked up her hand, kissed it. 'Didn't you say that the calm was unnatural, maybe meant she wasn't fighting?'

'That's the thing.' Alex took away her hand, sat up a little way. 'I didn't come away today feeling that Frankie *was* fighting.' She paused. 'I came away feeling she might be frightened.'

'Of what?' Jude sat up too. 'Bolin?'

Alex shook her head. 'I don't think so.'

'Maybe she's afraid she'll never get back to normal,' he suggested.

'Maybe.'

'Or having another stroke.'

'I'm sure she's scared of that. Most people are.'

'Or maybe,' Jude said, 'she's afraid of getting better in case Bolin leaves.'

'I hadn't thought of that,' Alex said. 'It's possible.'

'One thing's for sure,' Jude said, and drew her back down. 'You can't do anything about it tonight.'

'Can't do anything about it at all,' she sighed, snuggling close, 'unless she tells me about it.'

Chapter 65

'So are you ever planning to tell me?' Bo asks suddenly, out of nowhere, the following Saturday morning.

It's grown cooler, she's been feeling better, less afraid. Wondering if she's been imagining things or at least building them out of proportion.

But then now, out of nowhere, *this*.

They're in the kitchen, and he's been making toast for a while, building a stack of slices, like crooked crumbly tiles, and Frankie's noticed, off and on over the last week or so, that he's been getting restless, and she supposes he must be missing real work, the physical labour of it, and maybe one of these days he'll want to be off out to some job or other, and she isn't sure how she feels about that.

And now that question.

'What?' she asks.

'How you got here,' Bo says. 'Got this place. This fancy house.'

'Told you,' she says, her heart rate speeding up.

'Yeah, yeah,' Bo says. 'Mrs Bailey went off to Canada and left you in charge.'

Frankie shakes her head, points with her left index finger to her throat, something she often does now when she doesn't feel up to the effort of talking.

'You can talk,' Bo says, 'when you want to.'

He's right, of course, her speech is getting better, and there are times when it is simply easier not to bother, and Bo always could read her well, Frankie remembers, with bittersweet pain.

'I've been opening her letters,' Bo says. 'Lots of bills piling up.'

He brings the toast to the table, sticks the plate down next to the Flora and jam.

180

Frankie is well aware that this new line of conversation is bad news. Part of the ugliness that's been coming back, the stuff she's been keeping at arm's length.

Brain's length.

She doesn't shake her head again, just keeps her expression blank.

'We haven't really talked about bills,' Bo says. 'What you supposed to be doing with them, babe? Getting them paid or sending them to someone else?'

Frankie gives a small, still slightly one-sided, shrug.

'She know about your stroke, does she, this Mrs Bailey?'

Frankie doesn't answer.

'That's a no, is it?'

'Yeah,' Frankie says.

'Funny kind of arrangement.'

She shrugs again.

Bo pauses before his next question.

'What about the van in the garage?'

Inside Frankie's head, something stirs, not quite a pain, but something nasty.

'Door was locked,' Bo says, 'but I wanted to stick my truck in there, so I opened it, had a look.' He waits, watching her. 'Bit of a botched job, the re-spray.'

Again she doesn't answer.

'What you been up to, Frankie?' He waits again. 'Been up to something, that's for sure. Cleaning for people one minute, all done up the next. All those posh clothes up there in those nice, clean wardrobes.' He glances up at the ceiling, then back down at her face. 'Not your wardrobes.' He pauses. 'Not so clean any more either, dust getting in.'

He watches her for another moment, and then, looking satisfied, transfers his gaze to her hair. 'Highlights could use a touch-up.'

He reaches out, touches a few strands, and she tries not to cringe.

'That's more like it,' he says, and suddenly he's harsh. 'The Frankie I remember. The woman who loved me so much she couldn't stand me to touch her.' His eyes are harder. 'What you been up to, Frankie?'

'Don't know,' she says.

'Handy,' Bo says. 'Fucking convenient, in fact, wouldn't you say?'

181

She's starting to tremble, her mouth quivering.

'That an act, too?' Bo asks.

There are tears in her eyes.

'Better be careful, hadn't I?' he says. 'Don't want to give you another stroke.'

Chapter 66

'Alex, it's David.'

The call came on Thursday morning, early, while she was still up in the bedroom getting dressed.

'Suzy's in hospital,' David told her. 'Pneumonia.'

'Oh my God.'

'Don't panic, Ally,' David said. 'She'll be okay, but I know you always want to be told about anything like this.'

'Yes,' Alex said, calming down. 'Thank you.'

'No chance of you coming up, is there?'

'Every chance,' she told him. 'Where is she?'

'Royal Brompton.'

'I'll make some calls.'

'I'll tell her,' David said.

'Better wait, in case I hit a snag,' Alex said. 'Anyway, we both know she'll grumble about our making a fuss. Just give her my love for now, and tell her to do whatever she's told.'

'That'll be a first,' David said.

Less than three hours later, having rescheduled and reallocated various appointments for the next two days, Alex was on the London train. She had intended to drive, but when she'd told Jude what was happening, he'd pointed out that her mind mightn't be on the road, and that it wasn't just Suzy who needed her these days.

'Don't misunderstand me,' he said. 'I do think you should go, but I want to make quite sure you come back to me in one piece.'

He had initially offered to drive her, but Alex had told him he was already worn out with the job, and they were forecasting the

183

heat returning, and she didn't want him trekking back and forth for no good reason.

'Anyway, I like the train,' she added.

'Maybe,' Jude said, 'if you're still in London on Sunday, I could come up.'

Alex said she would love that.

Chapter 67

Frankie's getting really scared again.

It was true, in a way, what she said to Bo yesterday. She doesn't know exactly what she's done, can't remember everything, doesn't want to, because she knows it's bad, definitely bad. And remembering about Bo and her before, in the old days, is more than enough for her to cope with.

The things he used to do. The way he used to force her to kiss him, over and over and over again, making her feel sick, except that puking would have been much worse, so she had had to endure it, *had* to.

She remembers now that she used to wonder why real sex was bearable, how come she could cope with that, even like it sometimes. She supposes it was because she loved him so much, because deep down she was still, despite her psychiatric problems, a woman in love; or maybe Bo being inside her, really inside her, was beyond her coping, too much for her to think about. Like not thinking about internal organs and your own blood, which you can never clean properly, whatever they write in magazines about cleansing and purging and other disgusting stuff – though she did use to give herself douches when she could, when Bo was going to be out for long enough, because she knew how disgusted he'd be if he found out.

She remembers the first time Bo realised how she felt about the kissing.

'Tell me how you feel, babe,' he said, kindly. 'If you love me, you can tell me anything, trust me with anything.'

So she did. Said it wasn't him, it had always been like that, with every man or boy who'd ever kissed her, and there hadn't been

185

many, there hadn't been *anyone* for years and years before him, and she'd hoped, more than he could imagine, that it might be different with him, okay with him, because she loved him so desperately.

'But it isn't?' he said.

'No,' she admitted, miserably.

'Tell me exactly how it is,' he said, saw her shake her head. 'You have to tell me, babe, or I won't believe you love me. I'll just think I'm no different to all the others.'

So she told him that too. That it felt disgusting. Dirty. Sick making. The wetness, the invasion of her cleanness, the putting of germs into her – he already knew about her problem with germs, she said.

Bo went very quiet for a long time after she finished telling him, and she remembers feeling so afraid.

'So my kissing you makes you feel sick and dirty,' he said, at last.

'It's not you, Bo,' she said. 'Please, you have to believe me about that. I love you so much.'

'But my kisses make you want to puke,' he said.

She didn't say any more, knew she'd told him far too much, knew there was nothing she could say to make it better. And then he left her, went out through the front door of the Barkingside flat and didn't come back for five days. And Frankie came close to killing herself during those five days, thought she'd lost him forever, hated herself, wanted to die because she'd hurt the man she loved, because she was a sick, twisted, mad person.

And then, when he came back, and she was filled with relief and shame, he said very little, just drew her close and held her tightly, and even now, even with all the blanks still confusing her memories, she can still recall the wonder of that moment, feeling his warmth against her again, the sheer comfort of his big, strong body.

That was when Bo pulled away, just a little, and put his hands on either side of her face, and Frankie knew, immediately, what was coming, and there was nothing she could do about it, not if she wanted to keep him.

And he began to kiss her. The longest, deepest, tongue-invading kiss of her life. And he didn't stop, wouldn't stop, not even when she began to moan and try to pull away, just went on kissing her,

186

and Frankie had never, thank God, been raped, but this had to be close to it, worse than rape, for her, and still he went on, and when she gagged, he went on, and when she struggled, he pinned her against a wall, jammed himself against her legs so that she couldn't kick him, and went on and on.

And afterwards, he watched her run to the bathroom, stuck his foot in the door so she couldn't be private, even then, so he could watch her throw up, witness her wretchedness and revulsion. And he waited till she was able to look up at him again, and he said only one disgust-loaded word:

'Charming.'

Chapter 68

Watching the JCB digging out footings at the retirement home-to-be in Hove on Friday morning, Jude found there were still two extraneous things preying on his mind, one welcome, the other less so.

Thinking about Alex was still a source of constant pleasure–even missing her a semi-luxurious emotion. Missing her meant he cared as much as he'd thought he did; missing her meant he could anticipate her return.

The intrusion into his thoughts of the house on Winder Hill was less welcome, certainly more irritating, particularly as Jude still had no real understanding of why his mind kept on returning to it. Alex's feeling that Frankie had seemed in some way frightened hadn't helped, he supposed, except that the house had been nagging at him before that, hadn't it? And perhaps it was, after all, just those damned cracks that were still troubling him, just his builder's instinct warning him they might be symptomatic of a more serious problem.

'Forget about it,' Alex had said last time he'd raised the subject, after which they'd gone to bed and made love and he had, most decisively, forgotten. But she was in London now, which meant that come tonight she wouldn't be around to take his mind off it.

And for some reason, he thought as he donned his hard hat after lunch, he still didn't really believe that his anxiety *was* connected to the cracking.

Which was why he had already more or less made up his mind that if he had the energy, this evening, after another day's work in this awful wilting weather – and the heat had come back, just as they'd forecast – and if he didn't feel up to painting tonight, and if Roz Bailey's house was still bugging him, he would drive over to Rottingdean and take just one more look.

Nice woman, Mrs Bailey. Which was probably what lay behind this; the fact that he had liked the lady, and was therefore concerned that her house might be falling apart, and that the people taking care of it for her might not be up to the job.

Probably, that was it.

Chapter 69

If it had stopped there, Frankie thinks she might have survived. But after that, there was this terrible rage in Bo, this disgust, this need to punish her for what he regarded as a personal insult.

The kissing became just a part of it. He began to go out of his way to make sure she knew he was sleeping with, and kissing, other women, sometimes hookers – though Frankie used to tell herself that couldn't be true, because she knew that tarts disgusted Bo almost as much as homosexuals did. He talked about '*them*' a lot, always had, but once he realised that dirty talk in general upset her, he talked even more frequently about 'homos' and 'dykes' and what they got up to, how filthy it was. And Frankie could count herself lucky, Bo said, that he wasn't like some men, didn't fancy the idea of sticking his prick up her arse, so that was one thing she didn't have to worry about because he'd rather die than do that.

'Aside from that,' he said, 'I can't afford to be too choosy now my own woman's done her best to give me a fucking complex—'

'You haven't *listened* to me,' Frankie tried pleading.

'– so if I don't go out and find a few other women to appreciate me, I'm just going to lose all my confidence, and surely the main thing,' he taunted her, 'is me still coming back to you after.'

For the longest time, Frankie thought that was still true, that she needed Bo with her more desperately than she hated the things he did and said to her. And anyway, the *saying* didn't matter, she told herself, words were nothing, it was the *doing* that was driving her crazy.

'You know you're driving me crazy,' she told Bo once.

'Craz*ier*, you mean, nutbag,' he said.

He took her to a tattoo parlour next day, drove her all the way

190

to a place in Soho because he said it was the *best*, made her have a dirty man with filthy needles brand her with that black rabbit on her shoulder, told her that bunnies were symbols of madness. And when she wept and protested, he pointed out that he was having it done too, and surely even she had to see that meant he still loved her, and if she didn't agree to this then he'd know, once and for all, that she didn't love him.

Chapter 70

'David had no business scaring you like this.'

Suzy's first words when Alex had arrived in her room on the second floor of the Royal Brompton, and it was, apparently, true that the antibiotics had already begun to kick in, as a result of which she was feeling better than she had.

'He didn't scare me,' Alex said, 'he just told me.'

'If he hadn't scared you, you wouldn't be here.'

'I knew you'd be fine.' Alex looked at her friend, at the pretty face, thinner and paler than she'd seen her for a long while, the blond hair spikier than ever after fever and pillows. 'I just wanted to be here for you.'

'You always are,' Suzy said, then added, with a grin: 'Still no Jude?'

'Some of us have to work,' Alex said, knowing that their long-distance conspiracy over the photograph album had alleviated Suzy's concerns, and thinking how pissed off those cold-hearted burglars would probably be if they knew that their handiwork had done just a smidgen of good. 'He sends his love.'

'Thank him,' Suzy said, and then her forehead creased. 'He's not the only one with commitments. How many patients did you have to let down to get here?'

'Not let down,' Alex told her easily. 'All being taken care of.'

'That's all very well,' Suzy said, 'but David should have kept his mouth shut.'

A feeling struck Alex, at that instant, that something was wrong, something that had nothing to do with Suzy's pneumonia, and yes, she knew all too well that Suzy tended, like her hair, to spikiness when she was ill, became tetchy and cross when her

192

vulnerability was accentuated, but still . . .

'You okay?' she asked, gently, knowing better than to make a big deal of it.

'Never better,' Suzy answered. 'Give or take the odd infected lung.'

'David all right?' Alex pressed lightly. 'Apart from fretting over you?'

'David's fine,' Suzy said. 'Don't stress, Ally.'

Something was wrong. Decidedly so. A row, at least.

Just a row, obviously, just a quarrel because Suzy was extra low. All couples fell out, after all, even she and Matt had fought now and then, and Lord knew Suzy and David were the most rock-solid couple she'd ever known.

Which made anything more than that unthinkable.

Chapter 71

Bo was a kind of sadist, Frankie learned the hard way. Though by the time she came to realise that, she also knew that she was finished. Her OCD was out of control, the cleaning her only remaining comfort, the one thing that helped her to survive from day to day, helped her keep some semblance, some illusion, of control.

She cleaned and tidied their flat morning, noon and night, and her obsessions and compulsions just served to goad Bo, to feed his cruelty. If she tidied a room, he messed it up again. If she disinfected a kitchen worktop, he dropped food on it and then, perfecting his art, he soiled it with snot or spit, or put his shoes on the kitchen table, watched her face and then, seeing he'd achieved his aim, he either laughed or stared at her with cold dislike.

He began his final push by urinating in various places. First, just missing the toilet bowl, then pissing in the shower and bath, after which he would tell her that it stank, and stand by to watch while she scrubbed with bleach, over and over again – and then he'd repeat the exercise.

The first time Frankie lost it with him, she remembers now, was after she found out that he'd urinated in her favourite vase, right after she'd arranged daffodils in it – she loved daffs, the scent of them, their clean, beautiful shape, though as with all flowers, she was careful to change their water once a day at least and throw them out before they began decaying. But *that* day, when she realised what he'd done, she screamed, actually screamed, and hit Bo, and he hit her back, hard. And she knew then that they were coming to the end, and it was as if it was all filling her up, her OCD and his cruelty, and if it reached a certain point, filled up to

194

the very top of her head, if there was no more space to fill, then Frankie knew that would be it.

It was. Because Bo didn't stop at the pissing, he had to do worse. And he knew exactly what he was doing to her, she thought, with what brain she had left at the time, and it occurred to her that perhaps he was going mad too, in his own way, that maybe she'd done that to him, had driven him to it, because he'd always been sweet to her before she'd confessed to him about the kissing. So probably what he was doing, she thought, was taking her to the edge of the highest mountain he could find in their little war zone, and getting ready to push her over, because he'd had enough of her, wanted shot of her.

And he did it.

Took her pillow into the bathroom and smeared shit on it.

The last straw. The final act of their relationship.

She went berserk, literally, they told her later. Though she has no memory at all of exactly what happened, what she actually did. It's all gone from the moment of finding out what Bo did to her pillow, to coming to in the unit, the *place*.

Without Bo. With strangers, doctors and nurses and orderlies and other patients, mad as herself.

In the nut-house, where she belonged.

And when she came out, Bo was long gone, and so were all her possessions, and whether he'd taken them or chucked them out she never knew, and other people, more strangers, were living in their flat in Barkingside, her past obliterated.

And since she had to do something, earn a living, occupy herself, Frankie did the only thing she knew how to do well, went back to being the best damn cleaner anyone could possibly have asked for.

And now she's here, in this beautiful house.

Though even with all those other memories flooding, *burning* back, she still can't remember quite how she got here.

Not quite. Not exactly what she did, or why.

She knows it was bad, knows that much. And now that she's remembered everything about Bo's dark side, she knows it's only a matter of time till *he* finds out the truth.

And she wonders how bad that will be.

195

Chapter 72

As it turned out, Jude had been too tired the previous evening to think about going out again, but by Saturday lunchtime, having done the food and grocery shopping for both the flat and cottage, and still waiting to hear if Alex was coming home or if he was to drive up to London next day, he felt unable to settle to painting or anything halfway useful.

And the house on the hill was still gnawing at a corner of his mind.

So he left the flat, got in the Honda and drove to Winder Hill.

He stopped outside the house, glanced up at the sky, saw that the clouds he'd woken up to that morning really did seem to be building up to something, and maybe, with luck, the big storm they'd been tentatively forecasting for several days might finally be on its way.

And then, just as he turned his attention back to the house, the front door opened, and Mike Bolin came out, a cigarette stuck in one corner of his mouth, walked towards his dark green Toyota pick-up truck, and saw Jude.

Jude opened the door and got out. 'Afternoon.'

'What you doing here?' Bolin asked.

'I was passing,' Jude said.

'Oh, yeah,' Bolin said.

'Yes,' Jude said, easily. 'How's Frankie doing?'

'Not bad,' Bolin replied. 'Coming along.'

'Small world,' Jude said.

'Isn't it,' Bolin said, and started to turn away.

'One thing,' Jude said.

'Yeah?'

Jude raised his right arm, pointed to the cracks on the conservatory wall. 'Suppose you've already seen them?'

Bolin glanced at them and nodded.

'Just thought I'd mention them,' Jude said. 'In case.'

'Sure,' Bolin said. 'I'll take a look, soon as I get a chance.'

'Probably a good idea,' Jude said. 'If you need some help, I could—'

'I can manage,' Bolin said shortly.

'Course you can,' Jude said. 'Send my best to Frankie, won't you?'

'Sure,' Bolin said, and turned away.

So that was that, Jude told himself as he got back in the Honda and drove away.

Nothing more to be said.

Chapter 73

Frankie's in the kitchen when Bo comes in.
'That artist bloke was outside,' he said. 'Alex's friend.'
'What'd he want?' Frankie asks.
'I think he thinks the house is cracking up,' Bo says.
The word '*cracking*' sets off an instant pain in Frankie's head.
Outside, thunder rumbles.

Chapter 74

'They say I can go home tomorrow,' Suzy, out of bed and sitting with David, told Alex when she arrived at the hospital after lunch.

'How lovely.' Alex gave Suzy a hug, then kissed David's cheek. 'You must be relieved.'

'Very.' He stood up. 'Take my seat, Ally. I'm going to find Suzy a decent cup of coffee.'

Alex saw unmistakable discomfort in his eyes, just before they slid away from her gaze, and felt a thud of confusion and dismay in the pit of her stomach.

'Perhaps you could find one for Ally too,' Suzy said, stiffly.

'Of course,' David said, and went.

Leaving them alone.

'Okay,' Alex said, after a moment. 'What's going on?'

Suzy didn't answer.

'Tell me,' Alex said. 'Please.'

'David's having an affair.' Suzy looked at Alex's stunned, horrified face. 'I know. Doesn't seem real, does it?' Her mouth pulled into a sad, small smile. 'Over a year now.'

'You've known for a year?' Alex was incredulous.

'Just three months,' Suzy said. 'The affair's a year old.'

Alex felt suddenly fogged, as if something fundamental in her world had come adrift, supposed that it had, then instantly, angrily, reminded herself that this was not about her; this was about her beloved best friend and sister-in-law.

'That means you knew,' she realised, 'when you came down last time?'

'That's right,' Suzy said.

'But you didn't say a word.'

'No.' Suzy's mouth pulled again. 'Sorry.'
'Don't be silly,' Alex said.
'Wasn't ready to talk,' Suzy said.
'No.' Alex reached for her hand, shook her head. 'God.'
'Yes,' Suzy agreed.

Chapter 75

Frankie hasn't seen Bo for over an hour.

He wheeled her into the living room after Jude Brown left, then brought her a cup of tea and said there was something he needed to check out.

Said something again about cracks.

'One of the conservatory walls,' he said.

Which triggered the pain again.

And something worse. Another memory, more recent than the old bad things.

Uglier. Terrifying.

And then it was gone again.

And so was Bo.

She knows he went outside a while ago, but after that she heard him moving around again somewhere inside the house, and then there was silence, and she called his name, and her voice was still not very strong, but loud enough for him to hear from another room.

'Bo!'

Nothing. No reply. No more sounds since then.

She could, of course, go to find him, can propel her chair well enough with her good hand, getting stronger from her secret exercises; could even try the hated walking frame if she wanted to, thinks but isn't quite certain, that it's still out in the hall.

But she doesn't want to, and she isn't sure why.

Why she's suddenly so terribly afraid.

But she is. It's creeping into her now, like something thick and sickening being injected into her veins, travelling slowly around her body and up into her mind.

Don't, she tells herself, fighting to stop it, close it down.

A new flash of memory sears behind her eyes.

Black plastic.

Frankie feels bad.

'Bo?' she calls again.

But he doesn't come.

Chapter 76

'Suzy's physio,' Alex told Jude on the phone shortly after four that afternoon. 'David's been having an affair with her *physio* for a whole year – I just can't take it in.'

'Is that allowed?' Jude was shocked. 'Not that ethics are really the point.'

'I don't know what to do for her.' Alex had come outside the hospital, was pacing wretchedly up and down the pavement on Dovehouse Street, her mobile clamped to her ear, her long linen jacket swinging with each furious turn. 'I know what I'd like to do to *him*.'

'Is he going to go home with her?' Jude asked.

'So far as I know. Though I'm not sure Suzy really wants him to, and I don't imagine he really wants to either. It's all so awful, Jude.'

'Would she come to you, do you think?'

'She might.' Alex went on pacing. 'She's going to have to take some more time off from her job anyway, and I could take a bit of leave – though you and I were hoping to go off somewhere, weren't we?'

'We can go anytime,' Jude told her. 'Suzy's your family, and if coming to you is what she wants—'

'I don't think she knows what she wants.'

'Then maybe you should stay in London till she decides,' Jude said, 'and you'll let me know what I can do for you – make calls, whatever you need.'

Alex calmed down a little after that, stood still for the first time, near the pub on the corner, and listened as Jude told her, briefly, about his encounter with Bolin at Frankie's house.

'I thought you'd decided not to go back,' she said.

'I wasn't really planning to,' he said. 'But then I couldn't seem to settle to much else, and I was missing you, and the house kept on needling me, so I went.'

'What happened?'

'Not much. I told Bolin about the cracks, and he said he'd look at them, and I asked how Frankie was, and he said she was coming along, and I left.'

'So now you can forget about it,' Alex said.

'I suppose so.'

'What does that mean?' She felt irritated.

'Nothing,' Jude said. 'You won't be forgetting about Frankie, will you?'

'Of course not. She's my patient.'

'With a bloke hanging around who neither of us thinks is much cop.'

'Despite which,' Alex said, 'he is caring for her. Anyway, if I chose not to treat anyone with relatives or friends I didn't much like, I'd have very few patients and certainly no job.'

'I miss you,' Jude said, almost abruptly.

'Me, too,' Alex said.

'Good.' He paused. 'Not the right weekend now for me to come up.'

'Not really.'

'I'm sorry,' Jude said. 'I look forward to meeting Suzy.'

'Soon,' Alex said.

Chapter 77

The storm that's been rumbling around for hours has finally broken.

Frankie has not moved, her wheelchair still in exactly the same spot in the living room. She's certain now that Bo is in the house.

In the conservatory.

She's heard sounds, of furniture being moved, and other things, and part of her wants to go in there, to see for herself.

To confront him, and her fears.

Except that the fears are stronger, so she just goes on sitting, waiting.

For him to come to her.

Chapter 78

In the flat on Union Street, taking another look at the photograph of his old miniature of Roz Bailey's house, Jude felt a sudden, powerful urge to work.

Not on Alex's portrait; with her away, he found he wasn't in the mood for it. Yet this urge was strong enough to make him put up a new canvas and begin right away, working with charcoal. And he knew, already, that it was going to be a dark painting of the same house, but on a night of the kind this was soon likely to turn into, with wild weather lashing at it.

As he worked, he started thinking again about Roz Bailey, about what a nice, fun woman he had thought she was; open and easy to talk to, even, he remembered, about her gambling habit and the pleasure she derived from it.

Nice woman, he thought again.

And worked on.

Chapter 79

He comes back, at last, into the living room.

Doesn't speak to Frankie.

Walks past her chair over to the cabinet in which he's put a bottle of Jack Daniel's, his favourite, pours himself a large one.

Frankie turns her chair around, so she's facing him.

'Bo?' she says, quietly.

He takes a look at her, then gulps down his drink, all of it, and she sees his hand is shaking a little as he puts down the glass, pours another, and picks it up again.

'So now I know,' he says, finally, and, still holding the glass, sits on her bed.

His face seems paler than when she last saw him.

One of her bad feelings sears swiftly through her mind.

'Know what?' she asks.

Bo takes another drink, sets the glass on the carpet and lights a roll-up.

'Where'd you get it, Frankie?'

'What?' she asks, and her voice sounds almost normal, even though she's still not over her stroke, even though she feels as if someone has just taken hold of her stomach and is gripping it tightly.

'The box,' says Bo. 'The coffin.'

And with that last word, it comes back. *All* of it. Tumbling through space, crashing down onto her: Roz Bailey, the planning, her dying, *dying*, moving her into the coffin. And the plumber, too.

Bo is watching her face, and she can almost feel her own skin turning ashen.

'You okay?' he asks, then shakes his head. 'Can't believe I'm asking you that after what you've done.' He takes a drag of his cigarette, picks up the drink. 'I suppose that is Mrs Bailey, is it?'

Frankie nods, and now she's trembling.

'So who's the poor bastard in the plastic?' Bo asks.

She shakes her head. 'Don't know.' She feels suddenly sick, leans forward, grips the left arm of her wheelchair.

'You can cut that out for starters,' Bo tells her. '"Don't know." "Don't remember." Jesus, woman, last time I saw you before your stroke, you were a nutcase, but you weren't a murderer.' He takes another swig of his drink. 'It *was* you, I suppose? There's no one else involved?'

'No,' she admits.

'Why?' he asks. 'For the house?'

She nods again.

Bo stands up. 'Drink?'

'Not allowed,' Frankie manages, though those two words slur into each other.

'Not allowed to go round killing people either,' Bo says, pouring more sour mash whisky into his glass. 'Fucking hell. Fucking *hell*, Frankie. I don't know if I'm more shocked or impressed.'

Chapter 80

'Awkward for you,' David Maynard said, back home in Roland Gardens.

They were in the kitchen, Suzy's lovely adapted kitchen. All taken care of by David, her loving husband.

It was the first time Alex had been alone with him since Suzy had told her.

'Could say that,' Alex agreed.

'I'm sorry,' he said.

He had made a pot of coffee, but Alex had turned down his offer of a cup.

'Not me you need to say that to,' she said.

'Suzy already knows how sorry I am.'

'I can't do this,' Alex said flatly. 'I can't talk to you about what you've done, what you're doing, because I can't begin to understand it.'

'Nor can I.' David sat down at the table, slumping from the waist. 'I wake up every morning, in the middle of every night, and I feel as if I'm dreaming. I can't believe I'm doing this to her, because I still love her so much.'

'Please,' Alex said, violently. 'Don't. Just don't, David.' She stood up. 'I'm sorry I'm here with you tonight, and I wanted to go to a hotel, but Suzy asked me not to do that, not to make you feel worse than you already do. Can you believe that?'

'Yes,' David said. 'Of course I can.'

'Christ,' Alex said, and left the kitchen.

Chapter 81

'So how did it go?' asks Bo. 'You wanted the house, so you took it?'

Frankie doesn't answer, can't answer, is finding it hard enough just watching his face, searching his eyes for what she knows is there, deep inside.

'Why this house?' he goes on. 'Why this woman? Wasn't she clean enough for you or something?' He sees her wince. 'Well, I'm sorry, babe, but the Frankie I used to know was definitely barking, but the only killing she was into back then was fucking germs.'

Frankie whimpers, turns her face away.

'I don't understand how you, of all people,' Bo says, 'could *do* something like that. You've still got your thing, haven't you, your OCD? I mean, there must have been mess, there must have been blood or worse, it can't have been easy for you.'

Her eyes fill.

'Ah, babe, don't cry.'

She hears the gentleness, looks up with a flash of hope as he comes towards her, puts down his glass again, on the coffee table, crouches beside the wheelchair and takes her good hand in his.

'Not easy,' she admits.

'Can't have been,' Bo says. 'Making your own little DIY crypt, getting them down there, handling them. Not to mention living with them after, knowing they were rotting away.'

He feels her shudder, smiles, reaches up and strokes her cheek, sees her shrink away from his touch.

'That's more like it,' he says, and he's harsh now, the cruelty she was waiting for there, in his voice and on his mouth and in his eyes. 'More like the Frankie I know. My ever-loving Frankie who felt like chucking up when I kissed her.'

210

Chapter 82

Having got the house down in charcoal silhouette, Jude found he was not, after all, quite certain exactly what he was aiming for, could not settle to this either. And he'd spoken to Alex once already this evening, didn't want to bother her again, especially in light of what was happening with Suzy and David, and they'd agreed they'd talk in the morning, and missing her was fast becoming less pleasurable and more painful.

He abandoned the canvas, pulled on his old leather jacket and went out. He liked his home turf in all seasons, hectic and quiet, but though this was Saturday night, the Lanes were unusually and unnaturally empty; the storm, he supposed, having pushed locals and visitors into pubs and restaurants and homes.

Where most sensible people would choose to be or, once there, to remain.

The rain was still coming down with a vengeance, the wind, as Jude turned into Ship Street, packing a hefty punch, the intermittent thunder claps sounding almost like cannons being fired out in the Channel. Yet Jude felt nothing but relief at being out in it, enjoying breathing in the already fresher air.

Going nowhere in particular, he thought, until he came to King's Road, almost at the sea, and suddenly remembered Roz Bailey once telling him that her favourite casino had been in Regency Square.

Just a few blocks away.

The doorman, wearing a long dark green raincoat and matching hat, eyed Jude's aged, cracked brown leather jacket and jeans as he passed him and went through the creamy Ionic pillars of the

211

Lansdowne, into the club's mahogany-walled, red-carpeted entrance hall.

Getting ready to bounce him, Jude decided, and smiled at the dark-haired, smartly-suited young receptionist identified by her name tag as Mariella.

'Don't worry,' he told her, quickly. 'Not planning on coming in.'

'Members only, sir.' Her tone was friendly, her brown eyes less so.

'That's fine.' Jude decided against using her first name. 'I've just dropped in on the off-chance, wanting to ask about a friend who is a member.'

The woman smiled, but offered no other response.

'Mrs Bailey.' Jude wondered, briefly, if she was a Rosalind or Rosamund or any other variation, settled on what he knew. 'Roz Bailey.'

'Mrs Bailey's not in tonight,' Mariella said.

'I know that,' Jude said.

'I can't give out private information about our members, sir.'

'I'm not after anything like that,' Jude said. 'I already have Mrs Bailey's home address, but I haven't seen her for a while, and—'

A couple came in behind him, lowering a large red and white umbrella, scattering raindrops over the carpet, and seeing the receptionist's welcoming smile and extended right hand, Jude stepped back to wait while the doorman took the umbrella and Mariella asked after their health and signed them in.

'I was just wondering,' he said, minutes later, as the couple stepped into the lift and vanished, 'how long it's been since you saw Mrs Bailey.'

'That would be private information,' she told him.

'Right,' Jude said. 'Fine.'

He was back outside on the pavement, debating whether to go somewhere for a drink or to go back to the flat, when the doorman, who had followed him out, nodded.

'Nice woman, Mrs Bailey,' he said.

'Very,' Jude agreed.

'Always taking time to have a chat.' The man smiled. 'I've missed her.' He nodded. 'I'm Bill,' he said. 'Bill Deacon.'

'Jude Brown.'

They shook hands, Deacon's grip strong.

212

'I think,' Jude said, 'she's gone to Canada.'

'Really?'

'You look surprised,' Jude said.

'I am, a bit,' Bill Deacon said. 'She didn't say she was going away.'

'Think she would have?' Jude asked, casually.

Deacon shrugged. 'She's never seemed interested in holidays, not like most of our regulars.'

'I don't think she likes flying,' Jude said.

'Don't know about that.' Deacon rubbed his rather bulbous nose. 'Where in Canada's she gone, exactly, do you know? Only I've got a mate in Toronto.'

'I think that's where she is,' Jude said. 'Big city.'

'I wasn't thinking my friend would know her,' Deacon assured him. 'I know it's a big city. But I remember him saying once – he likes the tables, too, you see – and I think he said they don't have casinos in Toronto.' He grinned. 'You'd think, if Mrs Bailey was going to go anywhere, it'd be Vegas or Atlantic City, or even Monte, wouldn't you?'

'I suppose so,' Jude agreed.

'One thing though, if it's true,' the doorman said. 'At least, she'll be glad to get back to Brighton.'

Chapter 83

'You know they can't stay down there, don't you?' Bo said.

He's been moving around almost incessantly and edgily, and Frankie recalls how being irritated or upset used to magnify his old desire to torment her.

'It's starting to stink,' he goes on. 'Haven't you smelled it, babe?'

Frankie's left hand flies to her mouth.

Bo watches her gag.

'It's all right,' he says, after a moment. 'I'll help you.'

Frankie whimpers.

'Good old Bo'll help you.'

Chapter 84

Still awake in the Maynards' guest room at two fifteen, Alex heard a phone ringing and sat bolt upright, terrified that something had happened to Suzy, was still frozen in the same position when, a couple of minutes later, David knocked at her door.

'It's Suzy,' his voice said.

Alex got out of bed, grabbed her dressing-gown, still dragging it on as she pulled open the door. 'What's happened?'

'Nothing's happened.' He was wearing a white T-shirt and black shorts, his fair hair dishevelled. 'She wants to talk to you.'

She took it in the kitchen.

'I woke you, didn't I?' Suzy's familiar, husky voice said. 'Sorry, Ally.'

'I wasn't sleeping,' Alex said. 'What's up?'

'I've decided I don't want to go home, after all. So if you meant it, if you don't mind, I'd really like it if you could pick me up as early as you can stand, and take me back to the cottage.'

'If you're sure that's what you want, darling.'

'If you'd rather not, or if you think Jude might not—'

'Jude suggested it,' Alex cut in decisively, 'so don't start. I just want you to be sure.'

'I'm not sure about anything right now,' Suzy said. 'But I do know I need some time out, and if it can't be with you, I'll—'

'Suzy, stop it,' Alex told her. 'How early?'

'Early as you like, please, Ally.'

Getting off the phone, Alex considered calling Jude, but then she saw the oven clock – 2.23 – and thought better of it.

At least one of them deserved a little sleep.

215

Chapter 85

Back home again, Jude had dried off and eaten a sandwich before taking another look at the new canvas.

A good beginning. He liked it.

Enough to pick up another stick of charcoal.

And drop it again less than fifteen seconds later.

'No point,' he'd said out loud.

Not up to working, not now.

So he'd gone to bed.

Dreamed his old Scott dream.

Their mother's car rolling over him, her face and her screams.

Then the sight of his little brother's body.

He woke up sweating, as always, got up, took a shower.

Knew he wouldn't get back to sleep.

Got dressed again.

It was two-thirty.

Now what?

Chapter 86

'Sooner the better,' Bo tells Frankie.

He's pacing back and forth in the living room, smoking, psyching himself up, though he stopped drinking a long time back, after his fourth Jack Daniel's.

'Bloody hell,' he says. 'Bloody, fucking hell.'

'Sorry,' Frankie says, feeling marooned in her chair, trapped, almost too afraid to *be* afraid.

No bed for them tonight. He hasn't offered help, and she's grateful for that, at least, felt wary of being helped out of the chair and stuck in the single bed, found herself wishing, for the first time, that she hadn't rejected her walking frame so obstinately. Though as it is, she does have the chair, could move around in that if she wanted, if Bo lets her.

He did make them supper an hour or two ago – two chicken and mushroom Pot Noodles – stuck hers on her wheelchair tray with a cup of water, forked his way through his own and then, when she didn't touch hers, did the same with the second. She couldn't face food, couldn't stomach it, was nervous of drinking the water in case she had to ask him for help getting to the loo.

'Sorry,' she says again now.

Bo makes a scornful, snorting sound. 'I should just get the hell out.' His pacing whips up the air as he passes her, ruffles her hair a little. 'Just leave you to it, that would serve you right.'

Now she feels the fear, truly feels it.

'But it's a nice house,' he goes on. 'So I've decided I'm going to get rid of the one in the plastic.'

'Swann,' Frankie says.

'What?' Bo stops pacing, confused.

217

'He was called Andy Swann,' Frankie says. 'A plumber.'

Bo thinks of the space under the conservatory floor, remembers the pipework.

'Got too close, did he, poor bastard?'

Frankie nods.

'His van then, in the garage?'

Another nod.

'Shit,' Bo says. 'Shit, Frankie.'

Chapter 87

Still raining, still storming, as Jude came back out into Union Street.

Entirely deserted now.

He walked, quite slowly, over to Middle Street, where the Honda lived in the precious space he'd managed to scavenge in lieu of payment for a series of miniatures of his landlord's five favourite properties in Friston, Hove's Palmeira Square and inland, up in the bosom of the Sussex Downs. Ed and Eva Hauser had told him at the time that he was nuts, that he ought to have taken hard cash and raised his profile in the business, but given that a parking spot in the Lanes – permanent enough, at least, to see him through to the termination of his flat's lease – was pretty much gold dust, Jude had accepted his landlord's offer and been well pleased.

The Honda jeep was not, as sometimes happened at night, blocked in, so he took that as a kind of vague sign of higher approval, unlocked the door, got in, started the engine, waited for the windows to demist.

Asked himself, briefly, what he thought he was doing, got no sensible answer, and drove out of the space towards King's Road.

Turned left.

Heading for Rottingdean again.

Chapter 88

'Coffin should be okay for some time,' Bo says. 'Maybe forever, who knows, you did well there, getting steel. But I've got to get your Mr Swann out right now, stick him in my truck, get shot before things get worse.'

'Where?' Frankie feels sick, cold and drained.

Bo doesn't answer, and she knows him well enough, remembers him well enough, to see he's running on adrenalin now, disgusted and freaked out and excited all at once. And Frankie wishes she hadn't remembered, wishes she was still muddled and lost, wishes she didn't feel now that she could almost read his thoughts; but she *knows* he's having trouble believing that it's her, dumb, screwloose Frankie, who's actually done this thing, who's killed two people to get herself a fucking house.

And the thing is, too, since she *has* got away with it this far, and since no one's come looking for either Roz Bailey or the plumber, then maybe this really could be her house for keeps. *His* house, she's sure Bo's thinking now, if he plays it right, which he will, won't he, given that *he*'s not off his head and, worst case scenario, he could still always piss off, couldn't he, and leave her to the law.

The realization of what he's just told her hits her properly for the first time.

The horror of it, of moving *it*, too much to bear.

'Where?' she asks again. 'Where will you take him?'

Chapter 89

The storm had subsided a little when, pulling up a couple of hundred yards down from the top of Winder Hill at four minutes past three in the morning, Jude saw lights on all over the ground floor and swiftly, instinctively, turned off first his lights and then the engine.

Again, more forcefully this time, he asked himself if he knew what the hell he was playing at, sneaking around in the dead of night outside someone else's home. Felt, suddenly and unpleasantly, his never-quite-forgotten past in the courts and the youth custody centre, like sharp fingers down his back. It had felt like prison at the time, but Jude knew that prison would be worse.

He shuddered, reminded himself he had no illegal intent being here.

Then experienced a sense of sudden, disproportionate vindication as the front door opened and Bolin emerged, just as he had the last time Jude had come to Winder Hill.

Except that this time as Bolin walked towards the Toyota pick-up, leaving the front door open behind him, there was something different about him, about the manner in which he was moving.

Furtively.

You can talk, Jude reminded himself.

Bolin got into the truck, started the engine and moved it about three yards, edging its wheels up onto the pavement and stopping again, the back of the vehicle right up close to the gate between the privet hedges bordering the back garden.

Jude sank down deeper into his seat and watched as Bolin turned

off the engine, got out of the truck, opened the rear, left the flap
hanging down—

– and then went back into the house and closed the door.

Chapter 90

Frankie's in the hall now, as Bo comes in and shuts the door.

Feeling sick. Wanting to scream.

Because he really is going to do this thing.

'Fuck's sake, woman,' he says. 'I don't know why you're looking like that. It's me, not you, having to carry a sack of Christ-knows-what.' He sees her face turn even chalkier. 'You must have known what would happen to him.'

'Don't,' she pleads.

'Maggots, you nutbag,' Bo says. 'Fucking maggots.'

She makes a strangled, choking sound.

'Puke now, babe,' Bo says, 'and I won't be the one cleaning you up, right?'

'Please,' Frankie begs, and starts to weep.

'I'll be leaving the back way.' He turns towards the conservatory, then hesitates, turns back. 'You'd better be grateful to me for doing this for you.'

'But what are you going to do?' she asks, still crying.

'What's the matter, babe? Don't you trust me?' Bo smiles. 'Got no choice, really, have you? Bloody fruitcake killer, sectioned once already.'

'Don't, Bo.'

'You're dribbling,' he says, disgusted.

She tries to wipe it away, but it's on the right side of her chin, and with her co-ordination still off, she misses a bit.

'Want some help?' Bo raises his hands for her to see. 'Not very clean, mind, fresh from moving your plumber.' He walks back towards her chair, holds both hands palms out towards her face and, as she whimpers, he shrugs. 'Please yourself.'

223

'Bo,' she says, quieter now, more defeated.

Turning back towards the conservatory, he stops again.

'Grateful, right? For keeps, Frankie, or as long as I want you. If I ever do want you again, that is, which is bloody unlikely, looking at you right now.'

And then he's gone.

Chapter 91

Still sunk low in the driver's seat of the Honda, his eyes trained on the front door of the hilltop house, Jude heard a sound, tilted his head, caught a flicker of movement from the back garden.

Bolin – the shape of his head and broad shoulders unmistakable above the line of dark hedges – was coming out of the conservatory.

Three seconds later, and the gate in the middle of the hedgerow opened, and he stepped out onto the pavement, carrying something.

Something large.

It was too dark, and Jude was too far away to see Bolin's face, but it seemed to Jude from the stiffness of his back and the angle of his arms, elbows scarcely bent, that he was doing his utmost to keep his burden at arm's length from his body. And it was so quiet in the road, and Jude's window was wound down, which was why when Bolin's left trainer slipped off the edge of the kerb, and the man lost his balance, almost fell, almost dropped his load, Jude heard his muffled, gasped curse, heard what sounded to him like desperation.

And then whatever it was he was carrying—

– and Jude had caught a pretty good glimpse of its shape in the lamplight, knew what it *looked* like, did not want to think about it, did not want to *believe* it—

– was laid down in the truck, and the back flap was raised and locked into place, and Mike Bolin got into the driver's seat, started the engine again, turned the truck around and drove past Jude's jeep and away down the hill, past the other elegant, sleeping houses and round the corner.

225

Jude waited several seconds before he was ready to sit up straight.

And then he started his own engine.

Following.

Chapter 92

Frankie is in the conservatory.

First time since the stroke. Even before the memories started coming back, she realises now, she was avoiding coming into this part of the house.

Bo's put the rug back over the trapdoor, the cane chair over that.

Everything back in place.

All back in place now in her head, too, even things from much further back in her life, some of them things that maybe paved the way to the getting of this house.

Another kind of compulsion.

The compulsion to *have*.

She remembers, suddenly, back when she was very young and friendly with Ann Mackeson who lived next door, wanting Ann's toys. Lots of children covet and, Frankie knows, even steal other kids' possessions, but she wonders how many feel as desperately as she remembers feeling about Ann's things. As if she had to have at least *some* of them, that if she didn't have them, something terrible might happen.

Gottahavit.

Even back then, as a child: *gottahavit, gottahavit*, round and round in her head.

And then there was the nail.

Frankie shivers. That's one she's always tried extra-hard to forget, that particular episode from the early Frankie-the-nutbag chronicles, and she feels sick again, her head hurts just thinking about it.

About the day, in her early teens, when she went to see a film about Jesus, and started wondering how it might feel to have a nail

227

driven through your hand – and that had been a compulsion, too, no doubt about it. Except, of course, being Frankie, she had to go out and buy a box of brand-new nails and then boil the one she was going to use first. And the sight of her own blood made her faint even before the pain really hit home, and maybe if she'd hit an artery – she doesn't know if you *have* arteries in your hands – but if she had, she might have bled to death while she was still in her faint.

Pity she didn't, she thinks now.

Chapter 93

It was clear to Jude, as he continued to follow Bolin, who drove inland first up Saltdean Vale, then turned the Toyota around and headed back onto the South Coast Road, that the other man had no real idea where he was going.

The storm was gathering strength again, seeming to suck power from the looming blackness over the Channel, the lightning ever more awesome, the thunderclaps louder and closer, rain swamping the windscreen and hammering on the roof as Bolin sped through Peacehaven, where the A259 became the Brighton Road on its way to Newhaven.

'Beachy Head,' Jude said aloud, abruptly, making his first real guess as to where the other man might be making for.

The rain pounded harder, and he turned the wipers to double speed, screwed up his eyes to try to focus more sharply on the road ahead.

He had remembered, right at the outset – as soon as he'd allowed himself to accept the mad idea that he actually was following a man – that police in novels tended, when tracking suspects, to keep at least two vehicles between themselves and their quarry. But at around four in the morning on these almost deserted roads, that was easier said than done, which meant he was having to keep well back so that Bolin wouldn't notice him, which meant, in turn, that he was in constant danger of losing sight of the truck.

Good job too, he could imagine Alex saying, if she'd been with him. Though if she had been around to counsel him earlier, they'd presumably have been tucked up in bed together right now, either in Union Street or at the cottage, and he was already beginning to

229

wish to hell he'd done what she'd suggested, and simply forgotten all about Roz Bailey's damned house ...

Newhaven and the semi-comatose port had come and gone, the roads in the one-way system near the docks slick with surface water, and the Seaford Road was dark as pitch for a long while till it became first the Buckle Bypass and then grew urban and just a little busier before it turned into the Eastbourne Road, denuded of the buildings that Jude had found fleetingly consoling. Seven Sisters Country Park, beautiful in daylight and full of walkers, loomed darkly desolate to left and right as he trailed Bolin's rear lights, bushes and trees banking the road – and then suddenly, as lightning tore into the sky, Jude looked to his right and there was the sea again, the crests of rough waves savagely silvered, the Cuckmere River meandering towards it. And then they – Bolin a good distance ahead, but always visible – were approaching Friston, and Jude recalled a happy few hours there last year, sketching a beautiful old flint-walled church, and the contrast between that day and this night struck him sharply, almost sickeningly; and he wondered again what exactly was pushing him to this extreme, remembered again his bad days as a teenager, asked himself if this piece of impulsiveness had some link to that time, if some odd liking for a dark side had remained buried in his subconscious, was re-emerging now.

And then, on the other side of Friston, the Toyota swung round a bend way ahead of him, and Jude followed slowly, doggedly, resisting the temptation to put his foot down, thought to himself wryly that he was getting better at the game, until, rounding the same bend, he realised that the road ahead was black and deserted, not a red rear light in sight.

'Bloody hell,' Jude said aloud, sure that he'd lost him – but then suddenly it was there again, coming the other way, *towards* him, headlights piercing the night, dazzling, almost blinding him – and Jude felt his stomach lurch as the Toyota passed him, though Bolin did not appear to so much as glance his way as he flashed past.

Drive on, Jude told himself, *don't turn around*. He thought again about what Alex would say, didn't need her to tell him he ought to simply keep going in this direction until the next junction or roundabout, then turn around and go back home to Brighton and forget about the house on Winder Hill and Mike Bolin.

And what he had put into the back of his truck.

Not my problem.

Except that if it *was* what he'd thought it looked like, then that meant Frankie was living with . . .

You don't have the slightest idea what *it means.*

Probably nothing of any real significant, he told himself impatiently. Or maybe the thing that Bolin had laid down in the back of his pick-up had been some kind of dodgy goods or materials, and maybe he was looking for some place to dump them, or maybe he was just on his way to see someone, make a delivery.

At four in the morning?

The trouble was, there was no escaping the fact that Jude knew what the bundle had *looked* like, and though, to be honest, he supposed he might not have been getting this involved if Alex were not hooked up in Frankie's life, Alex *would* be back soon, would be going to Winder Hill again to visit Frankie. Which meant that, paranoia notwithstanding, Jude did want, very much, to know what Bolin was doing.

He saw the East Dean turn-off at the very last minute, stood on his brakes too hard, skidded, managed to correct the skid, then swung in, turned around and put his foot down, knowing he might have left it too late, might have lost Bolin. And around the next bend, he found himself behind a camper van, and now there was no chance of Bolin glimpsing him, nor any damned chance of Jude catching up with the truck.

The camper van turned off to the left.

Nothing ahead of him again except the empty A259, nothing but sheeting rain needling almost like sleet in his headlights, and then, in the next lightning flash, the broader, darkly beautiful picture of tree silhouettes bent almost double in the wind at the edge of Seven Sisters Country Park, all thrashing blackness now. And the next thunderclap came only two seconds later, and the speed of the windscreen wipers was almost dizzying, and Jude was certain now that he had lost the Toyota for keeps.

And then, suddenly, braking on a decline up ahead, he saw it again; hint of red glowing lights first, hazy through the rain, then the truck itself.

Jude sneaked a swift glance in the rear-view mirror, took his foot off the accelerator, slowed the Honda right down, his heart rate speeding up instead; and he wasn't entirely sure now if he'd wanted to see the truck again or not, but there it was, and Bolin

231

was braking again, and, an instant later, he turned sharp left on a bend, sending up spray.

Jude checked behind him again, saw nothing, slowed down to a crawl and realised that they were at Exceat and that the other man had made his turn into a small road beside a bus stop.

Jude passed the turning slowly, saw that the truck had come to a halt a little way into the blackness, took the jeep on a bit further, saw an access road to one of the car parks that served the Country Park, pulled in and killed the lights.

He took a moment, trying to orientate himself. He had never walked in the park, but he had once met a friend nearby and taken a look for future reference, recalled being told about forest trails on the other side of the main road and, on this side, walks through the Cuckmere Valley to a camp site and its quiet beach.

Now what?

Jude turned the Honda around, tucked it close to a fence near the road, turned off the engine, pulled his mobile phone out of its holder, stuck it firmly in the inside pocket of his leather jacket, and removed the key from the ignition.

It jangled on its key ring.

No noise.

Reaching down, he put the keys under the mat, opened the door and realised, as the full volume of the storm assailed him, that keys were probably the last thing Bolin was likely to hear.

God, it was dark.

The big flashlight he kept in the back was a non-starter unless he wanted to advertise his presence, but there was, he remembered, a tiny LED torch in the glove compartment.

Better than nothing, he told himself, reaching for it.

Not much.

Chapter 94

Having long since given up on any hope of sleep, Alex got out of bed again, put her dressing-gown back on, wandered into the kitchen, found David, still in T-shirt and shorts, sitting hunched miserably over at the table, and felt angry with herself for the sudden, unexpected rush of pity she experienced.

'Can't sleep either?' He sat up a little straighter.

She shook her head.

'Cup of something?' David asked.

'No, thank you.' Alex paused. 'Has Suzy told you she wants to come with me to the cottage?'

'Yes.'

She looked at his wretched face. 'Sorry,' she said, despite herself.

'Me, too,' he said, and began to weep.

Sympathy drained out of her instantly.

'Think I will make myself some coffee,' she said, and went towards the kettle. 'You?' she asked, picking it up.

'I never meant this to happen, Ally,' David said.

'Exactly how,' Alex asked, 'is that supposed to help Suzy?'

Chapter 95

Crazy.

Jude stood in the pouring rain, peering into the blackness, glad of only one thing, that the black sweater he'd just happened to pull on over his dark blue jeans, and, of course, his trusty old leather jacket, might be helping keep him less visible.

There.

About twenty or so yards away, the truck, lights off.

Bolin out of the vehicle, standing in front of it.

If he could see Bolin, then that meant Bolin could see him.

Except that the other man was occupied, busy doing something.

Lightning flashed, and Jude saw that Bolin was opening a five-bar gate, then froze as the big man looked around before he got back in the truck, turned his headlights back on and drove, very slowly, over a cattle grid and through the open gate.

'Shit,' Jude murmured.

Whatever the hell Bolin was up to, he had Buckley's chance of keeping up with him on foot.

But if it *was* a body, he couldn't just give up.

Crazy was not the word.

Call someone.

Jude felt the small, slightly comforting weight of the phone in his pocket.

Too soon to call the police. He supposed the station at Seaford might possibly send out a patrol car to check a report of a motorist driving into the country park in the dead of night. But if Jude started trying to explain what he *thought* he'd seen Bolin putting in the back of the Toyota, or the fact that he'd already been driving around for God knew how long in pursuit, then it

234

was more than probable he'd be dismissed as a crank.

And then whatever Bolin was up to, no one would ever find out.

He waited a few more moments, till he knew for sure that Bolin wasn't going to come back to shut the gate, and then he walked up to it, saw that the road ahead was pale concrete and quite visible, watched the Toyota's lights moving slowly, but steadily, away along the road into the night.

And began following again.

Chapter 96

'You still don't understand,' David Maynard said to Alex.

'Did you expect me to?'

All remnants of pity had evaporated entirely a while ago, at the moment when he'd attempted to tell her about the physiotherapist.

The other woman.

'I don't want to know,' Alex had said, her voice hard, stamping on his effort. 'I'm not interested in her, or in you, come to that, not any more.'

'All right,' David had said, and fallen silent.

'Do you want Suzy back?' she asked now.

'Of course,' he said.

'Is it over?'

His hesitation was brief. 'Yes.'

Too long.

'I don't believe you,' Alex said.

'Nor does Suzy,' David said.

Chapter 97

Jude wondered, during this now, infinitely more wretched, pursuit, with the storm still cascading stinging, cold water onto his head, into his eyes and down his neck beneath his leather jacket and sweater, if Bolin had, after all, had this place marked out all along – though if that was true, why had he wasted so much time driving so many miles out of his way? Had Cuckmere Haven been one destination on a list, or was this just a spur of the moment impulse that had come to Bolin as he'd driven past for the second time that night?

Another possibility sprang to mind as Jude trudged along the road that ran some way to the left of one of the river's oxbow bends, sticking as far as possible to the side of the pale concrete to minimize the risk – albeit ever-decreasing as the vehicle got further away – of being spotted by Bolin in his rear-view mirror. Had the other man known he was being followed? Might he actually have been toying with Jude since leaving Winder Hill?

Unlikely, Jude decided, wiped rain out of his eyes, saw that the Toyota was already too far away for him to see more than tail lights and, when the road became winding, the headlights too, almost lambent in the rain. Safer, he supposed, than being too close, except that whatever Bolin's plans were right now, if the truck got much further away, his mission would probably be over and done with before Jude caught up with him.

Mission.

Body dumping. Perhaps.

Turn back.

Sanest option by far for a man with half a brain.

No way was he going to catch up with Bolin now.

237

But if the bundle *was* a body, a human being, and if Jude did turn back for the sake of warmth and safety, or even stopped to try reporting his suspicions to the police, then he was more convinced than ever of the risk that no one else would ever know what Bolin had done.

Still crazy to go on.

If you had half a brain, you'd be dangerous.

One of his stepfather's sayings.

Bloody right, too.

No going back now

He told himself to concentrate.

A walker here, he recalled hearing his friend say that day over their drink, could easily reach the sea in around thirty to forty-five minutes, which meant that a truck would take no time at all.

Jude reckoned he'd probably been walking for about fifteen minutes.

'Christ's sake,' he muttered, 'walk faster.'

Chapter 98

Alex would have said that she and David had reached an impasse. Except that, truth be told, the impasse had been not so much reached as collided with the instant Suzy had broken the news to her about the affair.

She had not, until now, considered herself an unforgiving person, though she had, of course, always realised that some things were simply unforgivable.

Not *simply*, from David's perspective, but certainly from her own, the situation was crystal clear. Suzy was not only her best friend and family, she was also a very special, remarkably courageous and utterly loyal person, and Alex knew she would have gone into fiercest battle with anyone trying to hurt her.

It was just that she would never have believed that David, of all people, would have been the one to do such a thing.

He had attempted again to tell her about his lover.

'I've told you,' she had responded. 'I don't want to know. I don't want to know a single thing about her, not even her name, *especially* not her name, unless you want to risk my reporting her for gross misconduct, or whatever the official term is for screwing a patient's husband.'

'God, Alex,' David had said, growing even whiter.

Which was when she had seen that the other woman really mattered to him, which had made her despise him more than ever.

Hate him.

She couldn't recall ever really hating anyone, not even the driver whose lorry had killed Matt, because he had, poor man, looked so anguished at the inquest.

First time for everything.

She had left him in the kitchen, gone to her bedroom, taken a shower in the ensuite bathroom (one of the things David – considerate, loving David – had insisted on doing specifically for Alex, wanting his wife's best friend to feel welcome and comfortable when she came to stay), then dressed, in comfortable chinos and a T-shirt, packed her bag, stripped the bed and sat in the armchair by the window, waiting.

Morning could not come soon enough.

She thought about Jude, sound asleep in his platform bed.

A good sleeper, better than her, except when his nightmare troubled him. She watched him sometimes, when he drifted off first, liked seeing the last vestiges of tension slip away from his face.

Suzy had been so suspicious of him, and Alex had been angry with her for that, though she'd realised all along that it was only her friend's love for her that had made her that way.

Though maybe, if she thought about it now, it was her own husband's betrayal that had thrown all Suzy's trusting mechanisms out of kilter.

She got out of the armchair, looked out of the window onto the little paved courtyard with its ramp up to Suzy's and David's own bedroom.

The moon was up over London, silvering the top of the four small evergreens in their terracotta tubs, and she wondered if the moon was up over Brighton too; then remembered that Jude had told her that the storm they'd been forecasting had already broken.

She imagined him again, in bed, hair tousled, and smiled.

Looked forward to being with him again.

Good feeling.

Chapter 99

Frankie's doing her exercises.

The ones she worked out for herself.

The ones she hoped might help her feel less of a victim.

She's left the conservatory, didn't like being in there, is in the kitchen right now, using a can of baked beans as a weight.

And one, and two, and three ...

Trying not to think about where Bo is.

Or what he's doing.

But it's not working.

She didn't really expect it to.

She's not that far gone.

Not yet.

Chapter 100

It happened just a minute or so after Bolin, still impossibly far ahead, had stopped and got out of the truck to open another five-bar gate, then got back in, driven through and taken a right turn. And even from this distance, Jude could see, from the way the lights on the Toyota suddenly appeared to be bouncing, that either the road had come to an end or Bolin had, for some reason, left it and was now encountering rougher terrain.

Jude might have thought the tearing, cracking sound a part of the storm, if he had not, a split second later, seen the Toyota's tail lights lurch sideways: and, for a moment, he thought it was just another piece of uneven ground throwing Bolin slightly off course, or perhaps even an optical illusion of his own thrown up by too long spent straining his eyes into the implacable night.

The lights lurched again, the truck seemed to rear upwards, then rolled diagonally, like a red-lit domino four tile, and came to a halt.

No illusion, Jude realised, though it was several minutes more, because of distance and the noise of the storm, before he heard the sound.

Wheels spinning.

Bolin's truck was stuck, had hit something and then got itself bogged down.

Jude took a breath and let it out again, saw it steam and curl and vanish, then began moving again, more rapidly, more purposefully, aware that this was his only real chance of catching up with Bolin. Aware, too, that if he wasn't damn careful when he came to the end of the concrete road, he might go the same way as the pick-up and come off a whole lot worse.

He'd almost perfected the use of his tiny, but powerful torch by now, aiming its beam on and just a short way ahead of his sodden city boots, glancing up every few seconds to ensure he was still on course for the Toyota, then focusing down again.

Easier, for now, to move without as much fear of being spotted, at least while the sounds of spinning and grinding told him that Bolin was fighting to free the truck from whatever was gripping its wheels.

Thick mud, probably, or even a bog. Jude thought or imagined he could smell what he took to be bog or marsh, wondered at the speed with which it seemed even a city builder could grow accustomed to the country night, to different scents and sounds.

Don't kid yourself.

No such thing out here in the night, in this bloody *weather*, as instant on-the-job tracker training, and even a hint of over-confidence was a sure way to potential disaster.

There was one sound, though, that he was quite certain of.

Growing louder now with every few yards.

Water.

Not the sea, no waves crashing, but something more active, more violent, he thought, than even the swollen rushing river.

Concentrate.

One step at a time.

The Toyota's engine whined like a creature in pain, and an instant later, in the first lightning flash in several minutes, Jude saw the truck move, rock, almost seem to make it out of whatever was holding it fast, then lurch back again.

He imagined Bolin cursing, smiled into the dark, lost his own footing, stumbled and fell onto his knees.

'Shit,' Jude swore under his breath, and then, knowing he had not hurt himself, resisted the urge to stay where he was for a moment longer, finding the wet, hard ground beneath him crazily inviting, realizing almost for the first time how exhausted he was, thinking of his bed, of his mattress and duvet.

Alex's arms.

Up ahead, the Toyota whined and shrieked again.

And made its escape.

Jude got up quickly.

Began moving again.

Chapter 101

Alex, back in the armchair by the window in the guest room at Roland Gardens, was asleep and dreaming.

Of a picnic somewhere beautiful, a wild, green place near the sea, cucumber sandwiches and scones and cream and jam and a dish of moussaka all laid out on a white cloth on the grass.

Matt and Suzy and Jude sitting on one side of the cloth, all smiling at her, alone, on the other side.

No one speaking, just smiling.

She felt warm and happy and safe, the way a fortunate child felt, sometimes, with close, loving family.

And then, first Matt and then Suzy stood up and walked away, without a backward glance, and something in Alex felt surprised and glad that Suzy could walk so easily, but even so, the good feeling began to seep away as they vanished.

Jude got up.

'No,' Alex said, in the dream. 'Please.'

'Got to see a man about a house,' Jude said.

Lifted his hand and was gone.

Sitting in the chair in Suzy's guest room, Alex woke with a start.

Chapter 102

Jude had come to the open gate and the end of the concrete road, realised, as his boots sank into mud, that cold and wet as he already was, he'd be damned lucky if all he came away with after tonight was a chill or even pneumonia; both happier alternatives to breaking a leg or drowning in a bog or being struck by lightning.

Or encountering, maybe even fighting, Mike Bolin.

No real contest if that happened.

He knew now that the tearing sound he'd heard just before the Toyota had lurched and stuck fast had been another gate, a flimsier wire affair that Bolin had clearly driven straight through, probably accidentally.

He also knew that the truck had got stuck in thick mud, below the incline on top of which it was now parked – or 'balanced' was more the way it looked from Jude's perspective, about thirty or so feet away down in the long grass.

Not just an incline, Jude now believed, but the bank of whichever body of water he had begun hearing a while back. And maybe it was the river, after all, or perhaps Bolin's truck was poised on the bank of the canal that he suddenly vaguely recalled being told ran through the park to the sea. From the noise filling his head now, it sounded ferocious, hardly surprising if the tide was in, and, presumably, with the torrential rain still pounding down and feeding it, it was deep as well as wild.

Deep enough for Bolin's needs perhaps.

The Toyota's headlights were still on, engine still running, and, so far as Jude could tell from his uncomfortable skulking place down on his knees – ready to get down on his belly if Bolin

245

glanced his way – it was about as close to the water as it could safely be.

The driver's door opened, the internal light came on, and Jude froze as Bolin got cautiously out of the truck and walked around to the back, stepping carefully in what Jude guessed had to be a mess of slippery mud and grass. The big man's frame was illuminated suddenly in another lightning flash, his dark hair blown into a curling halo by the wind, and Jude held his breath because those flashes were now both friend and potential enemy if Bolin did look back down the bank stoop, rather than high and see him.

No chance now of explaining his way out if that did happen.

Plenty of apprehension, certainly, yet no real regrets either, for Jude was simply too ensnared now by his need to know, to witness what Bolin was going to do.

The storm lit up the Toyota and the other man again as he reached into the back of the pick-up and lifted out the black plastic body-sized bundle.

Get closer.

Jude crawled a few feet to his right, stopped, looked for a spot further along the bank where he could clamber up and get a better view, saw, as the sky lit up again, a gap in the reeds at the top another twenty or so feet on.

Just about far enough away to be safe, he hoped, wriggling into position.

Close enough to lie flat on his belly and observe, quite clearly now, courtesy of his ringside seat and the Toyota's headlights, and he found that his own night vision had sharpened over the past hour, even with the rain needles in his eyes.

On the canal side, he saw, the top of the bank was little more than three or four feet above the water, and if he'd been a betting man, Jude would have laid odds on Bolin choosing the sea and, most probably, one of the many cliffs along the coast. Though maybe the storm had fed his need to find somewhere more obscure; maybe that was why he'd taken such bizarre-seeming pains to reach this spot; maybe he had feared either being blown over or just standing at the edge of a precipice being lit up like Blackpool in the midst of his crime.

It happened, in the end, very quickly.

Bolin carried his burden carefully back past the truck, treading

246

gingerly over the treacherous, slippery ground, moving right to the edge.

And then, getting down on his knees, he laid it down.

It.

Jude saw Bolin take a swift, darting look behind him, once over each shoulder, and foolishly, given the still insistent, agonized howling of the gale and the noise of the rushing water, Jude held his breath again until the other man turned back to his task.

Picked up the big bundle again—

(and Jude was as sure as he could be now that it *was* a body, though his mind still recoiled from the acceptance of that)—

and heaved it out into the black heart of the canal.

Even with all the rest of the noise, the splash as it hit the water felt almost deafening to Jude.

Bolin was still on his knees, his shoulders heaving, and Jude supposed that the big man was recovering from the physical effort rather than psychological stress.

Taking time out, perhaps, after a job finally completed.

At last, Bolin got up, looked down into the dark, turbulent water.

No trace remaining.

And then, apparently satisfied, he turned around and trod, very slowly and carefully, head well down, back to the Toyota.

Jude waited

Until Bolin had closed the back and was inside the truck, door closed. Until he had reversed down the bank, skidding a little, but getting back onto the flatter ground without further mishap.

Until the Toyota had turned around and begun its journey back, through the first gate it had, not so long ago, smashed through, then through the next still open five-bar gate and back onto the winding concrete road.

Back towards civilization.

Jude waited until the rear lights had begun to fade out. And then he waited several moments longer, finding himself quite blind at first, the luxury of those headlamps stolen away again, waiting for his vision to settle.

Finally, he moved. Got off his belly, first onto his knees, groaning a little – and Christ, he was even colder and wetter than before, would not have believed that possible – then back up onto his feet.

247

Began to make his way to where Bolin had stood, easy enough to spot, the reeds and long grass flattened by the truck's wheels and the big man's boots, but God, it was slippery, the mix of grass and leaves and mud making it lethally so, and if he slipped now, so close to the edge . . .

He planted his boots as solidly as he could, half ruined as they were, built for pavements, not hiking; bent cautiously and peered down, saw nothing but fast-moving blackness, and standing here at this point, he could hear the sea, still quite a distance away, could picture the awesome, thrashing wildness of it.

Forget the sea.

He felt instinctively for the phone in his jacket pocket, knew he was nearly ready to use it now, wished for something solid, something *real* to show them, tell them about.

Keep looking.

The storm obliged him, threw a sheet of fresh, fleeting brilliance over the water, and Jude saw that the canal was probably forty to fifty feet wide and deep looking, probably at its deepest, as he'd thought, thanks to the rain.

Saw, too, that whatever the bundle had been, it had vanished without trace.

Gone.

No hope of retrieving it.

This whole night, this madness, for nothing, after all.

He wasn't sure, for a moment, if he wanted to laugh or cry.

Thought of the long journey back to the car park and the road.

Crying seemed the better option.

Pointless.

He sagged for a moment, then straightened up, turned around, trained the small, bright beam of light from his torch onto the ground around his feet, and began to step carefully away from the edge. The wind gathered momentum again, whipped hard against his ears, the rain lashed diagonally onto his face, and Jude tucked his chin down and shivered.

He neither heard nor saw him until it was too late.

Bolin.

A foot away to his left, and Jude saw that the other man had done what he had, earlier, had clambered up the bank just a few yards away, waiting for the right moment.

'Couldn't keep your nose out, could you?' Bolin said.

Lightning flashed again, and Jude saw the arm coming, saw the rock clutched in the hand just in time and ducked. It struck him on the left shoulder, hard enough to make him shout with pain, and he had no weapon, only his fists, so he swung with his right and landed a punch to Bolin's left eye.

'Fuck you,' Bolin snarled, and the rock was still in his hand, and this time when he swung, it was right on target.

The smash against the left side of Jude's head was louder than the clap of thunder that had preceded it by a second – and then, for a moment or two, he heard, *could* hear, nothing at all, and he was aware of falling, of going down, could see the other man coming at him, could feel himself being half lifted, half dragged back across the rough, slippery bank, back towards the canal, and there was nothing he could do, he was too dazed, too *gone*, to fight back.

'There you go, faggot,' Bolin said.

And pushed Jude over the edge.

Into the water.

Still conscious, *just*, as the black ice blanket closed over his head and sucked him down, swamping into his mouth and nostrils, down into his throat, choking him.

Drowning him.

Alex, he thought.

His eyes were closed against the salt, sweeping in from the sea, and her face was there, the blue of her eyes and her softly boyish cap of dark hair.

And then Scott was there too.

Coming, he told his brother, giving in.

And then his left knee touched something, and Jude opened his eyes.

Saw it, illuminated, even down here, below the surface, by lightning.

It.

The worst sight he'd ever seen.

The *worst*.

If he had not already been drowning, if his lungs had not already been filling with thick, black, salty canal water, if his heart had not already been about to explode, Jude thought he might have died of terror.

Yet seeing it, *him* – he thought it was a man, had been a man –

249

seeing him seemed, somehow, to restart Jude, and it was almost, he thought with an inexplicably blithe awareness, like being jump-started; he felt a kind of electric surge pumping new strength through him, enough to allow him to kick with his legs, flail with his arms, push himself up, *up*, fighting against the current and the pulverizing weight of water.

His head broke through, found the world again, the night, and Jude opened his mouth to try to breathe, but he couldn't – he was choking, still drowning, and he began to weaken again, but then something   that same *thing*, that poor once human – brushed against his groin.

Jude screamed, and his screaming cleared the way for air.

The *thing* touched him again, something soft, leaning into him.

His cry was unintelligible, beyond words.

He flailed towards the bank.

Towards land.

Chapter 103

'Now what?' Bo asks Frankie.

She watches him fingering his left eye, cut by Jude's punch and already starting to turn all colours.

He arrived back a while ago, soaked through and covered in mud, slamming the door behind him, not a word for her, only a look of pure rage before he went upstairs and banged another door. From the hall down below, Frankie heard the sound of the shower running long and hard in Roz's bathroom – *her* bathroom – Bo's now, and God, how she *hates* that. Though maybe, she thought then, recognizing his need to wash, maybe after what he had done, what he had carried, dealt with, *maybe* he might have just a tiny fragment of understanding of how it felt not to be properly, decently clean.

He's down here again now, back in the living room, hair still damp from the shower, wearing a black tracksuit, and he's just finished telling her about Jude, and Frankie can see, looking at his strained face and still haunted eyes, that if he was freaked out when he took his first look under the conservatory floor, now he's way beyond that.

'Why'd you choose that place –' she's curious, in spite of how bad, how sick she feels '– to get rid?'

'I didn't sodding *choose* it, you stupid cow,' Bolin answers. 'I was just so pissed off with not finding the right place – you'd think it'd be easy, but it's not. You chuck it over a cliff and you can't be sure it's going to land in the sea, and all the rest is bloody shallow beaches or too many houses and bungalows around, old people who can't sleep, nosing through their net curtains.'

'And you knew he was following,' Frankie says quietly.

251

'By then I knew,' Bolin says. 'Stupid bastard.'

She knows it was probably a game to him, knows that spooked as he was, he'll still have liked that part of it, playing with Alex's bloke, tormenting him; he'll have known that place would be okay for him in the truck, but not for Jude, on foot.

Poor bugger.

'Now what?' Bolin says again. 'That's what I want to know. Now fucking what?'

Frankie doesn't answer, doesn't dare.

'I'll tell you now what,' Bo says darkly. 'Now, thanks to you, I'm a fucking murderer too.'

Chapter 104

'Now what?' Jude asked himself and anyone or anything that might have been listening on this godforsaken night straight out of Stephen King-land.

Still alive, after scrambling up out of the water, thanks to the raggedy, broken concrete blocks that helped form the bank's edge, and to which his wounded, saturated city boots had somehow gripped hold despite the slithery, lethal mud. Heartily thankful *to* be alive, but so drained and shivering and freezing and wringing wet – and his head hurt like hell, too, and his shoulder, and he'd already emptied his stomach along with his lungs.

Worse things than that, far worse.

The certain knowledge that there was a man still down there in the canal, Bolin's victim, come half adrift from his plastic wrapping, and right now, maybe – only maybe, thinking of the force of the wind and currents down there – but *maybe* he was still hooked onto the piece of fractured concrete that had been clutching him when Jude had come face to gory face with him. Which meant that maybe, if Jude got help quickly enough, he could be brought up and out of the water before the current snatched him loose and carried him away, perhaps forever.

The sinking sensation in what was left of his stomach told him, even before his right hand began its search inside his waterlogged jacket, that the phone had gone.

Phone gone.

Torch gone.

No big surprise, he thought with an almost dead grimness, except that it meant the only way to get help now was for him to find his way back through the blackness to the road, to the Honda

253

and civilization. Virtually impossible, obviously, without so much as a beam of light to guide him. And even if by some miracle he did manage to make it back without collapsing or falling in the canal or the river or a bog, and if the phone in the old-fashioned box he thought he'd seen on the road near the car park, *if* it was working, it was going to take even more time to persuade the police that he wasn't some time-wasting nutcase. And even if they did believe him, it would surely take a whole lot more time for them to organize frogmen and Christ knew what else they'd need.

And by then the body would almost certainly be long gone.

So Jude knew what he had to do.

Get back to the water's edge and find a way, without having to actually get back into that killingly cold, powerful water, to get him out.

He had to try, had to.

And he had to do it now.

Chapter 105

'No choice,' Frankie tells him. 'You had to do it.'

'Thanks to you,' Bo says again. 'Except now I do have a choice, don't I? I can piss off and leave you to it, can't I, like I said before.'

'You can't,' she says, desperately. 'You wouldn't.'

'Why wouldn't I?' Bo says.

Because you love me, Frankie says in her mind, doesn't dare say it out loud.

'Thanks to you and Mr Plumber-in-Plastic, I can't even stick my own truck in the garage.' Bo shakes his head. 'And that's another thing I'll have to do for you: junk the number plates off that bloody van and get shot.'

'Sorry,' Frankie says.

'Fucking sight easier to just leave,' he says. 'Christ knows it's what you deserve, girl. That, and a lot worse.'

Chapter 106

No trees close to the canal, but the storm had deposited for Jude the gift of a thick, long branch, sturdy and craggy enough for him to keep a grip on, strong enough, he hoped, to stand up to some battering by the canal's current, and he had forced himself to move slowly, not to rush, take any more unnecessary risks, had located a section of wall a little further along that seemed closer to the water.

One goal at a time.

The first, finding *that* again, *him*, and getting it onto land.

Worry about the next step after that.

He was lying on his stomach again, back at the edge of the bank, wriggling out as far as was safely possible over the water, had dredged up just enough commonsense from his juddering, freezing brain to realise that if he were to actually get back into the water now, he would probably die of hypothermia, and then no one would ever know what had happened to him, let alone whoever that was down there.

'Please,' he said, out loud, into the wind and rain. '*Please*.'

The branch touched something.

Something.

'Oh, God,' Jude said, wanting to be sick again.

Not just because of the feel of it, but because he already knew that the branch alone wasn't going to do it, because he couldn't get the leverage he needed; because no mere branch could possibly be strong enough to wrench that waterlogged dead body off the concrete that had snagged it, let alone pull it out of the water.

Because, commonsense or not, he was going to have to get back in.

'Oh, shit,' he said. 'Oh, bloody, bloody shit.'

Do it in one go.

Get back in, keep a hold, somehow, on the bank and the branch, get straight to *it* and drag it up and out all in one go, because he knew he would be unable to endure any more than that.

And maybe, *maybe*, it was because he was already so frozen, so saturated, his mind so addled, but the curious thing was that as he lowered himself back into the water, it almost felt hot, as if it was *burning* him – but it was okay, it was going to be okay, because he was managing to tread water, and because he had already found it again, and the branch had located a hole in the plastic and hooked onto it, and Jude had found a decent foothold on a jutting piece of submerged concrete. And he had hold of *it* now, could feel, even through his numb fingers, that he was gripping plastic, he hoped to God it *was* plastic—

'Oh Jesus.'

And he began hauling at it with all his might, weak and pitiful as his might was by now, and Christ, it was so heavy, this man-thing, and Jude knew he couldn't think about what he was pulling up out of the canal, could not *allow* himself to think about it.

Just did it.

And, having done it, passed out.

257

Chapter 107

At six forty five, having been loth to remain in Roland Gardens with David a minute longer than necessary, Alex was already at the hospital, expecting a lengthy wait.

'All signed and sealed,' Suzy told her, fully dressed, bag packed.

'At this time of day?' Alex was impressed. 'How'd you manage that?'

'Drove them so crazy they obliged just to get shot of me.' Suzy paused. 'David okay?'

'Not really,' Alex answered.

'Good,' Suzy said unconvincingly, then pulled herself together. 'Let's get out of here, please, and get on a train. High time I actually got to meet your Jude dude.'

'If I can actually find him.' Alex picked up the bag. 'I called him as I left your flat, but his voice mail was picking up and his mobile wasn't responding, which I suppose means he's been called into work.'

'At crack of dawn on a Sunday?' Suzy said.

'I know,' Alex said. 'Must be some last-minute crisis.'

'He's a phantom,' Suzy said. 'A nice phantom, at least I know that much now.'

'Jude's definitely solid.' Alex smiled.

'Might be better off with a phantom,' Suzy said, wryly. 'Look at me.'

Chapter 108

'You never said,' Frankie says to Bo, 'how you knew I was in hospital?'

Bo napped for a half hour a while ago, but Frankie's had no sleep or rest, her dread of what's yet to come consuming her.

This question's been nibbling away at her for a long time. Almost from when he arrived at the Royal Sussex, but in the beginning she was too out of it and her speech was so poor, and then she went through that oddly peaceful, drifting time, not actually liking to ask anything that might have rocked her tranquil boat; and after that, when the past started coming back, she didn't dare.

But now, at this particular minute, they're sitting in the kitchen drinking mushroom Cup-a-Soups, and Frankie's actually managing to get hers down because she finds, suddenly, that she's hungry; and anyway, they're both taking a little time out from the main event, and though she knows it won't, can't, last, she feels almost, *almost*, able to pretend they're a normal couple.

'I saw them take you out of here,' Bo answers her question.

No prevarication. Straight down the line.

She asks nothing more, waits for him.

'Last few years,' he goes on, 'I've moved wherever work or the fancy's taken me. Didn't want to get stuck in one place, not after us.'

Us. She wonders, as he drains his cup, what's '*us*' means to him.

'And then, while I was working on the Brighton site – with the faggot – I went shopping for boots in Churchill Square, and I saw you.'

Frankie remembers him coming out of Clarks.

259

'You looked so different I couldn't believe it.' Bo shakes his head. 'So I followed you, saw you come in here, and I thought: she's cleaning here, and that was more like it, except you didn't come out again, like you would have – not for a few days, anyway.'

'You kept watch all that time.' The thought of that makes Frankie happy and scared all at once.

'So I thought: fuck me, she's got herself a rich bloke – except there wasn't any bloke here. And then you did come out, didn't you, went up Falmer Road, went off to work for the Levin woman, and you looked like you used to again, ordinary, like a cleaner. And I got to thinking: what's Frankie's game now?' Bo shook his head. 'And now I know, more or less, don't I? More than I want to. A whole shitload more.'

Chapter 109

Coming to in early light, sprawled face down on the wet mud and leaves and reeds, Jude began coughing up some of the filth that had lodged in his mouth and throat – and then remembered.

Wished he had not.

Wished to Christ it had all been a dream.

But, as he lifted his head and looked to his right, he saw all the proof he needed that it had not been. Was still not.

'Now what?' he asked himself again, out loud, and tried to get up, but the pain in his head and shoulder, and in his back and both arms too, was like fire – which was more than could be said for the rest of him.

Jesus, he was so cold.

He looked at his watch, but that said four thirty-three, which might, he supposed, have been the time when Bolin had knocked him down or tossed him into the water.

At least, thank God, the dark was gone, and the day looked, to his builder's early-start eye, as if it had been light for a while now, and the storm had passed, the air fresh and clean.

Enjoy that some other time.

He managed to sit up – and even that was tough going. He felt dizzy and sick and his teeth were chattering, and the damp that felt as if it had permeated his flesh, combining with the ice in his bones, seemed to be making his head hurt even more.

'Come on,' he told himself.

Time to leave that – him – and get some help.

That thought, at least, made clear sense, since, for one thing, Jude didn't know how much strength he had left, and for another, if he were to even try to move the body again, he'd almost

261

certainly be destroying whatever evidence might be left.

So now, all he needed to do was start walking back across what had, last night, been a nightmare and was, this morning, postcard-picturesque, get back to the Honda and find a phone.

'Piece of cake,' he said.

Tried to stand, slipped and fell.

Passed out again.

Chapter 110

'Sorry I can't answer right now,' Jude's voice told Alex, 'but don't hang up without leaving a message. Thanks.'

'Me again,' Alex said. 'Just to say we're here, at the cottage. Hope you're okay.' She paused. 'Call me, Jude. Please.'

They had arrived at Melton Cottage just after nine, and Alex had helped Suzy inside before checking her messages and trying Jude again both at home and on his mobile, and though she was doing her best to stay light about it, she didn't care for the knot that had begun tightening in her stomach because of his ongoing, unexplained absence. One of the many pleasures of their relationship, even in its early stages, had been the ease with which they had both freely elected to stay in regular touch. Jude often called her during work breaks, left brief, warm messages on her voice mail, never seemed in the least disconcerted if she did the same, said he liked hearing her voice.

It simply was not like him to disappear without explanation.

'He's probably just left his mobile at home,' Suzy said, reading her expression.

'You're right,' she said, except that the recorded message had reported that Jude's mobile was not responding, rather than switched off.

'I'm always right, Ally, you know that.' The wryness in Suzy's tone and face were painful. 'Specially about blokes.'

Chapter 111

'Need to go to the toilet,' Frankie tells Bo.

Third time she's asked him, and the Cup-a-Soup combined with several cups of tea have filled her bladder to bursting point.

'Fuck's sake, woman,' he says, 'haven't I got enough to worry about?'

'I'm nervous, too, Bo –' getting more so by the second '– and it makes me—'

'Bit bloody late getting nervous now,' Bo points out. 'You've killed two people, nutbag, and now you've sucked me into the same bloody boat, and *you're* scared. What about *me*, you stupid bitch?'

'Please,' Frankie says. 'Don't get angry.'

He makes a sound of exasperation, blows it out of his nostrils, shakes his head.

'I really need to go,' she says again.

She feels humiliation paint her cheeks red, and wishes now that she'd agreed to the commode they offered her when she first came home, because the chair won't fit through the door of the downstairs loo, so Bo has to help her; and she wishes, too, she'd made a bit of an effort with the walking frame, hadn't left herself so bloody dependent on the chair.

On him.

She wishes a lot of things.

'Please, Bo,' she says.

'For God's sake.' Bo lights his sixth roll-up since sitting at the kitchen table. 'Just give me five minutes' sodding peace and quiet to work out what I'm going to do next.'

Chapter 112

They'd had breakfast.

Scrambled eggs and toast and honey from a farm Alex had found with Jude a few weeks back, just a mile or two outside Woodingdean.

'Gorgeous,' Suzy said.

'Mm,' Alex agreed.

'So what's going to happen now?' Suzy asked.

'Depends on you,' Alex replied.

'I feel a bit of a wimp,' Suzy said, 'but the truth is, all I really want to do right this minute is go to sleep.'

'You're entitled,' Alex said.

Suzy was looking at her.

'What?' Alex asked.

'You're really stressing over Jude, aren't you?'

'Not really stressing exactly,' Alex said.

'Yes, you are,' Suzy persisted.

Alex shrugged. 'A bit.'

'So while I'm asleep,' Suzy said, 'go and find him.'

'I'm not going out and leaving you when you've just got out of hospital.'

'I'll be sleeping, dope,' Suzy said. 'And if I know you're sitting around biting your nails waiting for me to wake up, I won't be able to rest.'

'I don't bite my nails,' Alex said.

'Give me a break, Ally,' Suzy said.

She waited until Suzy was sound asleep up in the spare room, phone plugged in beside her, and then she let herself quietly out of

265

the cottage, got into the Mini, drove to Hove to Jude's building site – Sunday deserted – and then to the Lanes, where she saw that the Honda was not in its usual place, parked her own car on a double yellow line and ran to the flat.

She buzzed first – they both did that; Jude always rang the bell at Melton Cottage if he knew she was in, even though he had a key.

'Plain good manners,' he'd said to her, first time he did it.

One of the many things she liked about him.

Liked no longer a strong enough word, she realised now.

Feeling that more intensely as, getting no reply, she let herself into the house, went upstairs to his flat, and unlocked that door too.

'Jude?' she called, closing the door behind her.

The message could not have been much clearer if he had left a note. The blinds he sometimes drew at night still closed. The bed up on the platform rumpled, a pair of grey shorts on the floor beside it. The general uncharacteristic untidiness all pointing to a possibly hasty, probably unplanned waking and exit.

And the canvas on the easel in the studio area; barely begun, but there was no doubting the subject of the strong charcoal sketching, or the impression of stormy skies overhead and turbulent sea beyond the hill.

There'd been a storm down here last night.

And then, of course, there was the conversation she'd had with Jude yesterday afternoon about his having gone to Frankie's house and having seen and talked to Mike Bolin about the cracks in the walls.

Jude had said he'd gone there because the house had kept on 'needling' him and he'd been missing her and he'd had nothing better to do.

Alex looked at the new canvas, the clearest evidence that the house had gone on exercising his mind. Found herself wondering if perhaps that was where he had gone again, if he might have experienced a similar compulsion again in the early hours, and just given up on sleep and gone back to Winder Hill.

And if so, where was he now?

Probably nothing to do with the house or Bolin.

It was ridiculous to think it had; *she* was being ridiculous. Probably Jude had received a pre-dawn call from some friend or workmate in need, or maybe he'd just had an attack of restlessness and gone out for a run on the beach.

Still . . .

She picked up his phone, feeling intrusive, guilty, for checking his messages, then did so anyway, found only her own, then remembered Suzy's suggestion that he might have left his mobile at home and rang the number, but heard no tell-tale ring to back that up.

'Damn it, Jude,' she said out loud. 'Where *are* you?'

Over-reacting, she told herself right after.

Except that, irrational or not, her concerns had not been in any way alleviated.

On the contrary.

She debated going back to the cottage to check on Suzy, not liking to phone instead in case she was sleeping.

More practical, she decided, letting herself out of Jude's flat, to leave Suzy in peace, go to Rottingdean first, lay her unease to rest.

Then get on with Sunday.

Chapter 113

In the kitchen of the house on Winder Hill, Frankie gives a cry of dismay.

'What now?' Bo asks.

'Wet myself,' she says in a horrified, wretched whisper.

'God –' he screws up his nose and mouth '– you're disgusting.'

'Please,' Frankie says.

'Please what?' Bo says. 'You've done it now, haven't you?'

'Need you to help.' Her face is flushed with distress. 'Clean me up.'

'No way.'

'*Please*.'

'You were bright enough to set all this lot up, weren't you?' Bo's cold now, cruelly rational. 'Smart enough to kill a woman and get a sodding coffin down there and stick her in it, not to mention to kill off Mr Plumber.'

She stares at him, already mourning the passing of that almost companionable Cup-a-Soup breakfast they shared a couple of hours back, knowing now that it was an illusion.

*De*lusion, more like.

'You're the Queen-of-clean, aren't you?' says Bo, compounding it. 'So fucking go clean yourself up.'

Chapter 114

No sign of the Honda outside the house.

Just Bolin's green and very muddy Toyota truck.

Alex sat for several moments in the Mini, wondering if she should give up the idea of this highly questionable, almost certainly pointless visit, go straight back to Melton Cottage and wait for Jude to get in touch in his own time. Wondering if she was not only over-reacting, but possibly even encroaching on Jude's personal freedom.

Not her style, she liked to think, as a general rule.

But then she remembered again the canvas that Jude had left on his easel, his strong, continuing mistrust of Mike Bolin and his strange preoccupation with this house.

The fact that he'd told her last night that he missed her, would speak to her this morning. The fact that – Suzy's gentle joke about phantoms notwithstanding – Jude did *not* have a tendency to go missing unless it was for a good reason.

Alex looked at the house again.

Knew she had to go in.

Switched off the engine.

Chapter 115

'Can't stand this, Bo,' Frankie tells him.

Sitting there in her wheelchair, her knickers and skirt and the seat of the chair itself all soaked with her piss.

Stinking.

Filthy.

Unbearable.

'Bo,' she says again.

'Shut up,' he says.

'Please,' she appeals, 'don't make me sit like this. I can take a lot, but not this, you *know* that, Bo.'

She notes, even in the midst of this new horror, that desperation seems to be making it easier, rather than more difficult, to talk. Mind over matter, maybe.

You can talk when you want to.

Bo said that a few days ago, didn't he?

'Bo, please,' she says now.

'You going to stop whining,' Bo says, 'or you want me to shut you up?'

The doorbell rings.

'Who the fuck?' He gets up, goes out of the kitchen and into the living room, takes a quick look through the window, comes back into the kitchen.

'It's the Levin woman.'

'Christ,' Frankie says.

The bell rings again.

'Better answer it,' she says.

'You are joking,' Bo says, throwing her a look.

'You don't answer,' Frankie points out, 'she'll think I'm ill

270

again, maybe call an ambulance.' She pauses, fear making her mind keener for a moment, surprising her. 'And your truck's out front, isn't it?'

'Shit,' Bo says, goes towards the door. 'I'll get rid of her.'

'Be nice,' Frankie says.

'You stay put,' Bo tells her. 'I'll tell her you're tired and grouchy and some other time, right?'

Her own stench reaches Frankie's nose again, and panic returns, clutching her belly.

'Don't be long, Bo,' she says. 'Please.'

Chapter 116

Alex was wondering whether or not to ring again when the door opened.

'Oh,' Bolin said. 'It's you.'

'Sorry.' She tried not to stare at his injured eye. 'I didn't mean to disturb you, only—'

'Frankie's resting,' Bolin cut in. 'She's really tired this morning.'

'Okay,' Alex said, easily. 'So why don't I just look in on her, say hi, see if she needs anything, and then I'll leave her to rest.'

'She doesn't need anything,' Bo said, and began to shut the door.

'S'okay, Bo.'

Frankie's slurry voice came from somewhere behind him.

Bo turned around.

Using the moment, taking no time to consider, Alex stepped off the ramp, over the doorstep, and into the entrance hall.

Chapter 117

Frankie isn't certain why she did that.

Disobeyed Bo and came out of the kitchen.

It's not as if she really wants Alex in here now, she's afraid to have her here.

Though maybe she's simply more afraid of being alone here now with Bo.

Shouldn't have done it. Shouldn't have let her in.

Too late.

Alex *is* in, standing here in the hall, smiling at her.

'I just wanted to see you for a moment, Frankie,' she says.

'I told her you're tired, babe,' Bo says.

Fury in his black eyes, barely hidden.

'Just for a moment,' Alex says again.

'Okay,' Frankie says.

And wheels herself into the living room.

Chapter 118

Even if the hallway and living room had not looked so much more untidy than the last time she had been there, had not felt so truly unclean, the awful smell in the hall would have alerted Alex to the fact that something was very wrong.

That, and Frankie's face.

She looked ill, Alex thought, as the other women turned her chair around in the middle of the room, close to her bed. Ill, in body and mind.

'You're manoeuvring better,' she said, gently. 'But you don't look very well.'

'I told you,' Bo said irritably. 'She's tired.'

That kind of response from a carer was familiar territory to Alex. People struggling to manage, getting ratty, even belligerent, because of the great strain they were under.

'If things are getting on top of you both –' she spoke directly to him this time, very calmly and politely '– you know you only have to ask for a bit more help.'

'We know,' Bolin said. 'We're fine.'

'Frankie doesn't look too fine,' she persisted.

She took another step closer to the woman in the chair, and knew, instantly, that Frankie had wet herself, and her heart flew out to her because Lord knew that could be bad enough, humiliating enough for anyone, but for a woman with Frankie's OCD history . . .

She bent, slightly, towards her, spoke softly, privately. 'Would you like a hand getting to the bathroom, Frankie?'

She took off the lightweight belted rain jacket she'd slung on over her chinos and T-shirt when she'd left the cottage, laid it

274

over the back of one of the armchairs, turned back to Frankie, not even glancing at Bolin.

'I was about to take care of that,' he said, 'when you came.'

'Well, I'm here now,' Alex said, easily. 'So I might as well lend a—'

'You deaf or something?' Bolin asked. 'I said we can manage.'

'Can you?' Alex asked Frankie.

Frankie looked up at Bolin. 'Yeah,' she said. 'Course.' She managed a ghost of a smile. 'But thanks, Alex,' she added, 'for coming.'

'Yeah,' Bolin said, with an effort. 'Thanks. Didn't mean to be rude.'

'That's okay,' Alex said.

Bolin picked up her rain jacket, held it out to her.

'Thank you.' She took it from him, put it over her left arm, realised that Frankie's predicament had pushed Jude briefly from the forefront of her mind.

'By the way,' she said, casually, 'you haven't seen Jude, have you?'

Frankie made a small, involuntary sound, went white.

Alex looked down at her, her pulse quickening. 'All right?'

'She's fine,' Bolin said.

Alex kept her gaze on Frankie. 'Only I've been in London,' she said, 'and I haven't spoken to him since I got back, and—'

'Saw him yesterday,' Bolin said.

Now she turned to him, managed to seem surprised. 'Really? Where?'

'Here,' Bolin answered. 'Outside. Said he was just passing.' The irony was slight but noticeable. 'Asked if I'd seen some cracks in a wall.'

'Oh,' Alex said. 'Right.'

Nothing Jude had not told her.

She looked back at Frankie again. 'Sure you're okay, love?'

'Fine.' She sounded stronger, suddenly, sharper. 'I said.'

'Any other questions?' Bolin asked.

Sarcastic.

Alex looked at his injured eye again. That, and Frankie's reaction to her question about Jude, had really tipped the balance, was making her feel quite strongly that something actually might be wrong here, might be wrong with Jude.

275

'That looks nasty.' Her pulse beat faster again.

'It's nothing,' he said.

'Bo,' Frankie said, sharp again.

He ignored her.

'I'll see you out,' he said to Alex, walking ahead out of the room into the hall.

'If you need me,' Alex said to Frankie, 'just call.'

Frankie didn't answer, her eyes fixed on Bolin, out in the hall, as he moved to the front door and waited for Alex.

In her shoulder bag, Alex's mobile phone began to ring.

'Sorry.' She fished it out of a side pocket, hoped it was Jude, saw her home number on the display, wondered if it was Suzy calling to say she'd heard from him.

'Hi, Suzy,' she answered, moving out into the hall. 'You okay?'

'Absolutely fine,' Suzy said. 'Having a big yen for Häagen-Dazs.'

'What flavour?' Alex saw Bolin's impatient shake of his head.

'Surprise me,' Suzy said. 'Have you found Jude?'

'*Bo*.' Frankie's voice from the living room, calling him, insistent now.

'Not sure,' Alex said to Suzy.

'What does that mean?'

Bolin left the front door, moved past Alex, back towards Frankie, who was saying something, too softly for her to hear the words, though their urgency was clear enough, and it was interesting how Frankie seemed able to talk more freely when she chose, and something was happening here, Alex felt it, *knew* it now.

She looked at the front door.

Get out.

Instinct, nothing more, but powerful.

'Ally,' Suzy's voice said, 'what's happening?'

'Nothing.'

She took a step forward, but it was too late, Bolin was back, already between her and the door, and suddenly Alex felt the most pressing need to try to get some kind of alert to Suzy.

'You should ask David,' she said.

'What?' Suzy sounded confused.

'See what he'd do in the circumstances.' Alex was floundering, but it was the best she could manage with Bolin glaring at her.

276

Though at least he *was* at the front door, which meant he still wanted to get rid of her, which meant she would be able, in just a moment or two, to call Suzy back from the safety of the Mini.

'You've lost me, Ally,' Suzy said. 'What's going on?'

'Better yet,' Alex said, with sudden inspiration, 'get him to call one of his colleagues.'

'What the hell are you talking about?' Suzy demanded.

'They'll know what to do,' Alex said.

'Ally, this is weird,' Suzy said. 'What's going on?'

'Strawberry Cheesecake okay?' Alex said. 'Soon as I finish in Rottingdean.'

She ended the call, turned around to look at Frankie, couldn't see her, either in the hall or what little she could see of the living room, forced herself to turn back to Bolin with an apologetic smile.

'Sorry,' she said. 'Sick friend staying with me. Got a few hassles.'

'Join the club,' he said.

Get out now.

She moved closer to him, to the door.

'Anyway,' she said easily, 'thanks for letting me see Frankie.'

'No problem,' Bolin said, and opened the door.

Thank you.

'Tell her I hope she feels better soon,' Alex said.

Stepped outside and walked, as slowly and normally as she could manage, down the ramp onto the path and towards her car.

Chapter 119

'Shit,' Jude said, coming round again.

His head hurt, all of it, not just the wound. Every part of him hurt, and he was cold enough to want to lie down again and die.

Not till you tell someone.

He forced himself to sit up, felt dizzy, gritted his teeth, waited for it to pass.

Kept his eyes averted from the dead man.

Walk first. Then phone. First the police. Then Alex.

He had to look at the body then, *had* to make sure it was still there, that he had not, after all, dreamed that part of this nightmare. His eyes were sore and blurry, but the fuzziness was welcome as he looked and saw that it – he – was very much there, hideously pitiful in sodden, torn plastic.

He would have been sick again, but there was nothing left.

He looked at the loveliness all around him, remembered that he was in a beauty spot, a favourite place for walkers and, presumably, birdwatchers.

Lot of birds around.

Gulls, all kinds, swooping, screaming.

He envied them their wings.

Looked around for some early morning human life.

No one.

Lucky for them.

Get up, he ordered himself.

And this time, he managed it without falling.

Now walk.

Chapter 120

Alex's hands were shaking now as she took the car keys out of her bag, and she supposed it was reaction more to her wild, wholly unfounded suspicions than anything else.

Bolin had not stood in her way, had opened the door and let her leave, had *wanted* her to leave, had not wanted her in the house in the first place because Frankie wasn't feeling well and because he, presumably, wanted to be left in peace.

No crime there.

She stuck the key in the lock, gripped the door handle – heard his step too late, a split second before his hand, suntanned, much larger and unquestionably stronger, covered hers, prevented her from opening the door of the Mini, and Alex felt as if her heart was about to leap out of her chest as she turned to face Bolin, tried to mask her fear.

'You startled me,' she said. 'Creeping up like that.'

'Come back in,' Bolin said.

'Can't.' Alex tried to extricate her hand. 'Patients to see.'

'I thought you were going to get something for your sick friend.'

'I am,' she said coldly, her heart pounding. 'Then I have patients. Please let go of my hand, Mr Bolin.'

'Can't do that.' He prised her fingers off the door handle. 'Wish I could.'

'Let me go.' Alex stared around, saw no one on the hill to help. 'Let me *go*.'

'Shut up,' Bolin told her.

'This is ridiculous.' She tried to pull away, considered screaming, wondered if anyone would hear, if they would help if they did, and you heard tales these days of people ignoring others in trouble.

279

'Let me *go*.'

'Don't you want to know where your boyfriend is?' Bolin asked.

Swinging her leg back, about to kick him, Alex stopped dead. 'What have you done to him?'

He pulled her up close, and began to manoeuvre her up the path. 'Wait and see,' he said.

Chapter 121

The A239 looked, to Jude's salt- and wind-sore eyes, like some sort of asphalt oasis.

Two more heaven-sent visions besides: the public phone in its old green box, and the Honda, just where he had left it a million or so hours earlier.

He'd half expected the jeep to be gone, for Bolin to have moved it; could only suppose that the other man had seen no good reason to bother if he thought Jude was swimming with the fishes.

Swimming with . . .

The ghastly, mouldering face flashed before Jude's eyes again.

He shook his head, clenched his jaw, trudged towards the phone.

An old-fashioned expression came into his mind.

Done in.

All but finished, after his struggle back through all that spoiled loveliness.

He'd tried to distract himself during the long hike, to take in some of the beauty, hoping to lessen his pain and fatigue, to blot out the horror, and then, still hearing the shrieking, swooping gulls, he had wondered, suddenly, with sick revulsion, if there was anything of the vulture in them, if they might, perhaps, even now, be picking over that poor dead man's corpse; thought, too late, that he ought to have covered the body for protection, but he'd only had his leather jacket, and he'd known he'd needed that for his own survival, ruined as it was.

So much for distraction.

Phone.

The car park barrier that he was almost certain had been down last night was now raised, which presumably meant someone was around, and that was the most tempting idea, to go and find them, tell them, get them to take this over. But that, Jude knew, would just waste more time: persuading some well-meaning, normal person that he was not completely insane, that they needed to take action right away, call the police.

Which he could patently do himself, if the phone worked, and Lord knew he'd come this far . . .

He fished in his jacket pockets for coins, but they'd gone the same way as the mobile and torch, and his legs were very weak, and he wasn't sure how much longer he could stay on his feet, and the inside of the phone box had been vandalized and smelled like hell, but then again, so did he, and the phone itself did seem to be working, and anyway, he didn't need a coin to dial 999.

Except there was another call he wanted to make first.

A voice he found he quite desperately wanted to hear, before he got into the explanation game with the police.

He stuck his hand into the still soaking back pocket of his jeans, dug his fingers in and found a pound coin. He dragged it out, saw how the hand trembled with exhaustion, picked up the receiver again, stuck the coin in the slot and made the call.

Remembered, as the number was ringing, that Alex was in London.

Lifted his hand again, about to cut off the call when it was answered.

'Hello?'

The voice was female. Not Alex.

'Who's that?' His voice was hoarse.

'Is that Jude?'

'It is,' he said. 'Who's this?'

'Jude, thank God,' the voice said. 'This is Suzy.'

Chapter 122

Frankie is wheeling herself into the hall again as Bo comes back through the door, gripping Alex's arm.

'I was right, wasn't I?' Frankie stops the chair, physically exhausted, looks up at Alex's white face, at her furious, scared expression.

'What the hell is going on, Frankie?' Alex demands.

Bo kicks the front door shut.

'She knows, doesn't she?' Frankie says, ignoring her.

'*What* do I know?' Alex says.

'Shut up,' Bo tells her.

'She knows.' Frankie's statement is flat.

'Shut up,' Bo says again, to her this time.

'Will you please let go of my *arm*,' Alex tells him.

'Both of you,' Bo snaps. 'Just shut the fuck up and let me think.'

Alex looks from one to the other, picks Frankie again.

Weakest link, has to be.

'Frankie, listen to me,' she says, appealing to her.

'I don't have to listen to you,' Frankie says. 'You're not my therapist now, not my boss or *"client"*.' She manages to make the last word caustic, gathers a little strength from that. 'Nothing to me now.'

'I don't understand,' Alex says. 'But whatever it is you've got yourself into, whatever he's sucked you into, it'll be okay if we stop this now.'

Bo, still holding onto her, snorts derisively.

'You've been so ill, Frankie,' Alex goes on, 'no one's going to blame you.'

'Shut *up*,' Bo says again.

'That's right,' Frankie says. 'Bo's right.'

She wheels herself closer to Alex and Bo, and bravado or not, temporary upper hand or not, this is all costing her physically; she can almost feel her strength draining away again by the second, and in spite of all her secret exercising, now, when she really *needs* to be strong, she's hardly up to doing the slightest thing. And she can still smell her own acrid stink, that's the worst of it, and all she wanted to do before *she* came along, all she still wants to do more than anything, is get cleaned up, but this bloody nosy woman, this patronising cow, this *therapist*, is in her way, ruining everything.

'Shut the fuck up, Alex,' she echoes Bo, 'you stupid, stupid bitch.'

'You're not to blame, Frankie,' Alex says, desperately. 'They'll see that.'

'Think so?' Bo's jeering now. 'Think the cops are going to say "poor nutso Frankie and wicked old Bo"? I don't think so, not with dead bodies all over the shop.'

Dead bodies.

The words seem to judder in the air.

Frankie looks at Alex's horrified expression.

'Get rid of her,' she says to Bo. 'You have to get rid of her.'

He stares at her. 'This is getting so out of hand.'

'That's right, it is,' Alex struggles back into the conversation. 'So let's please just stop it right now.'

'You –' Bo yanks her up close again, takes her rain jacket from her, pulls its belt from the loops with his free hand, lets the jacket drop onto the carpet '– shut your interfering face.'

'What you going to do, Bo?' Frankie asks.

Bo doesn't answer, starts moving instead, startling Alex, dragging her with him towards the conservatory—

The phone in her bag starts to ring again, and Bo pulls the bag off her shoulder, takes out the phone, drops that on the floor, too, and stamps on it.

'Now they'll know something's wrong,' Alex says.

'I told you to shut up,' Bo says.

'Frankie, please,' Alex pleads, over her shoulder. 'Call the police.'

'Think she'll do that –' Bo's laughing '– and you're as barking as she is.'

Chapter 123

'For God's sake,' Suzy said to Jude on the phone, 'you have to call the police first, before anything.'

'Which is what I was going to do,' Jude said, 'till you told me Alex might be in there, in that house with Bolin.' There was a regular flow of traffic on the road now, and though his watch still said four thirty-three, he guessed it was probably after ten. 'But who knows how long it might take them to get their act together, and maybe if I can at least get back there before—'

'You're talking crap,' Suzy told him bluntly. 'All you'll succeed in doing is getting two of you shut up with a killer.'

'At least Alex won't be *alone*.'

'Oh, hell,' Suzy said, wavering. 'Oh, fucking hell.'

'I know,' he said.

'Okay,' she said, helplessly. 'So what am I supposed to do exactly? What's this non-plan of yours?'

'You're going to give me twenty minutes –' he thought about the distance, about possible traffic and his own physical condition, amended that '– make that half an hour.'

'Too *long*,' Suzy said.

'I'll need most of that just to get back to Winder Hill,' he told her. 'A half hour, Suzy, just so I can get to her, and then you call the police and tell them about Alex and Bolin and that poor bastard lying out there.'

'Ally first,' Suzy said, 'rotting corpses later.'

'Now I know why Alex loves you so much.'

'For God's sake, Jude,' Suzy said, 'be careful.'

'Thirty minutes,' he said, and cut her off.

285

Chapter 124

'For your information, Miss Do-Good-Bleeding-Heart,' Bolin told Alex, dragging her though the conservatory, across the tiled floor, past the cane furniture and chintz cushions, 'none of this is down to me. It's all been *her*, the good old Queen-of-Clean, lost her marbles and decided she needed her own palace to scrub.'

He halted by one of the armchairs, knocked it out of the way with his knee, then kicked away a white-and-navy rug, and exposed a trapdoor.

'What are you *doing*?' Alex's fear was gripping harder by the second.

'Only someone else was living in it,' Bolin went on. 'So good-old Frankie decided to clean her away, too, didn't she?'

He squatted, suddenly, almost hauling Alex off her feet, reached for the handle, heaved up the trapdoor and exposed blackness.

'No!' Alex started to panic as the stench from the hole hit her; the same kind, only much worse, that she'd smelled earlier in the hall. 'No!'

'Shut up,' Bolin told her.

She struggled, with all her strength, to pull out of his grasp, knew there was no hope as he dragged her to the edge of the cavity and shoved her hard from behind.

'*No!*'

Her scream cut off as she landed painfully on her knees, and she knew she hadn't fallen far, no more than about four or five feet, she thought, but it was black as pitch and filled with this terrible smell, and her new immediate terror was that he would shut the trapdoor and leave her down here in the dark.

'Please!' she cried out, then saw that Bolin was coming down after her, and fresh terror, even more powerful, seemed to clutch her by the throat.

'No!'

She tried to crawl backwards, away from him, then stopped, froze rigid, instinct telling her to stay close to the light, and saw that Bolin, too, was getting down on his knees, realised that it was because the ceiling was so low and, dear God, this was no more than a crawlspace.

'It's all right,' he told her.

'Please,' she said again. 'I don't—'

He grabbed her left arm and she cried out again as he dragged her further away from the opening and the light, and the sickening, cloying stench was filling her mouth and throat and nose, and this was worse than any nightmare, and she couldn't even try to fight him off now, because she had to, *had* to, clamp her free hand over her mouth and nose to stop herself from choking.

Bolin pushed her, abruptly and hard, and Alex fell over onto her back, and even then he didn't stop dragging at her, and she was aware of pain, but that didn't seem to matter; the terror, the *horror*, was winning hands down.

And then she saw it.

In the light from the open trapdoor now a dozen feet away.

A coffin, its shape unmistakable.

Alex felt her soul shrivel.

'Oh, no,' she said. 'Oh, please, God, no.'

'Want me to gag you?' Bolin asked.

'Tell me it's not Jude,' Alex said. 'Just *please* tell me that.'

'It's not Jude,' Bolin said, and dragged her right up hard against the coffin, slamming her shoulder against the steel. 'Now for the last time, unless you want me to do it for you, shut the fuck *up*.'

And as he tied both her arms, using the belt from her jacket, to one of the handles of the coffin, Alex did just that.

Beyond talking now. Almost beyond screaming.

Until she saw Bolin crawling away back towards the opening, straightening up and pulling himself out.

Until she saw the trapdoor starting to close.

Then she screamed.

Chapter 125

Once the Honda's heater had kicked in and Jude had managed to rub a little more life into his arms and legs, knowing he was in no shape to drive, knowing he was going to, regardless, he had made good time.

Until he'd hit a jam just east of Peacehaven.

Roadworks, jamming the road both ways.

He turned his head to his right, saw a woman in a VW stuck on the other side of the road, staring at him.

Knew what he must look like.

Like a nightmare.

She should only know.

The dead face came back into his mind.

'Go away,' he said out loud.

The woman in the other car shook her head and looked away.

Chapter 126

Suzy, upstairs in the spare bedroom at Melton Cottage, was looking at her watch.

Fifteen minutes.

Stupid, crazy, to wait any longer, to have waited *this* long. To wait even *one* minute to tell the police that her sister-in-law's boyfriend had fished a body out of a canal near the Channel. That he had, before that, been pushed in to join that body.

Except that what Jude had said about giving him time to get to Alex so she wouldn't be all alone, had made some kind of sense to Suzy. At least it had at the time.

There was, of course, still the possibility that Jude Brown was nuts. She didn't, after all, really know him, even if he had gone to the trouble of putting together that Matt-and-Alex photo album for Ally; even if Ally was in love with him.

But Alex's own weird phone call earlier had to have meant something, *had* to have been some kind of warning or even, she thought now, with hindsight and deepest foreboding, a cry for help.

'*See what David would do.*'

Something like that.

With David being the very last person in the world Alex would suggest Suzy sought advice from.

'*Better yet, get him to call one of his colleagues.*'

As a criminal defence lawyer, the police weren't exactly David's colleagues, pretty much the opposite; but what if that had been the best Alex could come up with in the circumstances she had found herself in?

Whatever those circumstances were.

Suzy looked at her watch again.

Sixteen minutes.

'Sod this for a game of soldiers,' she said.

And picked up the phone.

Chapter 127

Alex had stopped screaming again.

Partly because each time she opened her mouth, the stench was sucked into her throat, down into her lungs, swallowed into her stomach.

Partly because she knew that she badly needed to think, and screaming was going to stop her doing that, *and* was a waste of energy.

She knew she needed to calm down, take deep breaths.

No deep breaths, not in this.

Her mind was all over the place, not just racing, doing a bloody marathon.

One of the first things that had come to her had been that thank God this was her, not Jude, being tied to a coffin, of all things, because he would not have been able to stand it, might have lost his mind.

The next thing she had realised had been that if it was not Jude in there – and of course it wasn't, because whatever might have happened to him, whatever Bolin might have done to him, he wouldn't have had a bloody coffin ready and waiting, would he?

But if it wasn't Jude – *thank God* – who was it?

She'd already tried, and failed, to convince herself that the coffin might be empty. Failed because of the stink.

And the flies.

She hadn't noticed them at first because of the noise she had been making, and because of the dark. But now she couldn't *stop* noticing them, buzzing, crawling, flying all around her.

Roz Bailey.

Of course.

Oh, dear Christ.

'Jude,' she said out loud, as if he might hear her, as if she might reach him.

The realization about Mrs Bailey had brought her close to screaming again, but the foul air aside, if she made too much noise, it was possible that Bolin might come back down, and at least for now, she was still alive, but if she pushed that man too far, there was no knowing what he might do to her.

Her wrists hurt, and her arms were uncomfortable, *all* of her was wretchedly uncomfortable, wedged up against the coffin.

Don't think about what's in there.

Who.

She made herself think about Suzy instead, about whether she might have understood what she'd been trying to tell her; wondered if that had been her phoning her back again before Bolin had stamped on her phone.

Wait for Jude, she told herself.

Jude would come.

If he could.

292

Chapter 128

'Bo, what you doing?' Frankie calls from the foot of the stairs.

He went up there right after he came out of the conservatory, and since then she's heard him moving from room to room.

'What you *doing*, Bo?'

She's not feeling good now, not feeling good at all. First, *worst*, her own filth. But letting out that bit of anger against Alex didn't help much either, and therapist or not, she's finding it quite hard to get the sight and sound of the younger woman's terror out of her mind. It's not at all the way it would have been if her plan to take over Melton Cottage had worked out. Alex wouldn't have had time to feel scared then, any more than Roz Bailey or the plumber had.

Get rid of her.

Her words to Bo, so her fault, though she knows she was right, because what else could they do but get rid?

Yet still, Frankie doesn't like this any more.

She went looking for the walking frame a few minutes ago, because it wasn't out here in the hall where it used to be, and she found it, too, stuck right at the back of the coat cupboard, where there's no way she could get to it without help. And maybe Bo put it there because she said she hated it; and she *did* hate it, so maybe he was being nice, putting it out of sight so it wouldn't upset her. Except the physio and Alex too, once, said she just needed to try it for a while and then she'd change her mind, they said, get used to it, and it would be good getting back on her feet and, in time, she'd be able to manage without that too, and then both it and the wheelchair could become bad memories.

293

So Bo putting it away where she can't get to it might mean something else.

The opposite of helping her get better.

In her wheelchair, weak and pathetic and, now, utterly disgusting, means control for him, which is, of course, what Bo was always about.

Not *was*.

Frankie can hear him walking around up there.

Purposefully.

'I can piss off and leave you to it.'

He said that, didn't he, some time back?

Oh, God. Oh, God.

'Bo!' she calls again, yelling this time, but yelling makes her head hurt.

Bad pain, the way it hurt before her stroke.

So she stops yelling, stops calling.

Waits.

Nothing else she can do.

But she doesn't like it.

Chapter 129

Alex was wondering how long it would be till she lost her mind.

She, who had always hated enclosed spaces, who loved open windows, who'd never been all that keen on the dark, who liked curtains left at least slightly open, liked being able to see a chink of light under the door, was now sitting in unrelieved blackness in a space under a floor, tied to a coffin, with flies crawling over her and the worst smell in the world, the smell of human decay, choking her, making her want to be sick.

At least, in the dark, she couldn't *see* the coffin.

And better her than Jude, she thought again, as she had many times since Bolin had left her down here. Realizing, if any doubt had still remained, how much she loved him.

'Jude,' she said out loud again.

And began, at last, to cry.

Stopped again, after quite a short while.

She had often thought crying an over-rated pastime. Especially when there were more important things to be done.

Like trying to disentangle your hands from a belt tying them to a coffin.

Chapter 130

Not far now, traffic jam behind him.

Getting closer by the minute.

And no real idea what to do when he got there.

Jude supposed Suzy would have called the police by now, tried, as he drove the last half mile, to imagine what might be happening. A pair of PCs first, maybe, driving to Melton Cottage to speak to Suzy, check her out, see if she was a nutcase or not. Or maybe they'd already dispatched a car to Cuckmere Haven to look for the alleged body.

He doubted they'd be rushing straight to Winder Hill.

Which meant that, at least for now, he was probably on his own.

Which was what he'd told Suzy he wanted.

Not so sure now.

Not so fucking sure.

Calm down, Jude.

He couldn't even be sure Alex was there. Except that she had made that point of telling Suzy she was in Rottingdean, right after her weird reference to David and his 'colleagues'.

And Suzy had been trying to call Alex back when the phone had cut out.

Phones are always cutting out.

But Suzy said she had tried repeatedly since then.

Guessing game almost over now, anyway, because he was turning into the bottom of Winder Hill.

And he could see the house at the top.

The mud-caked Toyota in the drive, testimony to Bolin's confidence that Jude was safely gone, that even if his body were to wash up in time, there was no rush to clean the truck.

The Mini was right outside.

Jude pulled the Honda over to the side of the road, heart pounding.

Surely, if Bolin had done something to Alex, the first thing he'd have done was move her car so no one would know she'd been here.

Not the first thing, not if he had to . . .

Don't go there.

Maybe he hadn't done anything, maybe Alex was just sitting inside the house with Frankie, doing therapy exercises, and maybe Bolin, the man who'd dumped a body in a deep, turbulent canal and thrown Jude after it, was making them all tea.

In a pig's fucking ear.

Chapter 131

Bo comes down the staircase carrying two bags.

One of them a big, black hanger-type case Frankie's never seen before, since by the time he brought her back here from the hospital, he'd already unpacked and made himself at home.

The second bag's nicer, one of Roz Bailey's, brown canvas and leather.

Hers now.

'What you doing?' Frankie asks again.

'Leaving,' Bo answers.

She feels a big, dull, almost dead kind of thump in her chest.

'Clothes.' He reaches the bottom of the stairs, holds the black case higher, showing her. 'And cash,' he adds, raising the leather bag. 'Services rendered.' He pauses, screws up his nose. 'God, you stink.'

Frankie would like to scream.

'Take me with you,' she says, instead.

'Can't do that,' Bo says.

'Could,' she says, biting back tears, feeling like a child.

'Suppose I could,' Bo admits. 'But I won't.'

'Please, Bo,' she says, not too loudly, not wanting to make him angry. 'Don't leave me again.'

Because even though he's been the ugliest man alive to her at times in her past, because even though he still does things like hiding her walking frame and refusing to help her wash, he's still the only man she's ever loved.

And because, right now, he's also the only man who can save her.

'Too much of a liability, babe,' Bo tell her.

And walks past her chair into the kitchen.

298

Chapter 132

Alex kept telling herself she could do it.

It was hard going, unimaginably hard, and the foul air and dive-bombing flies were making matters worse, and the greater her efforts, the deeper the breaths she had to suck in and the warmer, the sweatier, she became.

More appeal to the bloody, *bloody* flies.

Yet though Bolin had knotted the belt tightly, she had found just a bit of wiggle room in the fabric itself, and Alex's wrists and hands were strong and supple, thank God, so she thought that, given enough time—

all the time in the world, maybe—

or not—

she might just be able to get at least one hand free.

Not might, she told herself angrily.

And went on working.

Chapter 133

Jude knew he was as ready as he could be.

He sat in the Honda a little way down the hill, trying to detach his mind from the various parts of him that still hurt like hell, wondering if Bolin had seen him from the house, if he was watching him, prepared for him. Looked at the crowbar now lying on the passenger seat, the closest, the *only*, thing he had as a weapon or burglarising implement; wished he were not so bloody conscientious about removing tools from the jeep when he wasn't working; and he'd only found the crowbar because it must have fallen out of his toolbag and got wedged into a dark corner.

A glass cutter might have been handy, or maybe a nice hard sledge-hammer.

Ready or not.

He wondered again about Suzy's dealings with the police, would like to have been able to call them now about Alex's car being outside.

No phone. No more time.

He caught sight of his reflection in the rear-view mirror, saw again why the woman in that car earlier had been staring.

He looked, with his dirty, bloody face and canal-slicked-down hair, like some 50s, B-movie monster from the deep.

He took a deep breath, opened his door.

Ready or not.

Not.

Chapter 134

'Do,' Frankie says, following him into the kitchen.

Moving the wheelchair is more of an effort than it was, *everything's* getting harder by the minute.

'Bo, please,' she says, still fighting not to whinge, knowing that always makes him worse. 'At least help me before you go.'

'I'd say I've helped you more than enough, wouldn't you?'

He opens the fridge, gets out a Bud, slams the bottle against the edge of the worktop and the top flies into the air, lands on the floor.

'Nursing,' he says. 'Cleaning. Body dumping.' He takes a long drink, removes the bottle from his mouth, his black eyes narrow and cold. 'Murder.'

'Clean me up,' Frankie pleads softly. 'Please, Bo. If you never do another thing for me after that, please, *please* help me with this last thing.'

Chapter 135

Jude was taking the back way.

The same route Bolin had used last night with the body.

Through the gate between the privet hedges.

If Bolin or Frankie were watching—

Too late to stop now.

He was in the garden, moving over the pathway to the conservatory.

He paused, bent, swiftly picked up a small rock from a flowerbed.

Crowbar in right hand, rock in the other.

One to lever a door or window, one to smash glass.

Or Bolin's skull.

Whichever came first.

Chapter 136

They both hear the sound at the same time.

From the conservatory.

'Thought you shut the trapdoor,' Frankie says, rattled.

'Course I fucking did,' Bo says.

The next sound's unmistakable.

Glass smashing.

'Fuck,' Bo says.

He puts down his Bud on the table, picks up a big Kitchen Devil knife from the sink, motions to Frankie to stay put and keep quiet.

And moves, very slowly, into the hall.

Chapter 137

Alex heard it too.

Muffled from where she sat under the floor, but almost definitely glass breaking, she thought.

Please God, please God.

Another fly landed on her lips, and she spat in disgust.

Began to fight even harder with the knotted belt.

Listening intently, desperately, while she battled.

Please.

Her right hand came free so suddenly, startlingly, that she could hardly believe she'd managed it.

She flexed the fingers, got the blood moving again.

Thank you.

Chapter 138

Jude stepped inside, jittery as hell.

Scanned the conservatory, left to right, up, down.

Looked normal.

Nice.

No one in it.

Still no real, sane plan in his head.

Except finding Alex.

And after the noise he'd just made smashing the glass door, if Bolin was in the house, then it wasn't likely to be more than another two seconds before he came storming in with a bloody arsenal of weapons, and even with his trusty crowbar, Jude knew he was in no physical condition to do more than dent the bigger, stronger man.

So, only one thing to do right now.

He took a deep breath.

'*Alex!*' he yelled.

Loud as he could manage.

Chapter 139

Untying her other hand, Alex heard him.

Knew it was him.

Joy and relief in equal measures.

Then fear.

'Jude!'

Her voice echoed in the black, stinking void.

She flexed both hands, rubbing the left with the right, tried to straighten up, and hit her head on the low ceiling.

'*Shit.*'

A whole squadron of filthy flies seemed to bomb her face, and for the first time she had the dubious luxury of being able to swat them away, before she got back down on her knees and started crawling towards the trapdoor.

Not exactly a chink of light, but a hair's breadth to tell her where it was.

She thought about what she remembered being overhead, recalled a rug and a chair covering the trapdoor before Bolin had yanked it open.

She didn't *think* she'd heard the sound of anything heavy being moved after he'd shut the door again and left her.

She closed her eyes for a moment, anything to help her focus, concentrate on remembering if she had seen anything, *anything*, in the conservatory that she might possibly be able to use as a weapon.

Remembered that there had been something.

Chapter 140

Bolin had heard Jude Brown's voice, then the Levin woman's responding, knew that the other man's priority had to be to find her.

He moved through the hall, the soles of his trainers silent on carpet.

Stopped to the right of the open conservatory door, and waited.

Any second now, Brown would call his bitch again, and she would answer, and the stupid faggot bastard would spot the trapdoor and bend down or even kneel down to get it open, and then . . .

The sound that came from behind him, startling him, was more than a scream.

It was a wail of sheerest terror.

Frankie, in the chair, was in the kitchen doorway, eyes torn wide.

'Fuck's sake,' Bolin spat at her.

'It's *him*,' Frankie cried.

He turned, saw what – who – she was staring at.

Jude Brown was standing, paralysed by her reaction, in the middle of the conservatory floor, bloody and filthy, and looking like—

'It's Swann.' Frankie was chalky white and trembling. 'It's *Swann.*'

'You *stupid* bitch!' Bolin yelled as he launched himself into the room.

Jude saw him coming, saw the gleam of the knife blade, swung the crowbar, knocked the knife out of Bolin's hand, but Bolin was faster again, the balance of power even more uneven than it had been last night, and Bolin grasped the crowbar, wrested it away

307

from Jude, raised it high in the air and then brought it down, striking Jude across his back, sending him sprawling.

'Should have drowned while you had the chance,' Bolin said.

And lifted the crowbar again.

Alex had heard Jude cry out with pain, heard the sound of someone – *him* – falling.

No more time. No more *time*.

Summoning every ounce of strength, she steadied herself, positioned her hands, palms up against the underside of the trapdoor.

Shoved upwards as hard as she could.

Light flooded in, dazzling her, overwhelmed her other senses, but she'd had time to plan while she'd been tethered below, and she was ready for that, screwed up her eyes, focused on using her hands and arms to haul herself up and out of the hole.

Get out and roll.

Moving targets harder to hit or stop.

First person she saw was Jude, on the tiled floor.

Then Bolin, standing over him, right hand raised, something in it – a poker, she thought, registering in the blink of an eye – ready to bring it down on Jude, except that the big man looked frozen, his shocked eyes on her instead.

And then he began to move again.

'*No!*' she screamed.

Jude's right hand snaked out, grabbed at Bolin's left leg, grasped a fistful of tracksuit and yanked hard at it, and the big man stumbled backwards.

'Bo!' Frankie cried out from her chair in the doorway.

Alex, knowing she had no more than a second or two and still disoriented, stared wildly around, seeking what she'd remembered, what she needed *now*.

Saw it.

Standing upright in the corner to her right close to some wilting orchids, tucked beside a small trowel and spade: a tool that looked like a small scythe.

Went for it.

Bolin, back on his feet, came at her, kicked her from behind, his boot catching her in the small of her back, and Alex fell, crying out with pain.

'Bastard!'

Jude felt his rage power him, give him the strength to fly at Bolin, who swung at him with the crowbar, smashed it against Jude's chest.

'Jesus!' Jude fell against the side of one of the chairs, slid down to the floor, the chair shifting with his weight, his face ashen.

One chance only.

Alex, scrambling back up to her feet, knew it was all they had. Tightened her grip on the scythe.

'Bo, look *out*!' Frankie cried out, a few feet into the room.

Bolin gave a shout of anger and lunged at Alex, who took a breath, half shut her eyes and swung the scythe, struck him on the forehead, cried out herself with the horror of it, the feel of it, the sight of the blood, heard both Bolin's and Frankie's simultaneous screams, opened her eyes, saw Bolin drop the crowbar, saw his hands fly up to cover the wound.

'*Bitch!*' he roared, suddenly, tried to come at her again, but the blood from the gash on his forehead was running down into his eyes, and he tripped over the crowbar and fell headlong, hard enough to make the floor shake.

'*Bo!*' Frankie screamed

'Oh my God.' Alex, shaking violently but still gripping the scythe, bent down to help Jude with her free hand, drew him back to his feet, felt his shudder of agony as she pulled at him. 'Oh my God, Jude.'

'Bo,' Frankie said again.

She says his name quietly this time, but the screamer's back in her head again, the one in the painting, the one that went away for a long time but came back when Swann died.

Back again now.

Screaming.

She tries, with an effort so great that her whole body trembles with it, to get out of the wheelchair and go to him. And then, suddenly, halfway up, she feels it again, the bad, bad pain, the worst of all.

She hears her own cry as if it's someone else's.

Puts her left hand up to her temple.

Feels herself going.

And crumples to the floor.

*

309

'Frankie,' Alex said, and began to move, instinctively, towards the fallen woman.

'No.' Jude's voice was soft and tense as he held her back, still sick with the new pain in his chest. 'Wait.'

He was watching Bolin.

Who seemed suddenly, impossibly, to have forgotten them and their fight and the high stakes of their fierce pitched battle.

To have forgotten everything but the woman now lying on the floor.

'Frankie, babe,' Bolin said, wiped the blood out of his eyes, crawled to her.

Put his arms around her, pulled her close, held her.

Alex took another step towards them.

'Wait,' Jude said again, still softly, insistently.

'I have to help,' Alex said.

'No.' Bolin did not look up, his voice different now, dull. 'No point.'

From outside, through the broken glass of the conservatory door, they all heard sirens; several, it seemed, coming closer.

Jude's eyes remained on Bolin, watchful, wary.

'Alex,' he said, quietly, 'come on. Let's go. Back way.'

'Please –' Alex spoke to Bolin '– let me try and help her.'

Bolin was stroking Frankie's hair. 'Too late,' he said.

'Alex.' Jude tugged at her hand.

'It's all right,' Bolin said from the floor. 'It's finished now.'

The sirens grew louder, then stopped.

They heard voices.

Then the doorbell ringing, a fist pounding.

'All right now, babe,' Bolin said to Frankie.

He held her close with one arm, felt with his other hand for a handkerchief in his pocket, found it and wiped away, with real tenderness, a streak of saliva still trickling from the right corner of her lips down her chin.

'She hates anything like that,' he said.

And then he kissed her, full on the mouth.

310

Chapter 141

Once the worst was over, wounds treated and healing, interviews and statements given, victim support offered, inquests opened and adjourned, bodies released by the Coroner, Jude poured his energy into arranging Roz Bailey's funeral, finding it intolerable to think of her having no one closer to care.

She had left no specific instructions about her funeral, or any preferences regarding burial or cremation, in the will that had shown up with a local firm of solicitors, but Alex had been to a patient's funeral at the Lawn Memorial Cemetery not far from Melton Cottage, and had been struck by the beauty of the place, all flat stones and rolling lawns and plenty of flowers, with farm-land backing onto it, giving a sense of space as well as peace.

'Bit like an American movie,' had been Jude's first comment.

'Not as lovely as an old churchyard,' Alex agreed. 'But Roz doesn't seem to have been affiliated to any particular church, and this does feel quite special, don't you think?'

Jude had visited the cemetery twice more before putting the suggestion to Roz's solicitor, who had offered no objections, and the money was available, and they could only hope that the lady herself would have approved.

Just a small gathering. Himself and Alex and Suzy; Bill Deacon, the doorman from the Lansdowne Casino; Roz's solicitor; Mrs Osborne, her next-door-neighbour from down Winder Hill, shame-faced for not having missed her; the Hausers, Jude's friends from the E Gallery, and Ray Cobbins, too, the last three there simply to support Jude.

Plenty of flowers. No police. Nor reporters.

'I hope,' Jude said, quietly, to Alex as they approached the grave, 'someone does something decent for Swann.'

'And for Frankie,' Alex half murmured, saw Jude's sidelong glance. 'I can't help myself,' she said. 'I still feel for her, in spite of everything.'

'I know you do,' he said.

They held hands tightly as the coffin was lowered into the ground, Alex knowing what that had to be costing Jude psychologically, and God knew it was bad enough for her, after her own ordeal. Not, of course, thankfully, the same coffin poor Roz had first been laid in – and if the police had learned where and how Frankie had contrived that grisly interment, they had not shared the information with Jude or Alex.

They were grateful, at least for the time being, not to know, knew they would find out soon enough when the inquests were reopened.

All that still to come, and then, when the slowly grinding wheels were ready, Bolin's trial; one or more, they weren't yet certain, knew that he faced several charges relating to Roz Bailey and Andy Swann, as well as to themselves.

They tried, back at work in the real world, to be as normal as possible, knew there was no real way to forget, but did their best to move on.

Spoke, now and then, about what remained to them both the most compelling mystery of all: the relationship between Frankie and Bolin.

'He must have loved her,' Alex said, remembering the tenderness at the end.

'Strange kind of love,' Jude said. 'Leaving a woman as fastidious as Frankie to sit in her own pee.'

'I think she loved him,' Alex said. 'Even if she was afraid of him.'

'Yet she was the killer,' Jude said.

'At least she was mentally ill.' Alex still felt sick, remembering. 'He tried to kill you in cold blood.'

'Trying to protect her, maybe.' Jude shrugged. 'Maybe.'

They fell silent.

'I don't suppose we'll ever know exactly why he took care of her,' Alex said after a while. 'Was it just for the house and the money, or is he some kind of sadist? Or was it love, at least in his fashion?'

'Hard to say.' Jude paused. 'He'd only packed for himself.'

'Including the bag of cash,' Alex said.

Jude shrugged again.

'I wish,' Alex said, after a moment, 'I could ask Frankie about their past.'

'You could try asking him,' Jude said.

She shook her head.

'I won't do that,' she said.

His dreams, since the horrors, had become worse than ever. Some nights they were as they had always been, about Scott and their mother, but at other times Jude dreamed a new version, in which he and Alex were lying in a grave between their coffins, with Frankie and Mike Bolin and poor, dead, ghoulish Andy Swann all staring down at them; and then Bolin started shovelling earth and filthy water down onto them, and the dirt blinded Jude, filled his mouth, and he woke up crying out and gasping for breath.

'It's all right,' Alex always told him, holding him close.

'I know,' Jude always said, angry with himself for being weaker than she was, wondering if perhaps, when it was all done, the trial over, too, and Bolin locked away, they might find real peace and normality.

'Long haul,' Alex said to him one evening, seeing that he was down.

'Together, though,' Jude said. 'So that's okay.'

She told him, soon after, that she'd missed her period, asked him if he'd mind.

Knew he would not.

They bought the test kit together, brought it home and waited, saw the fat blue line appear.

And the long haul grew a little easier.